GRAY BABY

GRAY BABY

A Novel

by Scott Loring Sanders

Houghton Mifflin

HOUGHTON MIFFLIN HARCOURT
BOSTON * NEW YORK * 2009

Houghton Mifflin is an imprint of Houghton Mifflin Harcourt
Publishing Company.

www.hmhbooks.com

The text of this book is set in Adobe Caslon Pro.

Library of Congress Cataloging-in-Publication Data

Sanders, Scott Loring.
Gray baby : a novel / by Scott Loring Sanders.
p. cm.
Summary: Clifton has grown up in rural Virginia with the
memory of his African American father being beaten to death
by policemen, causing his white mother to slip into alcoholism
and depression, but after befriending an old man who listens
to his problems, Clifton finally feels less alone in the world.
ISBN 978-0-547-07661-4 (alk. paper)
[1. Racially mixed people—Fiction.   2. Single-parent
families—Fiction.   3. Alcoholism—Fiction.   4. Grandfathers—
Fiction.   5. Kidnapping—Fiction.   6. Murder—Fiction.
7. Country life—Virginia—Fiction.   8. Virginia—Fiction.]
I. Title.
PZ7.S19792Gr 2009
[Fic]—dc22
2008036810

Manufactured in the United States of America
MV 10 9 8 7 6 5 4 3 2 1

For my father, who taught me to take on the world.
And for my mother, who taught me to give back to it.

Accomplishments have no color.

—Leontyne Price

Chess is the greatest game ever invented, because it only

looks like a game.

—Scott Kerns

I never believed in Santa Claus because I knew no white man

would be coming into my neighborhood after dark.

—Dick Gregory

"Poor Babes in the Woods"

My dears don't you know, not so very long ago

Two little children whose names I don't know

Were stolen away on a bright summer day

And left in the woods, so I've heard people say

And when it was night, so sad was their plight

The sun went down and the moon gave no light

They sobbed and they sighed and they bitterly cried

Till the poor little things, they laid down and died

And when they were dead, the robins, so red

Brought strawberry leaves and over them spread

And all the night long, they sang them this song

Poor babes in the woods, Poor babes in the woods

—Author Unknown

Chapter  1

"BUT HOW ARE WE GOING TO HEAR IT?" asked Clifton from the back seat. "That's what I don't get."

Mr. Carlson looked away from the road and over at his wife. Even though it was dark in the car, Clifton could still see their silhouettes as they smiled at each other.

"All we do, little man, is drive up to a parking spot in the field. There'll be posts on each side of the car. On those posts will be speakers. That's how we'll hear the movie. Ain't nothing to it."

Clifton looked out the window and thought about that. His mother, who was a bit of a worrier, had only recently decided that he was finally big enough to graduate from his booster seat (he'd just turned eight). The switch made him feel more grown up, but it also changed his perspective on things. For one, he couldn't see out the window as well. At the moment he was gazing at a splinter of moon that seemed to follow the car no matter how fast or slow his father drove. It might disappear for a moment when his father turned onto a new road, but usually, as soon as he made another turn, there it was again, stuck in the sky and keeping watch like a voyeur. Clifton's mind drifted back to the drive-in movie. "How will we see it if we're parked out in a field?"

Mr. Carlson lit a cigarette and cracked his window. From Clifton's vantage point, when his father sucked on the cigarette, the reflection of the orange cherry bounced off the windshield, oddly illuminating his face in the glass.

"They've got a giant screen set up. Not a screen like at the theater, but more like a huge wall," he said as he took a heavy pull from the cigarette. "You know, think of a wall at school that you might play dodgeball in front of. That's all it is. Just a giant wall in the middle of a field. There's a little stand set up at the opposite end of the wall. They got hot dogs, Cokes, popcorn, candy. That kind of stuff. Up above the stand is the little movie house. They got a projector up there that plays the films. It's just like a regular movie theater, only it's outside. There ain't too many left in the country, so this is a real treat." He took his hand off the wheel and sucked on his cigarette again, then turned and blew a stream of smoke at the open window.

Clifton enjoyed watching his father smoke. His large dark hands made the cigarette look like nothing bigger than a toothpick. When Mr. Carlson took a draw, he would squint slightly. Then a tiny wraith of smoke would mysteriously escape his mouth, only to be sucked up again by his wide nostrils. Clifton especially liked it when the smoke would pour out of his father's mouth while he talked. He looked like a dragon then. A big, black, muscular dragon, more powerful than any other man in the whole state of Virginia.

As his father put the cigarette to his lips, Clifton could just barely discern the raised and irregular welts that dotted his father's right hand and then traveled up his arm. They were smooth and seemed to shimmer in the faint light. He'd once asked his father about the scars, the way a curious young boy who doesn't know any better might ask a fat woman why she's so fat or a bald man why he doesn't have hair. But all his father had said was "Work accident. Got burned." And that had been the end of it.

"So what happens if it rains?" Clifton now asked. He was sucking on a McDonald's straw he'd found pinched in the folds of the back seat, aping his father every time he took a draw. "What do they do then?"

"Man, you're sure asking a lot of questions tonight," said Mr. Carlson, adjusting the rearview mirror so he could get a better look at his son. Clifton saw him smiling, the cigarette bouncing gently in his lips. "Ain't he asking a lot of questions, Sabrina?"

Mrs. Carlson looked over and smiled. Her smooth white skin, where it was pulled tight over her high, rounded cheekbones, shone as it caught some of the moon's light. Her long auburn hair was bunched in a ponytail and seemed to stretch her pretty face even tighter. "He's curious. It's good for little boys to ask questions."

"Better to ask than not, I reckon," said Mr. Carlson. He reached toward his door, cranked the handle all the way down, and flicked his cigarette out. A meteor shower of orange swooshed by the back window, much to Clifton's delight. The air, still warm but not unbearably humid like it had been during the day, filled the new Dodge with the fresh smells of late spring. Honeysuckle slipped into the car as sweetly as if a bee had brought it special delivery. Newly mown grass and the warm smell of a pine forest mixed with the honeysuckle, filling Clifton's head with wonder.

"So?" said Clifton.

"So what?"

"So what happens if it rains? What happens then?"

"Ain't nothing happens, little man. Darth Vader don't care if it's raining or not. You saw what kind of hell he gave Luke Skywalker in the first movie. It's only gonna be better in this one. That badass dude is gonna kick some tail again. He's gonna checkmate Luke's sorry butt. Ain't no rain gonna stop Darth Vader. The show must go on. Especially on your birthday."

Clifton chuckled. He now chewed on the end of his straw even though his father had already discarded his smoke. "You're the only person I ever heard of that cheers for the bad guy, Dad. Nobody but you likes Darth Vader."

"He's a badass, that's why. And he's black. That's another reason. Shoot, your mama likes him too." He took his eyes off the road to look at his wife. "Don't you, Bri?"

"I like Han Solo. Now he's one good-looking man."

"Han Solo? Hell. His best friend's a hairy ape that can't even speak English."

Clifton started laughing and so did Mrs. Carlson. "I could say the same thing about some of *your* friends," she said. "I think someone's a little jealous."

"I ain't jealous of nothing. Just remember, I'm Darth Vader and I'll kick Han Solo's butt from here all the way to Roanoke if he tries to mess with my wife."

Mrs. Carlson reached over and patted him on the knee. "I'll make sure to warn Han the next time I see him."

THE DRIVE-IN was on the other side of Crocket's Mill, on the outskirts, about twenty minutes from Clifton's home. It was a little off the beaten path, and there were several back roads that had to be traversed to get there. It was an oasis of popcorn, Goobers, and *The Empire Strikes Back,* all out in the middle of an abandoned cow field.

Once they reached the countryside and the prominent lights of Samford—the more populous city across the river from Crocket's Mill—disappeared, Clifton saw all of the stars shining, along with the moon that still tailed them. As he pressed his forehead to the window and stared out at the night, he felt curious and excited about the prospects of watching a movie outdoors. He couldn't wait to get there. However, he became instantly nervous and anxious when a flash of blue lightning caught the corner of his eye. His father had downplayed rain, but he hadn't mentioned anything about lightning.

"Oh, shit," mumbled his father, apparently having seen the lightning too. He readjusted the rearview mirror and began slowing the car. Gravel crunched and a stray rock popped up and hit the steel undercarriage with a loud thud directly beneath Clifton's feet. As Mr. Carlson rolled to a stop along the tree-lined road, a chorus of crickets and peepers began chirping so loudly from a nearby stream that it sounded as if they were sitting right there in the back seat.

"What's the matter, Jim? Why are you stopping?"

"We got the law on our tail," he said, throwing the car in park and killing the engine.

Clifton felt his heart beating in his chest. Looking out the side window, he saw the fat trunks of oak trees flashing blue as they eerily stood guard. A throng of dormant vines hanging off the branches made him think of the frazzled gray hair of witches. He got on his knees, turned around on the Naugahyde seat, which stuck to his bare, sweaty legs, and was greeted by the blinding high beams of the prowler. He put the edge of his hand across his forehead as if shielding the sun and saw the blue rooftop lights spinning and blinking. The click of Mr. Carlson's lighter caught his attention and then a moment later the sweet smell of tobacco overpowered the dank, earthy odor of the forest. Two uniformed men approached the back of the Dodge, one on each side. Clifton spun around and said, "Mama."

"It's okay, baby," she whispered as she glanced into the side mirror. "It's going to be okay."

In addition to the strange penumbra of blue light flashing through the woods, there were now two bright spots illuminating his parents. Each officer held a heavy-duty flashlight near his ear, blinding Mr. and Mrs. Carlson as they tried to see what was happening.

"Well, what do we got here?" said the officer on Mr. Carlson's side.

Because of the prowler's headlights behind him, Clifton saw the profiles of the two cops pretty well. The man who had just spoken was tall and broad shouldered. The hair that was visible from underneath his cap was dark but reflected spots of silver where he was just beginning to gray. Severe pockmarks covered his cheeks and chin as if someone wearing metal spiked cleats had stepped all over his face. The other man was much younger and built like a wrestler. An inch of Hitler mustache crept like a fuzzy caterpillar from underneath his nose.

"We're just heading to the movies, officer . . ." said Mr. Carlson as he read the name tag pinned to the man's uniform. "Officer Brader." He gripped the top of the steering wheel with both hands, sat upright, and turned to stare straight ahead through the windshield. The cigarette smoldered between his fingers. "Going to the Star Night, sir."

Clifton immediately noticed the change in his father. The change in his tone. The formality of his speech. He'd never heard him speak like that in his life. His dad almost sounded scared, which made Clifton become nearly frantic with apprehension. He'd never seen his father scared or nervous before. He hadn't even known it was possible.

"Why don't you look at me when I'm talking to you, boy?" said the pock-faced man.

"Sorry, sir," said Mr. Carlson, turning to make eye contact.

He drummed the grip of the wheel with his thumbs, causing the muscles of his forearms to ripple like pond water. His jaw tensed as he gritted his teeth.

"You know, we've seen you before. Driving your new car around Crocket's Mill with this white woman. You kinda stand out. We've been keeping an eye on you—did you know that?"

"Uh, no sir, I didn't," said Mr. Carlson. "But I haven't done anything wrong, have I? So I don't see what the problem is, officer."

"I'll tell you what the problem is. When I see someone like you driving a white woman around, I get awfully suspicious. You passed us a little ways back. Don't reckon you even saw us now did you?"

"No, sir," said Mr. Carlson. "I guess I didn't." He chuckled nervously.

"Well, we saw you. Recognized your car right off. Thought we'd see what you were up to. See why you were way out here in the country with this pretty lady. This pretty *white* lady." The officer turned his beam to Mrs. Carlson's face for a moment, then dropped it back to Mr. Carlson.

Clifton shrunk his turtle head deeper into the shell of the back seat but not so far that he couldn't see. He watched as his father took a draw off his cigarette. Then, instead of using the plastic ashtray by the radio, he reached over and flicked the ash out the window, directly in front of the scar-faced man who now rested his hands atop the door and windowsill. "That pretty white lady is my wife, if you gotta know. And I already told you, I was taking her and my son to the Star Night. It's his birthday. I mean, what the hell is this anyway? I thought it was 1980, not 1880."

Clifton became a little more at ease when he heard his father speaking normally again. He didn't like hearing, nor was he used to hearing, his father kiss up to anyone. But that feeling was short-lived.

Before Clifton knew what was happening, the officer opened the door, grabbed Mr. Carlson by the shirt, and tried to pull him out. "We got us an uppity one here, Randy," said the officer. "Get over here and help me."

In a split second, the other officer, who so far hadn't said a word, ran around the front of the Dodge and began to assist Scarface. But Mr. Carlson was a big, strong man. He'd played football in high school and now worked for an industrial pipe shop, making storm drains and sewer pipes. He didn't take kindly to being forced from his vehicle.

"Get your goddamn hands off me," he yelled. "I didn't do nothing." He squeezed Scarface's wrist, but the other officer pulled out his billy club and whacked him on the elbow. Hard. Mr. Carlson let go and yelped out in pain. The officers each grabbed an arm and ripped him from the car. In the struggle, the heavy door slammed shut behind him.

Mrs. Carlson began screaming frantically from her position in the front seat. "Get off of him. He didn't do anything to anyone. Please, I've got a child in here."

Clifton started crying and sank further into the back seat, crouching on the floor mat, where bits of dirt and tiny pebbles dug into his knees. He squeezed his eyes shut and put his hands over his ears. But despite his attempt to stopper the noise, the brutal thuds of two truncheons against his father's arms, legs, and back seeped through. Mr. Carlson let out agonizing yelps and tried to fight back, but the force of the clubs was too much.

Clifton heard a car slow down and then quickly speed up and disappear as the melee continued in the middle of the country road. And then there was a nauseating crack, like the snap of an ice-laden tree branch, as one of the solid hickory clubs connected with skull. The next thing he knew, his mother was in the driver's seat and had started the engine. He popped up and cautiously stuck his head above the seat as if peeking over a brick wall. His mother's hands shook so badly that she couldn't seem to put the car in drive. He looked back just in time to glimpse the officers struggling to stuff a limp body into the back seat of the prowler. The bright lights nearly blinded him, but he was able to see a man at each end of his father, one at his feet, one at his shoulders. Mr. Carlson's body bowed like a slack power line, and the butt of his jeans nearly scraped against the gravel. The officers were having a difficult time holding him up, as if he were a wet, rolled-up carpet.

A moment later, Mrs. Carlson had the car in gear and was about to pull away when Scarface hurriedly approached the door. "Looks like your husband had a little accident," he said, panting heavily. His elbows were ripped open, and trickles of drying blood were painted down the right side of his face. The sleeves of his brown starched shirt looked like the tattered ends of a weathered flag. "You best get your whore-ass the hell out of here and get that little half-breed home. These swamp monsters out here eat gray babies for supper."

The officer had looked directly at Clifton as he said those last words. Clifton shrunk back into his seat once more and tried to concentrate on the songs of the peepers through the warm night air. But they had gone completely silent. As if they were scared too. A moment later his mother, now hysterical, spun the tires in the dusty hardpack and sped off toward home.

Chapter 2

CLIFTON DRUMMED TWO PENCILS against the edge of his desk as he stared at the handful of other kids who were imprisoned with him. One boy sat in the corner, dressed from head to toe in black. Black combat boots, black pocket pants, and a black T-shirt with *The Dead Kennedys* written across the front. He had a small pair of tweezers and was busy plucking out all of his eyelashes. Not his eye*brows*, his eye*lashes*. He'd already finished with his right eye and was diligently working on the bottom row of his left. A tiny pile of black hairs sat on the edge of his desk, as if he were collecting them for some sort of experiment. There was another guy who looked normal enough, but Clifton soon found out that he'd mooned a substitute teacher on a dare. "I got ISS," he whispered to Clifton when the stern, lifeless monitor, who resembled a professional female wrestler, left for a moment to get a cup of coffee.

"But I got a dollar from every person in the class, so I ended up with like twenty-two bucks. A couple of chicks haven't paid up yet, but it was totally worth it."

And then there was Dweedle, who was a freshman and a year behind Clifton, but Clifton had known him forever. In fact, everyone—from the best-looking girl in the senior class all the way down to the biggest burnout at Crocket's Mill High—knew Dweedle. For one thing, his name was Dweedle. For two, he dressed and acted exactly like you'd expect someone named Dweedle to dress and act. He generally wore jeans or corduroys that were too tight and too short, which exposed yellow-stained socks when he wore sneakers, though sometimes he wore what can only be described as elf boots. They were bright green, went up to his calves, and were made of some sort of soft velour fabric. He was tall, skinny, and had a severe case of acne. Acne so bad that Clifton had a difficult time looking at him for more than a second or two. At the moment, he wasn't wearing his boots, but he did have a black cape tied around his neck that draped over the back of his chair. He was busy reading a *Dungeons and Dragons Monster Guide*. Probably reading, Clifton mused, about how to kill Hobgoblins or Harpies or some other weird creature that Clifton couldn't even begin to imagine.

Over the years, the one thing Clifton had learned about in-school suspension was that it was so boring that he was willing to talk to people he might not ordinarily talk to. Not that that was generally a problem for him. There weren't too many people that ever bothered to talk to him anyway, unless it was to call him names. Mostly it was "Skunk" or sometimes "Oreo" or "Salt and Pepper." The names didn't even bother him anymore. They used to, but the sting had faded years ago to where now he hardly even noticed. In fact, he sort of liked the name Skunk. He thought it was appropriate. He didn't smell, but he was both black and white, and, generally speaking, most people tried to avoid him at all costs. Which was the way he liked it. He'd found that he sort of enjoyed being a loner. At least, over time, he'd more or less convinced himself of that fact.

So while the monitor was busy picking lint off her sweatpants and sweatshirt, Clifton decided to say something to Dweedle. He sort of admired him in a strange way. Dweedle didn't care what other people thought. He was content doing his own thing and actually had a small faction of four or five friends that he played D&D with, which was four or five more friends than Clifton could claim. "Hey, Dweedle, what'd you do to get ISS?" he whispered while the monitor was grooming herself. "Kill a herd of Pegasuses or a dragon or something?"

Dweedle looked up from his manual and turned his head to the side. Judging by his overall appearance, anyone seeing

Dweedle for the first time would assume he had a high, maybe even feminine voice, but it was actually quite the opposite. He spoke in a deep, husky baritone that didn't fit with his image at all. "For your information, Clifton, there is only *one* Pegasus, so that part of your question doesn't even make sense. As for the other part, don't meddle in the affairs of dragons, for you are crunchy and taste good with ketchup." Dweedle turned back to his book without another word.

Since that was the end of the conversation, Clifton started playing everything over in his mind from the day before. For one thing, it had been a bad day to start with. It was his birthday, which was generally a good day for most people, but for him it marked the anniversary of his father's death. A death that had been ruled in the official police reports as "accidental while trying to subdue a violent offender." And even though eight years had gone by, and the events of that night had faded to some degree, when his birthday rolled around, the dark memories always came rushing back.

So Clifton already wasn't in the best of moods on his sixteenth birthday. And once he arrived at school, it only got worse. The first thing he found out was that he'd received a D on his geometry test. Then in gym class he learned that he was starting a four-week section on square dancing. It was then that everything really went south. For a moment, things actually looked like they weren't going to be too bad. He happened to get paired up with Julie O'Kane as his dance partner. Blond-haired and green-eyed, she was one of the prettiest girls in his grade. Besides being beautiful, she'd also always been nice to him, so he thought maybe square dancing wouldn't be so horrible after all. He remembered how years ago, shortly after his father had died, a couple of kids were picking on him in elementary school. They thought it was funny to clap the dusty erasers on his back, causing white marks to appear on his shirt. When he would turn in one direction, a kid would pop him in the back. Then he'd turn around again and the other kid would do the same thing. It was Julie who had come to his rescue. She had admonished both boys, and whether it was because of her stern demeanor or her good looks—even at nine years old—they had both hung their heads and walked away.

"Are you okay?" she'd asked, looking at Clifton with soft empathy.

"Yeah," he'd said, somewhat embarrassed at being helped by a girl. He brushed the white dust out of his wiry hair as she swept his back clean. "I'm fine. Thanks, though."

She had reached up and removed a streak that covered his arm. Ordinarily, if it had been anyone else, he would have instinctively pulled away. But because her touch was so gentle and her eyes so tender, he let her do it. "Your skin is so pretty," she'd said. "It's like melted caramel."

17

Clifton had smiled and walked away without a word, but he'd been grateful for her kindness.

BUT NOW, his joy at being paired with Julie for the square dance lasted only a second once he realized that Colt Jenkins was also in his group. Clifton mused to himself, as he usually did when it came to Colt, that he didn't know which was worse: being named Colt or being named Dweedle. He often wondered what their respective parents could have possibly been thinking. Had they been drunk in the hospital room while going over names with each other? But strangely, those parents had gotten their sons' names exactly right. Dweedle looked like a Dweedle, whatever that was, and Colt looked like he was supposed to be named Colt. But not because he resembled a horse. He usually wore tight jeans, tight T-shirts, and donned cowboy boots. If he wasn't wearing that, then it was cutoff jeans, flip-flops, and a Richard Petty baseball cap with greasy stains on the bill. Colt was a redneck, plain and simple.

Besides being a redneck, Colt was also the biggest lineman on the football team, mean as a blinded dog with a missing leg, and dumber than a sack of hammers. Big, mean, and dumb was a bad combination as far as Clifton was concerned.

It made him dangerous. He and Clifton had been going at each other since grade school. In fact, he'd been one of the kids with the erasers that day. Generally, Clifton could outfox Colt and escape most situations before anything serious happened, though they had come to blows on many occasions over the years. And when that happened, Clifton always came out the loser, though occasionally he'd get a shot in. But he was far better at taking jabs at Colt's mental deficiencies than actually punching him.

As Clifton's group circled up and began following the instructions given by the caller on the warped record, Clifton noticed Colt eyeing him. He had a feeling the blockhead had finally figured out who had recently vandalized his locker. The caller's words hissed and scratched over the PA system as the square dancers began bowing to their partners and neighbors. Clifton kept his eye on Colt as the dance began, smiling to himself as they went through the same motions they'd been doing since the first grade. When Colt locked his eyes on Clifton and stared him down during a do-si-do, Clifton couldn't help himself. He winked at Colt and puckered his lips. A second later, as he was promenading Julie all the way home, he felt a hard smack to his shoulder. He stopped and turned around, only to find Colt right in his face.

"Hey, Skunk," said Colt, "I got a little problem I need to talk to you about."

Clifton and Julie stopped as the rest of the students continued circling around them. He knew what was coming, but he decided that since he was probably going to end up in a fight either way, he might as well take advantage of the situation. It was a predicament he'd gotten used to over the years, and he'd learned that wit, if nothing else, was something most kids admired about him. He intentionally stared at the upper part of Colt's left arm, a forced look of bewilderment on his face. "Is it about that dickfor on your shirt?"

This took Colt aback. He looked confused. "The what?"

"The dickfor. It's right on your shirt," said Clifton, pointing at the top of Colt's thick shoulder.

Colt glanced down, looking for something that wasn't there. He examined his shirt for a moment, even stretching the end of his sleeve to get a better view. He looked back at Clifton and said, "What the hell's a dickfor?"

Clifton gave a sly smile at Julie, and she immediately cracked up as the loud music continued to swirl through the gymnasium. Colt stood there, dumbfounded, still trying to figure out what had just happened. Clifton grabbed Julie's hand and they quickly slid back into the circle. It took only a second before he felt his body snap forward as Colt stuck a meaty shoulder into his spine. He fell face-first and slid across the slick wooden floor, stopping near a blue stripe of foul line. By the time he rolled over onto his back, Colt was on top of him. Julie had been knocked to the side but managed to keep her balance. She yelled at Colt but he paid no attention. The screech of the fiddles and the caller's annoying voice continued loudly, and, as of yet, no gym teacher had noticed what was happening.

"Listen," spat Colt as he pinned Clifton's shoulders to the floor with his knees, "guess what I found in my locker the other morning?"

Colt's weight crushed Clifton's chest, making it difficult to breathe. He must have outweighed him by seventy pounds. Clifton glanced at Julie and caught her eye, if only for a moment. She was too busy pulling at Colt's arm, attempting to get him off, which unfortunately didn't help much. But Clifton did catch her eye, and that was good enough for him. "I have no idea what you found, fatboy," said Clifton. He wasn't scared and he didn't care. Messing with Colt had always been one of his favorite pastimes, though he knew he was going to get punched in the face if the teachers didn't break it up soon. He knew he should keep his mouth shut, but he couldn't help himself. "What'd you find—your mama's underwear? Didn't think those things could fit in your locker."

The punch connected on the pointy knob of cheekbone just underneath Clifton's left eye. It hurt like hell, and he actually saw little white flashes sparkle around him, just like in a cartoon, but he fought through the pain in order to keep smiling. He knew that smiling and laughing drove Colt insane.

"No, you little asshole, I found a brown lunch bag filled with dogshit. How'd you get in my locker . . . *Skunk?*" He emphasized Skunk as if it might cause extra pain. But it was the second punch that hurt far worse than the name. And then, out of nowhere, two gym teachers pulled Colt away.

THE GYM TEACHERS, of course, were two of the football coaches, which explained why Colt was nowhere to be seen in the ISS room that Clifton now found himself in. But as he tapped a pencil against the desk with one hand and probed the tender spot on his face with the other—one good thing about his skin color was that bruises didn't show up quite as prominently—he thought about what had happened the day before and smiled once again. He had seen Julie as he lay on the floor, looking down at him with what he liked to think of as admiration, though he couldn't be sure. For one, he hadn't exactly been seeing too clearly at that point, and for two, he was getting manhandled by two varsity coaches who pulled him to his feet and carted him to the principal's office. But he was pretty sure she had looked at him that way. That's how he had decided to remember it anyway.

The ISS monitor broke Clifton from his reverie. "Okay, come on," she said in a deep, nearly masculine voice. "It's time for the Balloon Ascent. Hello? Anyone home?" She rapped on the wooden door a couple of times to make her point.

Clifton looked up from his desk to see, much to his surprise, that everyone else had left the room. The monitor stood in the doorway, one hand in a fist against the open door, the other on the sweatpants of her prodigious hips.

"Come on, already," she said. "Even you hoodlums are set free for the Balloon Ascent."

Clifton slid his legs from under the desk and walked into the hall where he saw his fellow criminals leaning against lockers, waiting. Dweedle had one side of the cape draped over his arm, covering his mouth and chin as if he were Dracula. The punk rocker guy was repeatedly kicking the bottom of a locker with the toe of his combat boot, leaving black smudge marks. It appeared that his eyelash experiment had been a complete success. The normal-looking guy had disappeared altogether, blending in with the rest of the students who now filled the halls as they filtered their way through the exit doors on their way to the football field.

The Balloon Ascent had been the vision of the principal, Mr. Longsworth, who had decided that Crocket's Mill High School needed more school spirit. The whole promotion and buildup for the day had been going on for weeks. There were hand-painted banners in the hallways, flyers on the lockers, and a Balloon Ascent committee had even been created. At first, Clifton had found the whole idea to be pretty stupid. It seemed ridiculous to him that a group of high schoolers would stand around on the football field and let go of balloons. He had thought it was stupid, that is, until he found out how it worked.

This was the theory: Every student wrote his name on two identical index cards that had been stamped with the school's address, and then tied each card to the string end of a balloon. Each student got two balloons, one blue and the other gold, representing the school colors. Then, on the official day, so deemed April 21 by Mr. Longsworth, all of the students convened on the football field, each of them holding two helium-filled balloons. When Mr. Longsworth gave the word, they would let them go. What was supposed to happen was that when someone eventually found the balloon, whether it be in a different county or even in a different state, that person would hopefully mail the card back to the school by the May 21 deadline. Then, when it was determined whose balloon had traveled the farthest, that student would win a hundred dollars. There were second- and third-place prizes too.

What had really surprised Clifton as he had stood on the field, his two balloons banging against each other above him, was how much he had actually enjoyed the whole affair. It had been a perfect spring day, not too hot, and there hadn't been a cloud in the sky. When Mr. Longsworth had given the word from the bleachers over a hand-held megaphone, hundreds of Clifton's peers let their balloons go. The sky was suddenly clouded over with blue and gold as the balloons wiggled their way higher and higher. For a moment it had reminded him of the movie he'd had to watch in health class, where all the little sperm jockeyed for position to be first to the egg. The students had squirmed in their seats and snickered at snide comments to mask their own awkwardness. But what he had witnessed with the balloons was a thing of beauty.

Everyone had roared while watching the balloons climb. Though some balloons strayed from the pack when the breeze picked up, most stayed together as tightly as a flock of birds darting and changing direction for reasons that only they understood. Clifton had tried to keep his eye on his two balloons, but it didn't take long before they all seemed to meld into one. At least his balloons hadn't gotten stuck in the trees or power lines on the far side of the field like some others had.

As he had watched them slowly disappear and make their way over the mountains surrounding Crocket's Mill, he realized that he'd never wanted to win something so badly in his life. And it wasn't about the money, though that would have been nice. What it was, more than anything, was that he had just wanted his balloons to have a long and successful journey. He wanted to get word that they had traveled to Oregon or Maine or maybe Mexico or even Holland. To someplace foreign and exotic. And he wanted to be recognized as the one who had let them go, as if he'd masterfully solved the complex riddle of balloon release.

But as it turned out, he didn't win. In fact, neither of his tickets was ever mailed back to the school. The winning balloon was released by Barbra Cowherd, who was in Clifton's history class. The balloon had ended up in some town called Schooley's Mountain, New Jersey, nearly five hundred miles away, and the ticket was returned by a middle-school English teacher. He'd written a note saying he'd found the shriveled balloon tangled up in an azalea bush in his front yard. Upon hearing who the winner was, the thing that had hurt Clifton the most was that he'd been standing right next to Barbra when everyone had let the balloons go. Why was it that her balloon had made it that far while his had probably never even reached the county line?

But in one way or another, Mr. Longsworth did achieve his goal of boosting school spirit. That is, everyone wanted to participate because what could be easier than letting go of some balloons and then possibly winning a lot of money? And if nothing else, it had gotten Clifton out of ISS for part of the day.

THOUGH HE HADN'T won, there was still a positive outcome to the Balloon Ascent. The experience had given him an idea. Shortly after he'd found out the disappointing results, he'd decided to create his own Balloon Ascent of sorts. Instead of throwing away all of his mother's wine bottles like he usually did (seven bottles a week, every week), he'd decided to stash them in the lawnmower shed in the backyard. Then, at the end of that first week, he'd written different notes, stuffed them into the bottles, recorked them, and then carried them toward the Palisades in a cardboard box. As he walked with his bottles, he couldn't help but think of the first time he'd heard about the Palisades from his father. And also about the chilling details of the legendary Killing Pit.

Chapter 3

LAST AUTUMN'S DEAD LEAVES CRUNCHED under their feet as Clifton followed his father through the woods. The spring day was warm, one of the first since winter had officially ended a few days before. He kept his eyes focused on the leather heels of his father's work boots as he shuffled along the faint trail. From time to time, a thorny hand of greenbrier tried to grab his flannel, but other than that, the walking was flat and easy. Occasionally, when he would look up, glimmers of the New River reflected through the trunks of the oaks, sycamores, and scrubby white pines. Behind him, if the trees hadn't been in the way, he would have been able to see the rounded peaks of the Blue Ridge Mountains surrounding the valley.

Mr. Carlson had woken Clifton early on that Saturday morning. Clifton was confused and still half asleep when his father had said, "Come on, lazy bones. We're going for a hike. Your mama's already packed us sandwiches." Clifton had gotten dressed, brushed his teeth, and had barely downed a piece of toast before his father pushed him out the door. Mr. Carlson had a knapsack slung over his shoulders that held their food and water for the outing, and it swayed from side to side as they left their house on the corner and crossed Kamron Street—a street that during the week was dangerously busy and crowded with logging trucks and mill traffic. But on this Saturday morning, things on Kamron Street were slow. They quickly crossed and left their neighborhood.

Within minutes, they were walking down a calm residential road that was lined on both sides with big brick homes and perfectly manicured lawns. A fancy sign at the entrance to the neighborhood read WINDSWEPT HILLS. Somehow, the grass was already green and cut uniformly to match that of each neighbor's. Patches of crocus had popped their heads from thickly mulched beds, and tall stalks of unbloomed daffodils reached toward the sun, ready to open at any moment. A trio of Mexican men worked like bees as they scurried across one lawn in particular, setting up sprinklers and spreading fertilizer, which ruined the otherwise fine spring smell of the morning. Clifton couldn't help but think of his own scraggly lawn back home, only a few blocks away, which was still brown and dormant.

At the entrances to some of the twisty driveways stood concrete statues of lions or sleek racing dogs sitting atop pillars. The difference between the neighborhood on this side of Kamron Street and his own was striking. As Clifton walked alongside Mr. Carlson, with the top of his head barely reaching his father's bellybutton, he looked to the far side of the street to see a man getting a newspaper from his mailbox. The man wore a short-sleeve collared shirt with a tiny alligator or lizard—Clifton couldn't tell which—attached in the exact same spot that his father had *Jim* stitched in cursive on his blue factory shirt. His pants were red and white and looked as if they'd been fashioned from a picnic tablecloth. His arms and neck were bright pink as if he'd recently spent too much time on the golf course, and a circle of burned skin on the top of his head contrasted sharply with the horseshoe of white hair surrounding it. The man had the paper halfway out of the box when he noticed them approaching. He turned to stare at the two pairs of boots clomping along the asphalt. Mr. Carlson nodded at the man and said, "Howdy." Clifton mimicked his father with a smile and said the same. The man scanned Mr. Carlson's worn jeans and factory shirt for a second, looked at the boy at his side, then pulled out the paper nervously and headed back up his driveway without a word.

Clifton suddenly felt uncomfortable. When they'd distanced themselves from the driveway, Mr. Carlson said with a hint of disdain, "The folks that live over here are the big boys, little man. Most of 'em don't even work in Crocket's Mill. They're bigwigs that have fancy jobs in Samford but moved over here to get away from the city. But I was living in Crocket's Mill long before any of these houses were even built. When we were boys, we'd tromp through here when it was nothing but woods on our way to the Palisades. To jump off the rocks."

Clifton looked back to sneak another peek at the man. From the safety of his front porch, the man stared back at them with guarded suspicion. Though Clifton was still too young to understand why, he was perceptive enough to recognize that Kamron Street divided the two sides of Crocket's Mill as perfectly as a sharp blade through a ripe orange.

"Daddy, how come we're going to the woods this way?" he asked when they reached the end of the road. They were faced with a thick stand of trees along the bowled edge of a cul-de-sac. A trail eerily disappeared into the darkness of the woods. "Seems like it would've been easier if we'd just gone through town. I don't like it over here on this side."

Mr. Carlson kicked at the stone curb with the bottom of his boot and smiled as he looked down at his son. "Wanted to shake things up a little today, boy. Got something I wanna show you. And we can't get to it by going through town. Have to go through Mr. White Man's neighborhood to get to the Killing Pit." Mr. Carlson turned away and looked into the tall grove of poplars that stood like a platoon of skinny soldiers waiting for orders.

The Killing Pit. The name thrilled and haunted Clifton at the same time. He turned around and looked at the neighborhood behind him and then again into the depths of the foreboding woods. Just as the rich man's bald spot had contrasted sharply with the white of his hair, the fancy houses were doing the same thing in opposition to the backdrop of the menacing trees. And while the line of distant mountain ridges behind the houses took on a peaceful blue hue, a chill prickled Clifton's arms despite the warmth of the sunshine. "The what?"

"The Killing Pit," said Mr. Carlson. The smile had dissipated and his tone had gone stern. "It's something I want you to see. My own daddy took me to it when I was about your age, and I didn't never forget it. Now it's your turn."

The chill stayed with Clifton, and he felt nerves begin swirling in his stomach, mixing and churning. Something about that name, and his father's behavior, made him want to turn back.

"Come on, let's go. It's barely half a mile." His father stepped over the curb and was swallowed up by the darkness of the forest in a matter of seconds. Clifton hesitated for only a moment, then realizing he was all alone, darted into the trees to catch up.

As THEY VENTURED deeper into the woods, the only thing he saw around him were trees. Lots of trees. Whereas earlier, when the leaves had noisily shuffled around their feet, now the ground was covered with a soft blanket of dead pine needles that made the walking silent. In fact, everything was silent. No birds chirped, no squirrels bounded from branch to branch, the wind didn't even stir. And it was dark. Here and there, a column of sunshine worked its way through the canopy and shined a spot of light on the ground, but for the most part the branches and limbs had laced their twisted, gnarled fingers together to form a natural blockade. He stayed directly behind his father but would have preferred to have walked right next to him. The narrow path, however, didn't present that option.

After fifteen minutes of walking (the whole time of which his father never uttered a word) they finally stopped. He looked around to see why this particular spot was more significant than any other, but he couldn't distinguish anything out of the ordinary. But then he noticed a faint path that branched off the main one.

"Right over there is the Killing Pit," whispered Mr. Carlson. He squatted down so he was eye-level with his son. He took a sip from the canteen in the knapsack and handed it over. As Clifton took a drink, Mr. Carlson pointed to his right and whispered again. "Not too many people even know it's here. You see it?"

Clifton peered into the dankness of the woods. He didn't know why his father was whispering, but for some reason it made everything seem even creepier. More serious. Clifton whispered back, "No, sir. I don't see it."

"Look closer. See that dark circle over there by that stand of rhododendron?"

Clifton squinted even though his vision was perfect. At first, he still didn't see anything. But then, about fifty yards away, he did see something just above the ground that was circular in shape. The waxy green leaves of the rhododendron seemed to be protecting it. At first he'd thought it was just a pile of rotting logs, but now he realized that it was man-made. He nodded. "Yes, sir—I see it."

"That's the Killing Pit. If we went straight on down the main path, that'd bring us out by the Palisades. You know, those big rocks along the river I was telling you about that I used to jump from. But this way," he said, motioning with his head, "takes you to the Killing Pit. Come on, let's go take a look."

Clifton followed his father as they traipsed across the pine needles, their boots kicking and dismembering mushrooms from the damp earth as they went. A moist, earthy smell, an odor that could be found only in the deep woods, filled Clifton's head. He could almost taste the pine needles that seemed to be simmering with the warmth of spring. They were now following the fainter path, something that resembled an abandoned deer trail. When they reached the Killing Pit, Mr. Carlson stopped, though the trail kept on going.

"Where does this path go to?" asked Clifton as he stopped next to his father. He hadn't yet looked at the Killing Pit to his left.

"You don't want to go any farther than this. There's a little dirt road once you start heading down the hill. Then, if you cross it, there are a few scattered houses near the banks of the river. But you don't have no business going down in there." He then put his foot on the edge of the circular rock wall, which was about two feet tall and approximately twelve feet in circumference. It reminded him of an old well that he'd seen in a nursery rhyme book his mother used to read to him, except there was no bucket or crank above the hole. The stones were stacked neatly atop one another and covered in a slick green slime. When Clifton rested his foot on the edge, imitating his father, the sole of his shoe slipped right off.

"Careful, there, little man. That's about the last place you want to fall."

Clifton looked down into the black hole and at first saw nothing but darkness. They dropped to their knees on the forest floor and rested their hands atop the slippery rocks as they peered into the maw. After a few seconds of staring, Clifton's eyes readjusted. About twenty feet down, though it was nearly impossible to judge distance, he was suddenly able to make out a patch of blue sky sitting at the bottom. And then, when he moved his head, he saw the blurry reflections of both him and his father. Depending on how he focused his eyes, he could also see a layer of decaying leaves below the surface of the water.

"Here," said Mr. Carlson, holding a rock in his hand. "Drop this down there."

He grabbed the rock, no bigger than a tennis ball, and let it fall. The stone smashed his reflection, and a hollow *kerplunk* echoed its way up the shaft. The heads of Clifton and his father fractured into hundreds of tinier versions as the water rippled and splashed off the sides of the retaining walls. An acrid smell, like something from the bowels of a septic tank, drifted up and settled on the roof of his mouth and the back of his throat.

"What is this place?" He kept his eyes trained on the water as things slowly returned to calm. He could barely make out the rock resting on the bed of rotting leaves. "An old well or something?"

"No, this ain't no well. It's the Killing Pit. Back in the day, back during slave times, white men would sometimes bring a couple of slaves here. Even though slavery wasn't too bad in this part of Virginia, not like in the Tidewater or down in the deep South, it was still around. In fact, there's a grave on the other side of Samford, out in the country, where a slave owner was buried standing up because he said he wanted to watch over his slaves even after he died. But that's another story. With the Killing Pit, what they'd do is drop a rope ladder and then two slaves climbed down into it. Then they were forced to fight each other while the white men stood around and watched. They'd make bets on who would win. It was like a big party for them."

Clifton looked at his father and then back down into the pit. The walls were lined from top to bottom with moss and lichen-covered stones. Cobwebs clung to the sides, and thin-papered egg sacs hung lifelessly from the ends like shriveled balloons on weathered strings. Creeping vines snaked their way into crevices, their curled tendrils taking hold wherever they could.

"How did they know who won?" He tried to imagine two dark bodies slopping around down there, punching and pounding on each other, probably up to their knees in tannic rain water.

His father looked him squarely in the eye. The tight muscles along his jaw line twitched. The rims of his wide nostrils flared like a horse's, almost imperceptibly, as he repeated his son's words. "How did they know who won? Well, it's kind of like chess." Mr. Carlson had started teaching Clifton how to play chess when he was only four years old. His father wasn't necessarily book-smart, but when it came to a chessboard, he was a professor. Clifton felt pretty sure that his father, no matter what the topic of conversation, could somehow manage to tie chess into it. "In chess, only one man can win."

"Unless there's a stalemate," said Clifton proudly, trying to show off his knowledge. And also to ease the tension in the air.

"Yeah, but there weren't any stalemates in this game," said Mr. Carlson. The way he said it, the darkness of his tone, set the fine hairs of Clifton's arms on end. "Only checkmates. And in this case, the black side always lost."

"What do you mean?"

"When one man killed the other, Clifton. It was a fight to the death. The ladder wasn't lowered back down until they were sure that one of the men was dead."

Clifton felt another shiver pass through his body. Could he really be standing over a hole where men had once killed each other? He still didn't quite grasp the situation. "Why? Did the slave men not like each other?"

Mr. Carlson's face didn't change. It was as cold, as hard, as untelling as the rocks lining the pit. "No, boy, they might've liked each other just fine. But they liked life better, I reckon, so they had to do something unthinkable if they wanted to keep on living it. I've even heard stories of brothers having to fight each other down there. Those were bad times."

Clifton felt himself getting nervous and uncomfortable. He wanted to get out of the woods and back to the warmth of the sunshine. Back to the safety of his home and neighborhood. "They don't ... I mean ... they don't do that anymore, do they? White men don't come here anymore, right?"

Mr. Carlson, for the first time, looked away as if thinking deeply about something. He seemed to be staring farther down the faint path toward the hidden houses on the riverbank. "No, not anymore," he said. "Well, not exactly, anyway."

Clifton wanted to ask him what he meant, but somehow he sensed that his father wouldn't offer up an explanation. So instead, he picked a few acorns off the mattress of leaves and pine needles and dropped them, one by one, into the pit.

His father pulled out a cigarette from the pack in his shirt pocket and lit it. The smell of the smoke comforted Clifton. After a moment of silence, his father continued. "When my daddy first took me here, I was about your age. It was a different time than it is now, but it ain't all that much different. Daddy brought me here to make me understand the struggles that black people have had to overcome. He wanted me to see how you gotta fight every day of your life. Now don't get me wrong—things are better than they used to be. Way better. But it ain't perfect. And for you, little man, it's always gonna be a fight."

Clifton swallowed hard. He wanted to leave. He wanted to go home to the security of his mother's arms.

"See, it was tough for me, but it'll be even tougher for you." Mr. Carlson paused as if he didn't want to continue. "You know why?"

Clifton shook his head.

"Because you got a white mama and a black daddy—that's why," said Mr. Carlson. He kept grabbing clusters of dead pine needles and stripping them apart as he spoke, the cigarette knuckled in his right hand. "Ain't nothing gonna come easy for you. Now, your mama didn't want me to bring all this up. Begged me not to. But it's important. You gotta know this stuff. And the earlier, the better. Life ain't always fair, and for some it's more unfair than for others. It wasn't fair for the two slaves who had to fight each other while people stood above them, drinking whiskey and betting money on one or the other like they was a couple of banty roosters or wild dogs. You got me?"

Clifton nodded but he didn't really understand. That is, he understood what his father was saying, but he didn't understand how other human beings could have been so cruel and callous.

"Life's just like this Killing Pit here, boy. We all start at the bottom of it and then have to do all we can to fight our way out. And at any moment, even when things seem to be going fine, we can slip and fall right back down to the bottom. You remember that, okay? You keep this day in the back of your mind, just like I did after my daddy took me here. Always do the right thing, be kind and helpful. Don't ever slip down to the level of those men who once stood around this pit, watching others kill like it was a sport or something. But at the same time, don't ever forget that you always gotta fight. You got me?"

Clifton nodded again.

"They say if you dig through the rotting sludge down there, you'll find layers of old bones and skulls."

Finally, Clifton spoke. "Can we go home? You're scaring me, Dad."

Mr. Carlson stood up and started to flick his cigarette down the shaft. But then he hesitated as if he'd just thought of something important. He stubbed it out on the moist slime of the wall instead, where the tip sizzled like sweat on a hot muffler. He then flipped the butt into a copse of ferns that wiggled and danced in a nonexistent breeze.

As Clifton walked back through the woods toward home, with Mr. Carlson keeping a comforting hand on his tiny shoulder, hundreds of things filtered through his mind. Up until that point, he'd always thought of the world as a wonderful and happy place. He'd never once thought about his parents being from different races. To him, they were just his parents. Two people who loved each other and loved him unconditionally. He'd been colorblind and thankful for it. But now his view had changed. The world was full of different colors, and that wasn't necessarily a good thing.

And then, close to a month after his visit to the Killing Pit, Clifton's view of the world changed even further when he witnessed his father beaten to death by two white policemen.

So NOW, with his box of bottles that each held a message, Clifton walked through that same rich neighborhood toward the woods—the woods he'd entered only that one time with his father so many years before. He felt a disconcerting tug in his stomach as he left the neighborhood and an even more uncomfortable stab when he approached the side trail leading to the Killing Pit. The trail was a bit more overgrown now than it had been years before, yet it was still easily traversable. But he refused to veer off, instead sticking to the main path that led down the rugged mountainside toward the Palisades. For a moment he thought about making a detour and going to the Killing Pit, but for some reason he decided against it.

He was afraid that if he went too close, it might bring back solemn memories that he didn't want to relive. Going to the Killing Pit, he reasoned, might be too similar—in some strange way—to visiting his father's grave, which he'd done only once before. And once had been enough.

At the bottom of the hill, he crossed a dirt road, then a set of train tracks, and then climbed the steep outcrop of limestone that jutted out over the New River. The impressive rock formation stood like the spire of a castle. It stood, in fact, like a rook on a chessboard. It was from there, at the top of the Palisades, that his father had jumped with his friends as a boy on hot summer days.

After he reached the top of the promontory and caught his breath, he began heaving the bottles, one by one, over the edge. He watched as they whooshed by the sheer rock face, only to land with a loud splash a good thirty feet below. Then they bobbed down the river like a green crystalline flotilla, as if they were a motherless flock of baby ducks that he'd nurtured and then released. When one of the bottles caught a glimmer of fading sunshine, it was like a signal saying that it and the rest of the flock were going to be okay. Like a goodbye wave.

As the weeks passed and he continued to launch his bottles, it became his ritual to never leave the top of the Palisades until the last one had disappeared around the final bend. He'd found the bottle ritual to be a far better way of paying respects to his father than by standing next to a cheap headstone, the tablet poking out of the earth and etched with HERE LIES JAMES CLIFTON CARLSON. For some reason, knowing that his father had once jumped off those cliffs gave him a sense of comfort. Almost as if his father were now watching over him. At any rate, he found it to be far better than having to see his own birth date chiseled into a cold piece of stone.

THOUGH THE NOTES in the bottles were never exactly the same, they were always pretty similar.

Hello. My name is Clifton Carlson. I'm sixteen years old and I'm looking for something. I have no idea what I'm looking for, but I know it's something. If you find this note, that probably means you were looking for something too. I hope you'll write me a letter and tell me about your—self. Tell me where and how you found the bottle. Things like that. I mean, if you find it, then

*that means we're connected in some sort of way.
Maybe that's what I'm searching for, some kind
of connection. I don't know. But please write.
Thanks.*

After each note, Clifton signed his name and put his address at the bottom. He imagined that after his bottles reached the Gulf of Mexico, maybe they'd find their way to South America or at least Cuba. Maybe Haiti or something like that. But after several weeks of trying, he still hadn't received the first letter. By the time school let out in early June, and still his mailbox was empty every day, he decided he would've been happy to just get a letter from West Virginia, since the water from the New River actually flowed north before connecting with the Kanawha, then the Ohio, and finally the Mississippi. He'd even have been happy if he'd just gotten a letter from somewhere else in Virginia.

But then, two weeks into summer break, Clifton opened the mailbox, sifted through the bills and junk mail, and was readying for disappointment once again when he saw a wrinkled envelope addressed to him in sloppy, almost elementary handwriting.

Chapter 4

EARLIER IN THE DAY, before Clifton found the letter, the odor of stale beer and old cigarettes had hovered in the kitchen when he walked in to look for something to eat. It was a smell he'd gotten so used to that he didn't even think about it anymore. A couple of empty beer bottles were scattered around the table, many serving as receptacles for his mother's cigarette butts. A crumpled pack of Marlboro Lights rested on a dirty bread plate that was crusted with the remnants of Chinese food. Dried rice, resembling pellets of hard white mouse droppings, littered the table. By the looks of the mess, it appeared that his mother must have had difficulty finding her mouth the night before. Cockroaches scurried around the floor at his feet. Their antennae, bent and twitching, helped them to quickly find hiding places in the cracks between the wall and baseboards until Clifton disappeared.

He opened the refrigerator, hoping that maybe he'd find a little waxed carton of leftover sweet and sour pork or fried rice, but there was nothing. All he saw was a quart of milk, several bottles of wine, some bread, a jar of mustard, an open box of baking soda, and something grayish-green in a plastic container that had been sitting there for at least three weeks. In the freezer he found a frozen French bread pizza that he pulled out and stuck in the microwave. As the pizza cooked, he filled a glass with water from the sink and walked into the living room to turn on the TV.

Not surprisingly, he found his mother stretched out on the couch instead of in her bedroom, her head turned to the side and her mouth agape, sleeping soundly. The crimson throw pillow under her head showed a dark circular stain where a drizzle of spit had leaked from her lips. A thin blanket covered her upper body, but her pasty legs crept out from the bottom edge. Clifton couldn't help but notice that his mother looked old. She was still pretty in a way but looked prematurely haggard. Her skin hung looser on her face, and a pair of defined lines, not exactly wrinkles, stretched from the bottom of her nose to each side of her mouth. She'd aged in precisely the way that eight years of depression, drinking, and smoking will do to a person.

A glass and an empty bottle of wine sat on the corner of the end table, and an ashtray piled high with last night's contributions was in the middle, serving as the centerpiece. Mrs. Carlson's labored breath rattled from somewhere deep in her chest as Clifton grabbed the remote and turned on the television. He didn't bother to lower the volume, and it didn't seem to trouble Mrs. Carlson in the least. She stirred for a moment and said, "Hey, baby," in a rough voice before turning over and going back to sleep.

He flipped through the four available channels, but the only things on were early-afternoon soap operas. He wished his mother would turn the cable back on, but she'd claimed at the beginning of the year that they could no longer afford it. He eyed the empty wine bottle on the table and wondered where the money for that had come from.

He stared blankly at the screen as a buxom woman dressed in a low-cut nurse's uniform tried to clean the wounds of a man who'd crashed his motorcycle. Apparently the man had once been the nurse's lover, but he'd abandoned her for a fashion model. The nurse's dilemma was whether she should try to help him or just let him suffer for a while. In the end she decided to assist, but seemed to enjoy his pain as she applied rubbing alcohol to the deep abrasions on his handsome face.

When the microwave bell sounded, Clifton killed the television and went to get his food. He cleared away a space at the kitchen table, then ate his pizza as he stared out the window at the neighbor's dog. Bosco, half-black Lab, half-chow, sat chained to the metal post of a clothesline, his rounded snout fiercely gnawing at a large bald spot near the base of his tail. In the three years since Clifton's neighbor, Mr. Henderson, had gotten Bosco, he couldn't remember ever seeing the dog anywhere except right where he was at that moment. Day and night he sat chained to the metal post. He had worn a perfectly symmetrical circle around the post, and shooting off from the circle was a bare-patched swath of red clay that led to his doghouse. The entire area looked like the outline of a giant lollipop.

It was from Bosco that Clifton had collected the dogshit surprise that he'd left in Colt's locker. For his next attack, once school started back in the fall, he had thought about trying to scrape some fleas from the dog's back. He would collect them in a Ziploc bag and then somehow sneak into the football team's locker room and dump them into Colt's jockstrap. It was one of the many ideas, along with trying to come up with a library of insults about Colt's mother, that occupied him during his long, lonely days of summer. But that plan was still months away.

Often, he would stroll over to Mr. Henderson's yard while the man was at work and play with Bosco. It gave him something to do and Bosco seemed to enjoy it. *At least*, thought Clifton as he watched the dog continue to bite at himself, this time at his crotch, *the fleas give him something to do all summer. That's more than I can say.*

He finished his pizza and tossed the box into the overflowing trash can under the sink. Since he knew he'd eventually get scolded if he didn't take the bag to the trash can in the carport, he decided to go ahead and do it now and save his mother the breath.

He pulled the bag out and nearly gagged when something rank and rotten crept into his mouth and nostrils. It was as if he'd stuck his nose to an ashtray filled with cigarette butts and tuna fish oil and then tried to snort the whole mixture. He could nearly taste the odor in the back of his throat. He spun the bag around to close it, and hustled out the side door to the carport. A fist of mid-June humidity punched him in the face as soon as he left the comfort of the air conditioning. Beads of sweat instantly balled on his forehead.

The rusty steel garbage can sat in the corner next to his mother's beat-up Dodge. Holding his breath, he swooshed away the green-headed flies swarming over the lid with his free hand, grabbed the handle, and dropped the bag in. The can was nearly full, so he had to push down on the bag with both hands, as if giving it CPR, to make it fit. He forced the lid back on and then ran out of the carport to the edge of the driveway where he exhaled and then sucked in the hot, humid air.

Though it was still an hour before noon, it was already in the mid-eighties and the humidity near 100 percent. The air was so thick that it was truly hard to breathe; it was so thick that he could almost see it. Clifton chastised himself for not getting up earlier, but he'd fallen into a routine that he knew he'd regret once classes started. He'd been sleeping in to ten or eleven ever since school had ended. At the beginning of summer vacation, he'd promised himself that he was going to get up early while it was still cool and try to go fishing every morning down at the New. Then, once the day warmed up and became unbearable, he'd slip back to the sanctity of the air-conditioned house, take a nap, then go back to the river in the evenings and fish some more.

That had been the plan anyway. And though he did do that for the first few days of the summer break, it didn't take long to slide into a different routine. Part of the problem with waking up early was that his mother was usually still up drinking her breakfast. Mrs. Carlson worked across the river, doing third shift at the Volvo factory in the industrial section of Samford; she didn't get off until seven a.m. Then she'd come home and drink until she fell asleep. She'd sleep through the day, get up in the early evening, get showered and dressed, and then go back to work. She had no social life at all and had never dated anyone since Mr. Carlson had died, which was fine with Clifton. He didn't want some strange man coming into his life who might try to take the place of his father.

Although she had become less and less of a mother as he got older, he still loved her. And he knew she loved him. She still doted on him, worried about him all the time, and did the best she could with what she had. At first, once reality had set in and they'd both come to grips that Mr. Carlson wasn't coming back, she'd done her best to console him. But early on Clifton withdrew so deeply into himself that no one could get in—not even her.

He knew that his father's death was part of the reason he didn't have any friends. When he'd first gone back to school after the incident, some of the kids (still innocent enough at that age to show compassion instead of cruelty) had tried to reach out to him. But he'd refused their efforts by choosing isolation over friendship. He'd refused to accept the compassion they offered. So after a while, his classmates had learned to stay away, in the same way someone learns pretty quickly to keep a distance from a skittish dog. After a couple of years, he slowly began to pull out of his depression, but by then it was too late. His peers had gotten used to the idea that Clifton was a pariah, and, unfortunately for him, the barriers of adolescent cliques had already been established.

As he'd pulled out of his depression, accepting his role as a loner, accepting his father's death, his mother had begun to slip deeper and deeper into another world. It was as if she had given everything of herself during those first two years to make sure that Clifton was going to be okay. But once she realized that he was, she gave up on herself, knowing she didn't have the strength to save the both of them. She'd chosen to deal with her pain by hiding within the opaque walls of a bottle. A wall of glass that only seemed to grow and thicken with each passing year, like tree sap that congeals around a wound until the tree appears, at least to the casual observer, to be completely healed. But Clifton knew she hadn't healed at all.

When she was drinking, she'd often reminisce about the good times when her husband had still been alive. And as bad as that was for Clifton, it could have been worse. Thankfully, she wasn't a mean drunk. She never got violent. And as much as he didn't like her drinking, he also understood she did it because she was hurting.

So he didn't blame her. Instead, he blamed the two police officers, especially Scarface. He blamed them for everything. Even blamed them for things that they had nothing to do with. If a carton of milk spoiled, he'd sometimes get so angry that he might fling the container across the room, screaming and yelling profanities. If he made a mistake on a test at school, he'd sometimes fly off into an inexplicable rage, storming out of the classroom. Oftentimes, when he'd lie awake in his bed at night, he'd plot ways to get his revenge on the cops in the same way that he devised pranks against Colt. But whereas his mischief toward Colt was more or less harmless, his ideas concerning the cops were anything but. When he was old enough, he told himself, he'd get them back. One way or another, he'd avenge his father's death.

So he blamed the cops, not his mother, for everything that went wrong in his life. He understood that she didn't have any other family except Clifton and that she did the best that she could. It was just the two of them. She worked hard, paid the bills, and kept food on the table—at least she usually did. But at the same time, as much as Clifton loved her, he didn't like being around her when she was drinking. During the school year, he'd wake up and leave the house about the same time she got home from work. But during the summer, it was a different story. That's why his fishing plans hadn't worked out as well as he'd hoped. By staying locked up in his room until she passed out, he'd more or less fallen into a schedule of avoidance.

AFTER HE DISPOSED of the garbage bag and then sucked in a little fresh air while standing on the gravel of the driveway, he went down to the mailbox to see if anything had come. And that's when he found the letter. There was no return address, but the postmark was stamped Crocket's Mill.

Clifton ran inside, left the rest of the mail on the kitchen table, and then went to his room to open the letter. He sat on his unmade bed, looked for a moment at an outdated, wrinkled poster of Darth Vader holding a light saber—a poster that he couldn't bring himself to take down—and then slowly began opening the envelope. He was nervous and anxious. He couldn't remember the last time he'd received something in the mail. In fact, he couldn't really remember ever receiving anything in the mail except letters from school about his deviant behavior. And those weren't ever addressed to him, they were only *about* him. He'd always made sure to intercept those and had become an expert at forging his mother's signature.

He had once asked his mother why he never received anything from his grandparents on his birthday. It had been the first anniversary of the beating, and he was still having a difficult time dealing with things. His mother had taken him to the McDonald's over in Samford and then made a fresh batch of brownies to celebrate his birthday, trying her best to conceal her own misery.

"Why in the world do you ask something like that?" she'd said when Clifton posed the question. "Me and your daddy always tried to give you things."

"I was just wondering," he'd said as tears formed in his eyes.

"Lots of kids at school say they get presents from their grandparents on their birthdays. At Christmas and stuff."

Mrs. Carlson had turned away for a moment with a subtle, pained look. She brushed the bottoms of her eyes with her finger and said, "Both your daddy's parents passed when he was pretty young. I never met them. And my mama died of cancer shortly after you were born. And my daddy, well, he's just not around anymore."

"Where'd he go?" asked Clifton innocently, the way a child will do, not realizing that she didn't want to talk about it.

"I don't know, Clifton. He's just not around."

"How can't you know where your own daddy is?" he had asked, perplexed.

Mrs. Carlson let out a deep sigh. "Clifton, honey, this is the way it is. My daddy wants nothing to do with me, okay? And I want nothing to do with him. We don't talk anymore."

"How come?"

Tears formed at the corners of her eyes, and black streaks of mascara began trickling down her cheeks. "Because your daddy was black, that's why. He didn't want me marrying a black man. When I did it anyway, he disowned me. Hasn't talked to me in close to ten years."

Clifton stared wide-eyed at his mother. The whole idea of differences in race and the problems it caused, despite the talk he'd had with his father at the Killing Pit, still hadn't really connected in his young mind. "Why does that matter? Who cares?"

"Unfortunately, a lot of people care. My daddy happens to be one of them. It's not right, and it's ignorant, but that's the way it is, Cliffy. A lot of things in this world aren't right, but you just have to learn to deal with them."

Clifton paused for a moment as he absorbed his mother's words. "Don't you at least have some pictures of him? Or any of them? I've never even seen my grandparents."

"There's a picture of you and Mama on my dresser—you know that. You've seen it a hundred times. Taken the day you were born." She paused and wiped at her eyes again. "Taken shortly before she died. All of our . . . our other pictures were lost"—she hesitated again as if thinking deeply about something—"lost in the fire."

Clifton's eyes widened again at the mention of that. "What fire?"

"Don't be silly. I'm sure I've told you about that. Before you were born, your daddy fell asleep one night with a cigarette still burning. Nearly burned the whole house down. You remember those scars on his hand and arm?"

"Yes, ma'am."

"Well, that's how he got them. From a fire. He never liked talking about it. Embarrassed him. Anyway, we lost all our picture albums."

"But I thought he—"

"Now how about we get you some of those brownies for dessert?"

In his young mind, Clifton had felt confused as a faint memory of his father's scars tugged at him, but the promise of brownies easily superseded that thought.

But now he had a letter. A letter just for him. He felt foolish and childish, getting excited over something as simple as receiving a piece of mail, but he didn't care. He'd tossed those bottles in the river with hopes of finding something, and now that something had arrived.

Clifton felt his heartbeat increase as the sticky lip of the envelope peeled away. Inside was a piece of notebook paper, folded over on itself three or four times. Clifton pulled it out and began to unfurl it. Just like the address on the envelope, the black-inked writing was almost childlike.

Dear Clifton

I found your bottle and note. I live down on the river. Dont have a post address but I live on the river. If you know where the Palisades is, I live downstream. Or you can go to old Henrys dock take a left and walk the train tracks. Go a mile and my house sits on the hill. Its green. Aint no driveway but the house is green. Cant miss it really. Only one around except old Henrys. My names Swamper. Im 65 and mostly I fish. Hope to meet you.

Swamper

Clifton shook with excitement. Someone had found one of his bottles. It wasn't exactly from West Virginia or Cuba, but Clifton realized maybe this was better anyway. If someone in West Virginia or Cuba had found it, he'd never be able to meet them. But this was different. This man lived close by. He could actually meet the person who found it. He'd never even thought about that before. He'd figured he'd get a letter, write the person back, and then that would probably be the end of it. But now everything had changed.

He sat on the edge of the bed and read the letter again. He had a vague idea of where the house was. Of course he knew where the Palisades was, and he was plenty familiar with Old Henry's. Old Henry was a black man who had a small bait shop on the New River. Clifton had gone there many times with his father, and even now he'd sometimes go and get minnows when he couldn't dig up enough worms. For a dollar, Old Henry would let people fish off his rickety dock, day or night. One of the biggest catfish ever pulled out of the New was caught at Old Henry's. There was a faded picture of it tacked to one of the pine-slatted walls of Henry's shack. Old Henry stood on one side of the fish holding the end of a hickory branch, and a fat, bearded white man stood on the other end, both of them with big grins on their faces. The branch went through the gills of the catfish, and it appeared that the two men were giving it all they had to hold it up. The tail curled and swept the boards of the dock despite the men's best efforts to hoist it. It had always been Clifton's dream to catch a fish that big. Every time he went into the shop, he'd stare longingly at that picture while he waited for Old Henry to net him a bag of minnows from one of the holding tanks.

But now Clifton had a decision to make. He had no address, so he couldn't write this Swamper man back. If he wanted to correspond with him, he'd have to go to his house and search him out. *But should I?* he thought as he got off his bed and began pacing around his room. He stepped over wadded-up clothes that hadn't made it to the hamper, holding the letter as he read it a few more times. *What if he's some crazy man living out in the woods? What if he's some weirdo who wants to lock me up in his attic? Crazier things have happened.*

You're being ridiculous. Maybe, but remember that kid from over in Bent Mountain who got kidnapped by some wacko farmer a few years ago? Kept him hidden away in a potato cellar for a year and a half? Didn't feed him anything but bread, peanuts, and Kool-Aid? Yeah, I remember, but come on. This Swamper guy's probably just a lonely old man who found your bottle. He's just writing you back like you asked him to. He's sixty-five. What's your problem? My problem is I don't want to be the next kid in the news. That's my problem.

Clifton carried on similar conversations with himself for the next half-hour, playing out different scenarios in his mind. But finally he decided he might as well check out the house. He didn't have to go up to the door. He could just scout it out, maybe get a glimpse of the man, and then make a decision. Besides, his curiosity was killing him.

Clifton went outside and grabbed his fishing pole from the mower shed. *Just to make it look good,* he figured. He had two options on which way to go. Since he had a pretty good idea of where Swamper's house was, if he went toward the Killing Pit, it would take less time. However, if he went through town and toward Old Henry's, it would take longer but he would feel more comfortable. Besides, once he got to Old Henry's, he might be able to ask a few questions about this Swamper man.

Clifton set out down the sidewalk of Kamron Street, his

fishing rod over his shoulder and a plastic bucket hanging off the end of his rod like a hobo with a bindle. The logging trucks roared past him, one after the other, the sweet smell of diesel exhaust filling the air with every step he took. The poplar and oak logs teetered on the backs of the trucks, bouncing and jostling. Bits of bark and pulp littered the street, sticking to patches of rainbow-colored oil slicks as the trucks flew by on their way to the big lumberyards across the river in Samford.

A mile later, he entered Crocket's Mill proper. The town had once been a thriving mill community, with red-brick buildings lining the street on either side. But now, the mill had shut down and a lot of the stores had closed shop, moving across the river, where there was more business. Crocket's Mill still had a locally owned grocery store called Good Enough's, a bank, a couple of gas stations, a Popeyes fried chicken place, a hair salon, and a small post office that had been there since the 1800s. Most necessities were still available in Crocket's Mill, but at a much higher price than could be had if people decided to go across the river into Samford, where there was a Sears, a Kroger, a Kmart, and every fast-food joint known to man.

When Clifton reached the one traffic light in town, he crossed the street in order to avoid going directly past the police station. It had recently been renovated and had a brand-new blue and white façade that sickened him every time he saw it. Ever since the events of that night, whenever he went into town, he refused to cut past the police station. He'd always cross the street and turn his head, choosing to watch his own reflection in the plate glass windows of the antique shop and the now-abandoned hardware store.

He'd seen the pock-faced policeman from time to time—in a town the size of Crocket's Mill, it was impossible not to. Every time Clifton saw the cop, always from a distance, an intense hatred would swell inside of him. *Some day,* he would think to himself, *some day I'll get him back.* But more than the hatred, he felt fear. Scarface scared him more than anything else he could imagine. He knew what the man was capable of. He knew what kind of hate the man had inside of him. And that was also the reason, probably more so than any other, why he avoided walking near the police station. The thought of bumping into Scarface terrified him.

Once on the other side of town, he could see the New River slowly rolling along down below. In the distance was a steel bridge spanning the water that led into Samford. But he turned left down a side street well before that. If he'd taken a right, he would have headed toward the Star Night drive-in and been on the road where his father had been killed. So he gladly took a left.

It didn't take long before the cracked pavement turned to

clay and gravel. The rumbles of the logging trucks back on Kamron Street dissipated, now overtaken by chirping birds and the flittering of grasshoppers in a cornfield on the left side of the road. Behind the cornfields were the heads of the mountains, looming tranquilly in the distance. Bare patches dotted the mountainside where loggers had been clear-cutting. The sporadic patches were ugly and looked as if God had reached down with His fist and snatched up handfuls of trees. Like He'd been pulling weeds out of a huge garden. On the other side of the road, locust trees blocked his view of the river, their trunks laden with poison ivy and Virginia creeper. However, the locusts, and also the oaks and sycamores, helped cast some much appreciated shade. He walked on the edge of the road, looking down at the purple flowers of morning glory that smiled up at him from a ditch, their vines fighting against honeysuckle and goldenrod for prominence and precious sunlight.

A pickup truck rolled up behind him and slowed as it passed. Two white men, both scraggly bearded and wearing oil-smudged baseball caps, nodded at Clifton as he looked over. He waved, and the man in the passenger seat waved back. The truck stopped.

"You headin' to Henry's?" said the passenger, eyeing Clifton's rod. A wad of chewing tobacco swelled in his cheek.

Clifton nodded. "Yes, sir."

"Jump in the back if you wanna," said the man, gesturing with his head toward the bed of the truck.

"That's okay," said Clifton. "I'm almost there now."

"Shoot, son, jump on in. You look hot as hell. We're going there anyways."

Clifton hesitated for a moment and then said, "Okay. Thanks. I appreciate it."

He swept a line of sweat from his forehead and walked to the back of the truck, tossing his rod and bucket in before him. The reel clanged against the bed as he did so, resting against the men's rods and tackle boxes that were bungeed to the side. The bed was rusted-out in spots and there was no tailgate. He sat on the bump of a wheel well, facing the river, and held on to the sidewalls as the truck took off, spinning its tires a little and kicking up a fog of red dust. A plastic cooler sat in the corner, and a couple of crushed beer cans rattled and slid when the truck lurched into motion.

Clifton's body bounced and swung from side to side as the truck hammered over the ruts in the road. He smiled as he watched the white flowers of mountain laurel blur by, thinking that today was going to be a good day. The breeze flew in his face and cooled him. The man had been right: He *was* hot as hell.

After a couple of minutes of driving, the passenger slid the truck's rear window open and yelled to Clifton. "Hey, you mind grabbing me a beer?"

Clifton followed the man's eyes to the cooler. "Sure," he yelled over the whip of the wind. He scooted on his butt across the bed, opened the lid, and pulled out a can of Pabst Blue Ribbon that was buried in ice. He handed the beer to the man through the window.

"Grab one for yourself if you wanna," said the man.

Clifton politely declined, though the thought of something cold to drink did sound enticing, even if it was beer. He'd never tried alcohol before, mostly because of the way he'd seen it affect his mother. It was the same with cigarettes. He despised the smell that seemed to constantly fill his living room. He'd always enjoyed watching his father smoke, but his mother's habit disgusted him. And almost as if on cue, he caught a whiff of smoke trailing from the open window. Sure enough, when he looked into the cab, he saw the driver with a cigarette in his hand.

Five minutes later, the truck rounded a bend and then turned right down an even bumpier road that descended into a hollow toward the river. Henry's bait shop sat at the bottom of the road; its tin roof, turned orange in spots, reflected the bright sunlight. At the bottom of the hill, the truck bounced over the train tracks and then a second later they'd arrived. When the driver parked next to the only other car in the lot, Clifton stood up, gathered his gear, and jumped to the ground.

"Thanks a lot," he said as he came around to the passenger side where the man was getting out.

"Ain't nothing but a thing." He spat on the ground, leaving a stain on the clay like spilled coffee.

"Good luck," said Clifton.

"It's too damn hot to fish right now. Probably won't catch nothing. But a bad day fishing's still better than a good day working." He smiled, showing a bottom row of yellowed teeth. The bulge still protruded from his cheek, but he took a long swig from the can of beer anyway.

"Thanks for the ride," said Clifton, waving to the driver who was now at the back of the truck undoing the bungee cords. The driver, who was quite a bit older than the passenger, raised his hand and nodded but remained silent.

Clifton looked down to the end of the old, leaning dock where a solitary black man was sitting on an upside-down five-gallon bucket, holding a rod pointed at the clouds. Clifton put his own rod over his shoulder and decided that even if he didn't find this Swamper man, he could always come back to Henry's dock and do a little fishing. He had a feeling that the passenger man would probably keep him well entertained.

He turned toward Henry's shop, eyeing the sign that was

fastened to the graying boards of the gable above the porch. HENRY'S BAIT & TACKLE was written in faded block letters. The words were bookended with circular, red and white Coca-Cola emblems designed to look like bottle caps.

As he walked up the warped steps that bowed in the middle, a feeling of calm swept over him. A fat tabby sat on a bench, curled in a ball, and eyed Clifton with no interest whatsoever. He had always loved coming to Henry's, and as he thought about that, a brief remembrance of the first time his father had ever brought him there flashed across his mind. He had walked up those very same steps, probably no more than four years old, holding his father's hand and looking up at him like he was the greatest man on earth. He remembered being ecstatic about getting to go fishing with his father for the first time.

As Clifton set his pail down and leaned his rod against the walls of the shop, the memory didn't make him sad. In fact, it was quite the opposite. He now repeated to himself the same thing he'd thought earlier in the truck. *This is going to be a good day.*

Inside, the shop was gloomy. Sunlight tried to creep through the windows, which were mostly covered in dust on the outside and blocked by iron racks filled with fishing lures, leaders, and hooks on the inside. Despite the lack of light, the overhead fluorescents were turned off. A smell of mildew filled the room, combined with fried pork, which cooked in an oversize fryer in the corner. A transistor radio rested on the counter, and behind the counter sat Old Henry, rocking slowly in a wicker chair, staring at the radio with deep interest and making no acknowledgment that Clifton had entered. The radio buzzed and crackled and Clifton couldn't make out what the newsman said.

"Hey, Mr. Henry," he said rather loudly as he approached the counter. Old Henry had notoriously bad hearing, and the radio, which seemed to be turned all the way up, didn't help matters.

Henry looked up, slightly startled, and squinted at Clifton through the gray light. He pushed himself out of his rocker, his ancient hands squeezing the arms of the chair so hard that the tendons bulged out of his skin. He got up, now slightly hunched over, and slowly shuffled his frail body to the counter as he scratched the wiry gray of his head. His face was dark and wrinkled; it reminded Clifton of a dried-out riverbank after the sun had baked it for a summer. "It's damn craziness, is what it is," said Henry as he turned down the radio. Clifton couldn't tell if Henry was talking to him or just muttering to himself. "You hear what that man was sayin'?"

"No, sir. I just walked in."

"They gone and let that boy go that killed his two buddies a few years back. Probably wasn't no older than you at the time. Let's see, this was probably around 1976 or thereabouts. You probably wasn't even born then, huh?"

Clifton smiled and then nervously picked at the plastic of some wrapped crackers sitting on a counter rack. He crinkled the corner of the package and tried to straighten the display. "No, sir, I was born already. But I was just a baby then."

"Well, let me tell you, young'un. It was quite a little to-do goin' on around here back then. It happened down south, in Alabama I believe, if I got that right. This boy goes off and kills his two best friends. Murders 'em. A boy, same age as you, for no reason kills his two best buddies. Can you figure? And now they gone and let him go. They says he's all fixed up."

Clifton didn't know what to say, so he didn't say anything for a moment. Instead, he just shook his head and continued fumbling with the pack of peanut butter crackers. Every time he entered Henry's shop, he knew it would be an adventure, but the old man seemed to be more out of sorts than usual today. Finally, Clifton asked, "Why'd he end up here in Virginia if it happened way down there?"

"Well, that's why everybody was puttin' up such a stink. When the boy turned eighteen, he was supposed to move to a prison for adults. But their prisons was all overcrowded, so they shipped him up here with a handful of other no-good rascals. That Samford prison is private, you know, so they're willin' to take the scum from the bottom of an old johnboat if there's money in it. They don't give two hoots to hell as long as they're gettin' rich."

"Well, maybe he'll just head on back to where he came from."

"Seems to me that if a state can't control its own people, then they's the ones who got to deal with it. Don't seem right to ship 'em all up here. We got trash fillin' up our landfills from New York City on one hand, and murderers comin' from all over fillin' up our prisons on the other. And what do we get out of it? Nothin' but a damn headache if you ask me." Henry took a sip from a dark brown bottle that he pulled from underneath the counter. Then he put it back and rested his hands on the worn pine countertop. "I don't know what's gonna come from your generation. Goin' around, shootin' each other up, stabbin', doin' grass and drugs. You hear about it all the time over in Samford. And hell, seems like Roanoke's a war zone. Times was, if you had a problem with somebody, you went out back of the schoolyard and fought with your hands. Like men. You whupped him or he whupped you, and that was the end of it. Killin' your best buddies over nothin'? No, sir. Not when I was a young'un."

Clifton nodded. "Yes, sir. It's awful," he said, doing his best to placate the old man without smiling.

"Damn right it's awful," said Henry. And then, without any

warning, as if the subject were completely forgotten, he said, "They say it's gonna rain tomorrow. Should be good for the fishin'. You lookin' for some minners?"

Clifton hadn't been ready for the abrupt shift, but he was thankful for it. "No, sir, I got some worms. Thought I'd head on down the tracks a little ways and try down there."

Henry smiled for the first time, showing a perfectly white and straight set of dentures. Once the topic got on fishing, which it always eventually did, Old Henry's demeanor inevitably changed. "You headin' to Ward's Holler? If you are, go down to the old dam. That's a honey hole if there ever was one. Enough smallmouth and crappie down there to keep you busy. Big cats in the bottom. Like to hang down there under that busted-up concrete. Worms'll do you right down there."

Clifton looked to where the old picture of the giant catfish still hung on the wall, the corners folded over, the image faded and streaked with years of sun. "You think Ward's Hollow has got one like that lurking at the bottom?"

Henry smiled his biggest smile so far. "Don't rightly know, young'un. Fishin' ain't as good as it used to be. Times was, folks would catch 'em close to that size pretty often. Not so much no more. Ever since they stocked the river with muskie years back, fish've gotten smaller. Those mean bastards eat up everythin'. Now that's a fish that'll fight you, but you'll need some steel leader if you're gonna try for them. Got teeth like razors. And smart. But you never can tell. A few months back, some boy was out with his daddy using nothin' but a rinky-dink Donald Duck rod and hooked into a little red-eye. Next thing he knows, as he's reelin' in, a muskie comes and chomps down on the red-eye. Hook gets him right in the corner of the mouth. Ends up haulin' in a twenty-pound muskie. Didn't even have a steel leader. Damndest thing. On a Donald Duck rod. Can you imagine?"

Clifton smiled. "No, not really. Never seems to happen to me."

"That's why they call it fishin', not catchin'. You don't want one of them anyway. Meat tastes like hell. But the only way to make it happen is to get you a wet line. You go on down to Ward's Holler and give her a try. Or a little farther down to the Palisades. You know where that's at?"

"Yes, sir."

"Fish up against them walls. That's some deep water. Goes all the way down to hell. You got smallmouth all up in there. They love them ledges."

Clifton hesitated for a moment, contemplating whether he should ask about Swamper or not. He picked once again at a cracker wrapper and then said, "I was thinking about going a little farther down than Ward's Hollow. Somebody told me there was good fishing down by Swamper's place. You know where his place is at?"

Henry reached down and took another drink from his bottle. "'Course I know where it's at. Not too far past Ward's Holler but before the Palisades. On this side of the water but on the other side of the tracks. Sits on a hill. But the fishin' ain't all that good up there. Ward's Holler's where you want to go."

Clifton paused again. He scratched nervously at an itch in his scalp that wasn't there. "I guess you know Swamper then?"

Henry looked up for a moment as the two men who'd given Clifton a ride entered the shop. "'Course I know him. Known him all my life. He's one of them boys I fought in the school-yard once. 'Course we went to different schools back then, but I know him. He comes in here from time to time. Good enough fella, I reckon. Loves my cracklin. Says I got the best around." He winked at Clifton and said, "And he ain't lyin' about that."

"Hey, Henry," yelled the passenger man who'd entered and now stood by the section of the shop that contained swivels and lead weights. "You got any two-ounce sinkers? The triangle kind? I don't see 'em. Kmart was all out."

Henry looked away from Clifton, his hearing apparently a lot better now that the radio was off. "Kmart? What kinda crackerjack operation you think I'm runnin' here, son? This is a tackle shop. This ain't no Kmart. Course I got 'em. Just hold on a minute." He then looked back to Clifton. "You want

74

anythin', young'un, before I go help that blind, Kmart shopping son of a bitch over there?"

Clifton shook his head with a smile but then stopped. "Actually, yes sir. How about a cup of cracklin?"

"Now you're talkin'. My brother-in-law just slaughtered a hog a few days ago. Better if you kill 'em in the fall, but he don't give a damn. I'll get you a fresh cup." Henry went over to the fryer and dropped a basket into the oil, which immediately popped and snapped. A minute later, he scooped several ladlefuls of hot cracklin into a Styrofoam cup. He secured a plastic lid overtop and handed it to Clifton, his hands shaking slightly. "That'll be one dollar. Best damn cracklin in southwest Virginia. And that ain't no lie."

Clifton reached into the pocket of his shorts and pulled out one of the two dollars he'd swiped from his mother's purse before he left. He placed it in Henry's pink palm, and Henry put it in a steel lockbox underneath the counter, presumably next to his bottle.

"Thanks a lot," said Clifton.

"Come on back," said Henry as he walked toward the passenger man. As Clifton left the store he heard Henry say to the man, "Times was, you couldn't get no lead weights around here from anyone but me. Now with all them Kmarts and such . . ."

He closed the door, placed the cup of cracklin inside his

empty, wormless pail, and grabbed his rod. He glanced down at the solitary black man on the end of the dock who didn't look like he'd moved a muscle. He walked down the steps and then up the drive from where he'd come. When he got to the train tracks, he took a right, smelling the strong odor of creosote on the railroad ties as they stewed in the hot June sun. It can't hurt to go check it out, I guess, he said aloud as he began walking over the gravel between the ties in the direction of Swamper's place.

Chapter 5

AN OVAL OF SWEAT DAMPENED the neck of his T-shirt as he walked along the tracks. Patches of black tar on the ties cooked in the heat. The silver steel of the rails gleamed. *What am I doing? This is crazy. It's not crazy. This is why you tossed all those bottles in the river. Yeah, I know, but it's weird. So what's going to happen? I say, "Hello, I'm Clifton. I wrote the note," and he says, "Oh yeah, nice to meet you." And then what? What am I trying to prove here?*

A faint whistle in the distance finally awoke him from the conversation he'd been having in his head for the last ten minutes. When he turned back toward the train, though he could only hear it and couldn't see it yet, he figured he'd been walking for nearly a mile. And it had all been a blur. He'd been so entranced with talking to himself that he'd paid no attention to where he was going. For a moment, he had a sinking feeling that maybe he'd already passed the house, but then he reassured himself that he couldn't have missed it, despite the daze he'd fallen into.

When the rails began to shimmy and rumble, he hopped off the tracks and switchbacked down the steep gravel embankment to some thickets of rhododendron. Scattered at his feet were pieces of coal that had fallen from previous cars. When he looked back up toward the sloping bank, off to his right, maybe twenty-five yards away, a flicker of something caught his attention. It took him a moment to zero in on the movement, but when he did, and his eyes focused, in the shadows he located a doe, her brown tail twitching occasionally, showing glimpses of white. Her head was bowed to the ground as she foraged through the detritus of the forest. Clifton clicked with his cheek, as if calling a horse, and she sprang to attention. Her head shot up, neck extended, as she looked back toward him. She appeared to see him but didn't act alarmed. Clifton stood perfectly still and admired her grace and beauty. After a moment, she took a few steps closer to the base of the embankment before eating again.

The metallic squeal, like a fork against a car hood, got louder as the train rolled closer. Suddenly he realized that on either side of the doe, not more than four feet away from her, were two more deer, also rummaging for food along the forest floor. They had materialized out of nowhere.

The train whistled again, this time much louder, and the rumble and clicking along the tracks now began its rhythmic, hypnotic beat. One of the deer that had recently appeared, along with the one Clifton had first spotted, propped its head to attention when the whistle screeched, but the third one, a buck with only velvety nubs for antlers, continued eating as if he didn't have a care in the world. As the metronomic hum of the train got louder, the two alert deer effortlessly bounded up the hill and over the tracks to the other side. They stared at Clifton as they stood in the open sunshine a good fifty yards above him, their tan bodies perpendicular to the steep mountainside.

To Clifton's left, the engine turned the corner as the headlight peeked through the trees about a hundred yards away. When he looked back to the buck, it was no longer there. Up the hill, the other two deer still looked back in Clifton's direction. And then, just a little farther down the tracks, he spotted the solitary buck standing in the middle of the crossties, his head down and seemingly foraging for something, but for what, Clifton couldn't imagine. Clifton glanced to his left as the train drew dangerously near, then back to the deer, and repeated the process as if watching a tennis match. Clifton waved his arms and fishing rod, screaming, "Get off the tracks. What the hell're you doing? Get off the tracks."

He felt completely helpless as he watched everything unfold. As the engine screamed past him, the buck still remained stationary. The deer finally looked up, but the train was already on top of him. The engine skewed Clifton's view, so he didn't see the impact, but he felt just as sick as if he had. He couldn't do anything except watch as car after car flashed by in front of him. He could only wait futilely at the foot of the hill as the endless train kept rolling by. Brown painted steel, crested with mounds of chunked coal, whipped past him as bits of dust and wind stung his face. The leaves and branches of the rhododendron clicked against one another. When the rear engine finally passed and the train was swallowed by the mountain around the next bend, Clifton looked down the vacant and lonely strip of track. Everything had gone hauntingly quiet, just as it had been before the interruption. A few birds were singing, but nothing else stirred. He saw no sign of the buck, no mangled pieces, no destroyed and bloody carcass. He looked across the tracks and saw the other two deer, now standing next to some exposed granite a little farther up the hillside, feeding once more.

Clifton climbed the embankment and stood on the railroad ties, the thick, pleasant smell of creosote filling his nose once more. And then, just on the other side, in the bottom along the gravel and rocks that formed the foundation for the tracks, he saw the third deer—standing, his head upright, his velvet-covered antlers looking as soft as down feathers, his tail casually twitching, perfectly content as if nothing had happened.

The buck slowly clambered his way toward the other two, and when they'd regrouped, they trekked up the slope of the hillside as quietly as an owl on the wing, heading toward the plateau of the dirt road up above. Clifton kept his eyes on them, especially on the buck, until they melted into the landscape and vanished. He wondered if the buck had ever realized how dangerously close he'd been to dying.

As Clifton stood on the tracks, he looked around and soaked up the beauty surrounding him: the verdant woods of the forest; the cobalt sky sprayed with white cumulus clouds; the glimmer of the river below; the mockingbirds and cardinals now chirping away; the smell of cracklin emanating from his bucket. Maybe it was the day or maybe it was just the relief he'd felt from not having to witness the death of that deer, but either way, Clifton suddenly felt alive. He felt better than he could ever remember feeling.

When he spied a huge thicket of blackberry bushes running along the opposite side of the tracks, he dropped into the bottom. His feet spilled a little cascade of gravel and coal down the embankment in front of him, and then he immediately began popping the purplish-black fruit into his mouth. The sweet-sour juice trickled from his lips and down his chin as he voraciously picked and stuffed, picked and stuffed. He ate like a feral dog, and he didn't care. He felt alive and ready for an adventure. After ten minutes of gorging himself, he said aloud, as if talking to the blackberries, It's time to go meet Swamper.

Clifton grabbed his rod and pail and scrambled back up the gravel hill to the tracks. He set out walking again, probing between his teeth with his tongue for the little seeds that had gotten stuck there. When he rounded the bend where the train had disappeared, he saw the house.

Tucked into the steep side of the mountain, sitting in the middle of the woods without the slightest hint of a driveway, was Swamper's place. It was surprisingly similar to what Clifton had imagined: a tiny, boxlike, one-story structure with a porch that tilted to one side. A pair of dark, uninviting eyes—where the windows were—stared at him from the green face of the house, daring him to enter through the mouth of the open doorway. The back corner of the roof looked to be damaged by a windblown maple. The tree, which was still alive, leaned against the corner, its dirt-clodded root ball partially exposed. The rim of the brick chimney had all but crumbled away, and an orange slag line ran from its base, staining the scum-covered shingles. In the front yard, if it could be called a yard, was a square patch of turned earth that was Swamper's garden. Potato plants and the hollow stalks of onion popped from the ground in neat rows. The heart-shaped leaves of bean plants covered the far end, and scattered around the perimeter were young lettuce plants the same color as the fleshy pulp of a lime.

When Clifton stopped, his eyes followed the worn path of clay that led from the tracks and up the hill to the front steps of the porch. Clifton's palms were soaked with sweat and he felt his heart beating faster. *I'm not going in there. No way in hell. Screw this.* But before he could turn away and beat it down the line, an elderly man appeared in the doorway. He was tall and thin and had to duck below the door frame as he opened the screen door and walked out onto the porch. His jeans hung off of him loosely, and the sleeves of his flannel shirt were fastened at the wrists despite the heat. His skin looked red to Clifton, as if he'd spent most of his life outdoors, and his hair was as white as cake icing. It wasn't gray or silver, it was bright white. The man cupped his hand to his brow to cut the sun's glare and then craned his head forward as he spotted Clifton standing on the tracks. He lifted his other hand and waved. Clifton waved back with the tip of his fishing rod.

"Going fishing?" yelled the man, now resting a hand against one of the porch posts.

Clifton swallowed and said, "Yes, sir. I was thinking about it."

The man nodded and said, "It's mighty hot right now. Caught me a few this morning when it was still cool. You want something cold to drink? I got a few Coca-Colas in the icebox."

As was his instinct, Clifton hesitated. But then the voice in his head pushed him forward. *Well, go on. It's now or never.* Clifton couldn't understand why he was so nervous. He'd taken a ride an hour before from two perfect strangers who were far more imposing. He'd talked to Henry about fishing, cracklin, and about some crazy released prisoner who'd once killed his best friends. So why was he so nervous about meeting this man?

When Clifton didn't reply, the man spoke again. "You know, if you're trying to get yourself killed, ain't no better way to do it than to just keep standing right where you're at. Next train'll be by in twenty minutes."

Clifton looked down at his feet as he stood on the tracks and then smiled. "I guess you're right. A Coke actually sounds pretty good if you don't mind."

"If I minded, son, I wouldn't have offered you one. Come on up."

Clifton jumped down off the tracks and walked up the beaten trail to the foot of the steps. When he got to the porch, the man extended his hand. "My name's Swamper."

Clifton took the man's hand and shook it. He was surprised by the strength of his grip. "I'm Clifton."

Swamper looked deep into Clifton's eyes, studying them. "Thought you might be. Guess you and me is connected now, just like your note said." Swamper smiled as he released Clifton's hand. It was a warm smile, and it immediately wiped out all of Clifton's previous trepidation. He suddenly felt relaxed and comfortable. It was as if that one smile said they'd known each other their whole lives. "Take a load off and I'll get you that drink," he said, motioning to one of the two homemade shagbark hickory chairs sitting on the porch. "Guess we got some catching up to do."

Clifton set his gear against the house and took a seat. The chair creaked as he did so. He could hear Swamper fumbling around, and from somewhere in the house was the muffled sound of a radio. When a light breeze swept up the hill from the river, the warm, comforting scent of dead pine needles teased his nose. Though the house was a bit rundown, the property itself was beautiful. The house was cut into the steep side of the mountain, so Clifton had a sweeping view of the New River and the valley on the other side. The water flowed slowly under Swamper's dock, which stretched out for about fifteen feet from the muddy shore. Across the river was flatland and floodplain, covered in sycamores, oaks, and pines. A little farther back, Clifton could make out the perfect rectangles of cornfields in the distance, and also the black-and-white forms of cows that looked like four-legged dice as they stood in the open fields. And then at the horizon, off to his right and barely discernible, was the faint outline of some of the larger buildings in Samford. At the moment, as far as Clifton was concerned, the hustle and bustle of that city might as well have been a million miles away.

When Swamper came back out, he handed Clifton a miniature glass bottle of Coca-Cola. It fit his hand perfectly. It was ice cold, and when he took a swig, it immediately wiped away the dust and heat that had been collecting in his throat all day. He swished his second swallow around in his cheeks and dislodged the last bothersome blackberry seed.

Swamper sat down in the other chair and took a drink from his own bottle. "I can't stand to drink a Coke out of those plastic bottles they seem to put everything in these days. Can't stand it. Some things are just meant to be drunk out of glass. Milk is one. Coke's another."

"Yes, sir. It's awfully good."

Swamper looked out at the river and Clifton did the same. "Don't get too many visitors out this way. It's nice to have some company every once in a blue moon."

Clifton took another sip off the bottle. "It's beautiful here."

"Gets lonely sometimes, but I kinda like it." He nodded toward the doorway. "Got my radio to keep me company though. That's how I get most of my news. For some reason, I can't seem to get a paperboy to deliver out this way." Swamper didn't break a smile, and Clifton wasn't sure if he should laugh or not. Swamper recognized Clifton's awkwardness because he eyed him and said, "Relax, son. That was a joke." And that seemed to crack the ice. Clifton laughed and Swamper joined him as they both again looked out at the countryside. Other than the distant buildings of Samford, and a few farmhouses in the fields below, there was nothing else in sight that was man-made. "Was just listening to it right before you got here. Newsman was saying they just released this fella from the Samford Penitentiary. Apparently some of the old church ladies around here got their panties up in a wad over it."

"Yes, sir," said Clifton. "Old Henry was just telling me all about it."

"Old Henry Motley," said Swamper with a chuckle. "Hell, now that's a crazy old bastard. Nuttier than a fruitcake, but he's salt of the earth. I've known him all my life."

"That reminds me," said Clifton as he got up from his chair, now feeling more relaxed thanks to Swamper's easygoing demeanor. He went over to his pail and bent down. "I got you a present."

"A present? I don't need no present. Finding your bottle in the river was present enough."

Clifton grabbed the Styrofoam cup and handed it to Swamper. "Got you some cracklin. Old Henry said you loved it."

Swamper took the cup, removed the lid, and swirled it under his nose as if it was a glass of fine wine. He looked at Clifton and said, "I sure appreciate it." The look in his warm eyes told Clifton that he really meant it and wasn't just being polite. There were plenty of people who would thank you up and down if you handed them a rotting opossum carcass from the side of the road. Clifton had a feeling Swamper wasn't that way. He seemed to be a straight shooter, and Clifton liked that.

Swamper suddenly got up and went inside. He came back a second later with two fresh bottles of Coca-Cola, a stainless steel bowl, and a big smile on his face. "Can't eat cracklin without something cold to drink." He poured half the cup of greasy pork rinds into the bowl and handed them to Clifton. He kept the cup for himself. "Hot damn, they're even still warm."

They began crunching on the fried pork and sucking the grease from their fingers. Swamper slurped loudly, then moved the mishmash of pork from side to side in his mouth like working a plug of tobacco. Between bites he said, "Used to have a couple of neighbors upriver a little ways. But they're dead and gone now. Pretty much just me and Old Henry along this stretch."

Clifton nodded as he worked on a mouthful and wiped his hands along the sides of his shorts. "I live on the other side of town. Just me and my mom."

Swamper nodded. "Yep, I know."

This took Clifton aback for a second. How could he know that? With a quizzical look he said, "You do? How'd you know it's just me and my mom?"

The wrinkles on Swamper's face compressed together for a quick instant, as if he'd just put his lips to a carton of spoiled milk, but he recovered instantly. "No ... not about *who* you live with ... about *where* you live. You left your address in the bottle, you know?" He methodically popped another piece of cracklin into his mouth. "I've lived in Crocket's Mill all my life. I know where that's at."

Clifton smiled, strangely relieved. For some reason, he didn't want to have to bring up his father. Or his lack of a father. "I've got neighbors all over in my neighborhood. Must be nice to have the river down there and nobody to bother you."

Swamper spat a rubbery piece of fat into the air and over

the railing. "Like I said, gets lonely sometimes, but I wouldn't trade it. Used to walk down to Tommy's place and play cards and drink with him sometimes before he died. Shoot, we used to live high as hogs. He had a little locksmith shop in town next to where the bank is now. Worst damn locksmith that ever walked the earth."

"How come?" He watched as a blue jay swept down from the branch of a locust and snatched up Swamper's discarded fat. The jay landed for only a second, secured it in its beak, and then took off back to the branch.

"Problem was, Tommy was drunk most of the time. Used to lock himself out of his own shop about once a week." He began laughing from deep within his belly as he remembered his friend. His chest rattled with phlegm until he coughed something up and spat it over the railing. The blue jay immediately returned but quickly turned away, this time disappointed. "Damndest thing you ever seen. People calling him to come help get their keys out of their cars, and there he is, locked out of his own place. Can't even get his tools. He once had to call a locksmith over in Samford just to help him get into his own shop."

Swamper laughed so hard that tears began rolling down his face. Clifton joined him, suddenly realizing that this was exactly why he'd sent that message in a bottle. For the laughter. It must have been. When he'd been little, his father made him laugh all the time. He'd never thought about it before, but now, as the two of them sat on the porch, one of the things he'd missed for so long was laughter. Once again, just like on the train tracks, that feeling of being alive filled him.

"There was another fellow," said Swamper, "who was a doctor. Doctor Love was his name, which is sort of funny in itself. Better than Doctor Hate, I reckon. But that wasn't what was so funny. This was years ago, back when I was young, and he was an old coot by then. But he'd been the doctor in Crocket's Mill forever. But his problem was, he was sick all the time. And I mean all the time. Couldn't hardly ever get him to tend to nobody because usually he was laid up. It seemed like every other week, Mama or one of the other ladies was taking Doctor Love a pot of chicken soup. Some people reckoned he was probably faking because he couldn't cook."

Clifton found himself enthralled with Swamper's stories as he imagined Crocket's Mill in a different time. It seemed so foreign to him. Over the years, he'd more or less grown to hate the town and most of the people in it. It was in Crocket's Mill, after all, that his father had been killed. It was in Crocket's Mill that he'd had to endure taunting, verbal abuse, and the occasional beating from Colt and his buddies. But Swamper was painting a different picture; he was making it come alive.

"Who else?" asked Clifton. He took a long drink from his second Coca-Cola and said, "Any others?"

"Oh, there were plenty of crazies running around Crocket's Mill back in the day. There was Otto, who lived in town but had a tattoo parlor across the river in Samford. Out near the arsenal. Used to be an Army base there too, but they closed that down years ago. Best place in the world to have a tattoo parlor is near a military base. Nobody but a prisoner loves a tattoo more than a soldier. But if Tommy was the worst locksmith, there ain't no doubt Otto was the worst tattoo artist. Now he was a character."

Clifton felt himself warming. He was amazed by how quickly he'd gotten comfortable around Swamper. "Let me guess—he couldn't draw."

"No, he could draw all right, I reckon. Problem was, he couldn't spell. You ask him for an eagle, an American flag, a skull, something like that, and he could draw it up just as good as anybody. But if you asked him for something that had words, well, nine times out of ten he'd blow it all to hell. Guys would come in wanting to get their girlfriend's name put on their arm, and walk out with a different name altogether. I imagine they found themselves in a fair bit of trouble when they got home."

Clifton chuckled and said, "Yeah, I guess so."

Swamper coughed up another oyster of phlegm and hocked it over the railing. Then he reached into his pocket and grabbed a pouch of tobacco and a packet of rolling papers. He sprinkled some into the fold like a chef adding a pinch of salt to a pot of soup. He twisted the ends with a snap of his fingers and lit it with a Zippo.

For the next several hours, Swamper kept Clifton entertained. He continued telling stories about the old days while Clifton sat on the porch soaking up every word. He couldn't believe the fun he was having with someone who was old enough to be his grandfather. Maybe even his great-grandfather. But he was. And he liked that Swamper didn't ask him any personal questions. He also liked that he was laughing. Laughing easily.

Before he knew it, the sun had begun setting behind the house, creating a soft orange glow over the New. Ripples began springing up everywhere, as if a giant hand had just thrown pebbles across the surface. Smallmouth bass broke the skin of the river as they crashed through schools of frightened minnows. Upriver, from a hole in a deposit of limestone, big-eared bats funneled out by the dozens, skimming the water to inhale moths and hatching mayflies, their wings flapping furiously as they rose and then dived once more. Crickets and frogs began singing as the day lost its grip to evening. Across the fields, a small sliver of moon poked up over the horizon. After the paralyzing heat of the day, when everything had been dead, things were suddenly waking up and coming to life.

Clifton stood up from his rocking chair—the chair he'd hardly gotten out of all day. He stretched his hands over his head and said, "Well, I guess I better be heading home before it gets dark."

Swamper stood up and placed his palms on the small of his back. He pushed forward, causing his spine to pop and snap. "You want some supper? I got a little venison sausage I could fry up. Got plenty of catfish fillets if you'd rather."

"I appreciate it, but I better head on home." He wanted to come back again, but he didn't know how to broach the subject. Swamper saved him the trouble.

"If you get a notion, come on back tomorrow, just before sunrise, and you can help me pull my trot line. Usually got a few on there every morning."

Clifton was suddenly thrilled, but he tried not to show it. "Okay. What time?"

"Shoot, I'm usually up by four. Any time is fine, I reckon."

"I'll be here before sunrise," said Clifton, again trying to stifle the excitement but failing to do a very good job of it. He gathered his rod and bucket and started for the front steps.

Swamper nodded at the fishing rod. "You can just leave your gear here if you want to. Unless you plan on doing some fishing tonight."

"Well, if it isn't any trouble."

"Now what kind of trouble could come from a boy leaving a fishing rod on an old man's porch? You gotta stop being so polite to me, son. You're making me feel uncomfortable."

"Sorry, it's just—"

"There you go again. Nice manners is a fine thing with girlfriends and grandmas, but not with an old ornery son of a bitch like me. Makes me itchy. You got me?"

"Yes, sir."

"Tomorrow when you show up, you be relaxed and ready to tell me some dirty jokes or something. Tell me a story about the nasty things you're doing with all those little schoolgirls."

Clifton felt his cheeks warm as he turned to go down the steps.

"You know, Clifton, you could save yourself some time if you walk around the house and cut up that way. You know where the Killing Pit is?"

"Yes, sir."

"Well, take the trail behind my house up the side of the hill. Cross over the road and you'll see where the path keeps going. Can't miss it. It starts right next to a telephone pole.

Just follow that trail up the hill until it flattens out. Killing Pit will be on your right and then you should know your way from there. Save you a good thirty minutes."

Clifton looked out at the river that was quickly darkening, thinking that he didn't want to take a chance on getting lost in the woods around the Killing Pit. But at the same time, he didn't want to offend Swamper. Or maybe *offend* wasn't the right word. He didn't want Swamper to think he was a chicken. "All right. I'll see you in the morning. And thanks for the Coca-Colas."

"There you go again, being polite. But while we're acting all sweet and sugary to one another, thanks for the cracklin . . . and the company."

Clifton nodded. "See you bright and early."

He took off around the side of the house, sidestepped the hole that the giant clump of root ball had created, and immediately saw the switchback trail leading up the steep incline. The woods were dark, but as soon as he reached the road, things cleared considerably. He looked down the long stretch of road and then at the black oval where the path lay, inviting him into the woods. *Go on, you sissy. It'll save you thirty minutes. Yeah, but I don't know my way. It's getting dark. What if I lose the trail? You're such a pussy sometimes. Let's get home already. Yeah, but some murderer just got set free today. You've got to be kidding me. You think that out of all the places in the world he could be right now, he's hanging out in this stretch of woods? Well, yeah, actually I do. Come on, you're being ridiculous. He's halfway back to Alabama by now. Take the shortcut.*

Against his better judgment, Clifton decided to follow the path into the woods. He stepped across a rusted string of barbed wire that hung slack like an overburdened clothesline. As soon as he entered, things went quiet. He couldn't help but remember how dark it had been when he'd gone there with his father years ago, and that had been in the middle of the day. Once he got a hundred feet from the road, it was just like nighttime in the forest. He looked over his shoulder and saw the residual light calling to him from the road, but he decided to march on. He climbed the hill, keeping his eyes trained on the faint path that got harder and harder to see with every step. What he wouldn't have done for a flashlight at that moment.

His heart began beating faster, and he stopped every few feet to listen. He swore he heard branches cracking and things shuffling through the leaves. But every time he stopped, the sounds seemed to stop too. When he made it to the top of the ridge, the Killing Pit was off to his right. If he hadn't been looking for it, he'd have never even seen it; it just looked like a pile of black stones. For a moment, Clifton's mind began playing tricks on him as his imagination ran wild. *Is that the Killing Pit, or some sort of man hunched on the ground? What would happen if I was coming through here and didn't know about the Killing Pit? What if I fell in? No one would ever find me.*

And then Clifton heard a voice. A deep, longing, hollow voice that beckoned him. It was coming from the hole in the ground. His father's voice? *Help me. Someone, please help me.*

Clifton took off running, his hands flailing out in front of him as if he were a blind man. He ran as fast as he could under the circumstances, but, because of the low visibility, he couldn't run at an all-out sprint. When he saw a glimmer of lights sparkling through the trees, relief overwhelmed him. Once he made it to the clearing and onto the asphalt of Windswept Hills, he stopped running. He bent over and took a few deep breaths. *You're such a pussy, you know it? I know, I know, but I got freaked out. Voices, for God's sake. Give me a break.*

While he caught his breath, he realized that the few hours he'd spent at Swamper's had almost been like going back in time. He hadn't seen another soul except the wrinkled man on the porch. He'd listened to stories about the old days. It was as free as he had ever remembered being.

As his sneakers quietly slapped the pavement, as the cool of the evening settled over his head, as the porch lights lit up the huge houses that he knew he'd never get to enter, he was able to relax and think about the things he wanted to think about. About the great time he'd had today. About the connection he'd been responsible for creating by simply tossing a bottle in the river. About the possibilities of what awaited him tomorrow. And for the rest of the summer.

Chapter 6

THE ALARM CLOCK STARTLED CLIFTON when it buzzed on the bedside table. The red glowing numbers said five a.m. Though usually it was a chore to lift himself from bed, this morning he jumped up and immediately got dressed. He was ready.

He went into the kitchen, put a piece of bread in the toaster, and then looked into the living room where the television chattered. The room was covered in a haze of cigarette smoke, and his mother sat on the couch, staring blankly at the screen, a glass of wine in her hand. A late-night infomercial was on with a man trying to convince her to buy his amazing set of knives. Knives that could cut anything from an aluminum can to blocks of concrete. Still dressed in her work clothes, she turned toward him with that same blank gaze.

He looked back at her, confused, and said, "What're you doing home?"

"Hey, baby," she said. "I left early. Wasn't feeling too good. Had a bad headache, so I left at three. What're you doing up so early?"

He looked at the glass she held, wondering if that was what a doctor would prescribe. "I'm going fishing."

"Fishing? What about school?"

Clifton looked hard at his mother and shook his head. "I've been out of school for two weeks, Mom. It's summer break, remember?"

"That's right." She forced a smile, though it was clear she hadn't remembered at all. "I don't know what I was thinking." She reached for the bottle on the table and topped off her glass. "Who you going with?"

"Nobody. Just me."

"Well, if you catch a big one, bring it home and I'll fry it up for your supper."

"Okay, we'll see." He turned away to check on his toast, knowing full well that she'd never get around to cooking a fish even if he did bring one home. He buttered his toast and sat at the table, munching as quickly as he could in order to get out of there.

"I'm thinking about ordering these knives," said Mrs.

Carlson from the living room. "It's hard to find a good knife these days."

Clifton clenched his jaw. "Maybe you should go grocery shopping instead. We don't have crap."

"You watch your dirty mouth," she said over the hum of the television, but Clifton ignored her.

He put his dish in the sink, where a formidable stack had already accumulated, and headed for the door. "I'll see you later."

"Wait a minute. Can I at least have a hug? Seems like I don't ever see you anymore. Working at that shithole all the time."

Clifton rolled his eyes toward the ceiling. "Watch your mouth, Mom."

"Don't get smart with me," she snapped. He had noticed that lately she seemed to be more on edge than usual. Whereas before she was mostly a mellow drunk, now she seemed prone to mood swings that brought out an ugly side of her personality. "I'm still the adult in this house, whether you like it or not. You know what they pulled on us the other night?"

Clifton walked into the living room, sucked in his breath, and leaned over to hug her. He hated the way she smelled: like gear oil, cheap alcohol, and stale cigarette smoke.

"You know what they're trying to do now? You won't believe it."

"Mom, I gotta go. I'm late as it is."

"Those fish'll still be there," she said, a subtle look of hurt showing in her face. The crow's-feet around her eyes scrunched tighter. Clifton noticed that her complexion, which had always been so smooth, was gray and rough, almost scaly. And he didn't know why she was being so chatty. Usually, when he'd see her in the mornings, she hardly said a word. The wine generally made her drowsy and lethargic, but at the moment she couldn't seem to stop talking. "They want the swing shift to start doing forced overtime. Like I don't work there enough already. I'm getting tired of their bullshit."

Clifton released his mother and headed for the door. "I'm sure you'll work it out. I gotta go."

"You be careful," said Mrs. Carlson. "I love you."

But Clifton had already closed the door and didn't hear her.

The morning was cool and the black sky was just lightening to a deep blue on the horizon over the mountains. The faint bark of a dog sounded from somewhere in the neighborhood. Clifton wore only a pair of shorts and a T-shirt and thought for a second that he might need to grab a sweatshirt, but the idea of having to talk with his mother again dissuaded him.

He chose to take the shortcut through the woods by the Killing Pit despite the anxiety he'd felt the day before. It was getting lighter, not darker, so he decided to head in that direction. When he entered the Windswept Hills neighborhood, several fancy cars were pulling out of their driveways, their owners heading to work in Samford. A brand-new Mercedes passed him, the driver dressed in a suit and tie, sipping on coffee. A shiny Audi also passed, the driver similarly dressed. He craned his neck, looking at Clifton with suspicion.

When he entered the woods, the sky had lightened a bit more, and he was able to follow the path without much trouble. Birds chattered incessantly in the canopy above him. A small stand of beech trees to his right reminded him of the joke he planned to tell Swamper. He'd practiced it several times the night before as he lay in his bed, wanting to make sure to get it right. As he passed the Killing Pit and headed down the hill, he laughed at himself for being so freaked out the previous night. Voices? he said to himself. You're ridiculous sometimes.

At the bottom of the hill, he crossed over the barbed wire and came out on the dirt road where a sweeping movement to his right startled him. A deer stood in the road, eyeing him before it bounded into the woods. Clifton saw little velvet nubs poking from its head. Was it the same buck he'd watched almost get killed the day before? He didn't know, and he didn't really care. It was amazing how much better he felt when he knew the sun was on the rise. If it had been the reverse, he would have been nervous, but with the day quickly approaching, he felt nothing but excitement.

As Clifton traversed the winding path down to Swamper's, he saw a yellow light shining through the window of the house. Once on the porch, he tapped the edge of the screen door.

"It's open," said Swamper from inside. "Come on in."

Clifton opened the door and walked into the room. He was surprised that the inside was the exact opposite of the outside. The thing that immediately struck him was how neat and orderly the main room was. That, and the rich aroma of smoke that smelled like sausage. The sizzle of meat cooking in a frying pan caught his ears. From the kitchen, Swamper said, "You hungry?"

Clifton walked past a worn couch where a quilt was folded neatly and draped over the backrest. A desk in the corner had a few books stacked in a perfect row, and next to them were several pens sticking out of a coffee cup. A radio sat on the other corner of the desk, the volume on but turned down low. A man's voice relayed the morning news. In the other corner was a homemade chess table. The pieces, which looked hand-carved, stood at attention and ready for action. On the far wall, the head of an eight-point buck stood watch over the room. On the other walls were different varieties of fish, from several smallmouth bass to brook and brown trout to what must have been a thirty-pound muskie. On the hearth next to the fireplace was a fully stuffed wild turkey, its talons clawing a piece of driftwood as it perched on its mount.

In the kitchen, Swamper stood in front of the stove, a steel spatula in his hand as he turned over ground sausage in a cast-iron skillet. The grease popped and snapped, and a trail of gray smoke rose toward the ceiling. Above Swamper, on either side of the stove, frying pans and other utensils hung from hooks in perfect order. A shelf to the right held bottles of spices and condiments, all of them organized precisely. Order. Perfect order.

"How you doing this morning?" asked Swamper. "You want some breakfast?"

Clifton's first instinct was to decline, as he thought it the polite thing to do. But he remembered what Swamper had told him, and besides it smelled so good. He said, "Sure."

Swamper pointed his greasy spatula toward the table in the corner. "Grab a seat. It'll be ready in a minute."

Clifton sat down in one of the two chairs and watched him work. Swamper was too involved in what he was doing to talk. He turned the mound of sausage once more, then picked up the skillet and scraped the meat into a bowl on the counter, careful to keep the grease in the pan. He set the skillet back on the eye and quickly grabbed six eggs from a carton, cracking them with one hand against the edge of the iron and expertly dropping them into the hot grease. When they were ready, he slid the eggs out onto a plate with a deft turn of the skillet. Clifton realized he was watching a maestro at work. Almost on cue, four pieces of toast popped up from the toaster. A moment later, Clifton had three perfectly done eggs, sunny-side up, a pile of sausage, and two pieces of toast sitting on a plate before him, steam rising directly into his nostrils.

"Butter's on the table," said Swamper as he made his own plate. "OJ or coffee?"

Clifton was in awe, and it took him a second to respond. "Orange juice would be great. Thanks."

Swamper went to the refrigerator—an ancient thing that was short and bubbling out in the middle like the gut of a fat man—and grabbed the orange juice. The juice was in a glass milk bottle. "OJ's another thing that just tastes better when it comes from a bottle." He set an empty jelly jar next to Clifton, put the bottle on the table, and poured himself a cup of coffee. He then sat down and said, "Dig in."

Swamper took a bottle of Tabasco from the center of the table and turned it on his eggs. "Nothing better than bloody eggs," he said through a mouthful of sausage.

Clifton ate with abandon. It was the best breakfast he could remember eating in years. There wasn't much conversation as they both worked on their plates. The sound of a morning train rumbled outside, rattling the window like a strong wind. The screech of steel on steel got louder and then softer as it passed, producing the Doppler effect in Clifton's head. Finally, when they were both nearly finished, and Clifton was sopping up the last of the runny yolk with a corner of his bread, he said, "Something interesting happened to me this morning on the way over."

Swamper sipped his coffee and looked across at Clifton. A column of sunlight was just starting to seep into the window in the kitchen, highlighting the sausage smoke that still lingered in the room. "What's that?"

"When I was walking through the woods between Windswept Hills and the Killing Pit, I saw a beech tree." He felt his stomach dancing, the same way it did sometimes if he had to speak in front of the class. He wanted to get it just right. "And about ten feet away was a birch tree."

"A birch tree?" said Swamper, eyeing Clifton as he set down his mug. "There ain't no birch trees around here. They only grow in Yankee country."

"Yeah, I know. But yesterday you said you wanted a dirty joke. This is the cleanest dirty joke I know."

"Oh, okay. Roger that. Go ahead."

"So I see these two trees. A beech and a birch. And in between them, right in the middle, is this much smaller tree. All of the sudden the beech tree starts talking."

"Really?" said Swamper with a smile, raising his eyebrows.

"Yeah. It says to the birch, 'I think that little tree is a son of a beech.' And the birch tree says, 'No, it's a son of a birch.' So I'm just standing there as the two trees argue back and forth. Then, from out of nowhere, a woodpecker flies up. The beech tree says, 'Well, why don't we let the woodpecker decide? He knows trees better than anybody.' The birch tree agrees, so the beech says, 'Hey, Mr. Woodpecker, see that little tree there in the middle of us? I say it's a son of a beech, but he says it's a son of a birch. Can you tell us who's right?' The woodpecker nods his little red head and says, 'Sure.' He starts pecking at the tree, sending a loud *knock-knock* through the forest."

"So this is a knock-knock joke," said Swamper, smiling.

"No," said Clifton, his stomach tightening as he neared the punch line. "That's just the sound the woodpecker made. So anyway, the woodpecker taps at the tree for a minute and then he stops. The beech says, 'So, which is it?' The woodpecker looks at the two trees with a satisfied look on his face and says, 'It's neither a son of a beech nor a son of a birch. It is, however, the best piece of ash I've ever put my pecker in.'"

Swamper looked blankly at Clifton for a second, and Clifton immediately got nervous, thinking maybe he'd crossed the line. But then Swamper erupted in laughter. He laughed so hard that he started coughing again, just like the day before. He coughed so hard that his chest rattled through the kitchen like the windows had earlier. He got up and hurried to the sink, where he doubled over and spat chunks of something into it. He turned on the faucet to wash the stuff down, and then spat again.

"Now that's . . . what I'm talking about," he said between breaths. "No more of that polite BS." He wiped at his eyes with the corner of his buttoned sleeve and then leaned his head under the faucet for a drink of water. "The best piece of ash. That's a good one."

Clifton smiled, pleased with his effort. He grabbed his dishes and took them to the sink next to Swamper.

"Just drop 'em in the sink. I'll worry about it later," said Swamper, again dabbing the tears from his eyes. "Let's go check them lines."

Swamper refilled his coffee cup, pulled several Ziplocs from a drawer, and then they walked out to the porch. The sun was now just above the far off buildings of Samford, and the fields in the distance glowed like they were on fire. Specks of lazy cows lumbered in the morning dew. On the river, a faint fog was lifting as the sunshine burned through. The river itself didn't appear to be moving at all; it was a perfect glass tabletop.

Clifton followed behind Swamper down the trail. They crossed over the train tracks and then caught the trail again before walking onto the dock. A shroud of fog hovered just above Swamper's head as it drifted slowly downstream. On the far bank, a blue heron stood motionlessly, one foot raised, the other pillared in the water. It stabbed its beak in the shallows several times and then came up with a small fish—a bluegill, it looked like to Clifton. The bird then spread its wings and flew off silently, drifting downriver through a gauntlet of sycamores until it disappeared around the bend.

"See that rope tied to the post?" asked Swamper, pointing his handful of Ziplocs toward the end of the dock.

Clifton nodded.

"I got my trot line tied in to that rope. If we're lucky, we should have a few flatheads or channel cats waiting for us. Why don't you go down there and pull it in."

Clifton nodded again and walked to the end of the dock, Swamper following behind him. He went to his knees and grabbed the frayed rope.

"Pull it in slow, hand over fist. You should feel some weight on it if we got anything. But make sure to pull slow. Them cats are tricky and they'll flop right off if you ain't careful."

Clifton began pulling in the line and felt the weight on the end of it. He felt fish pulling and tugging as they fought against the hooks. It was like he was a little kid looking for Easter eggs. The excitement of the unknown filled him. As the first hook came to the surface, it was empty. He looked back at Swamper with disappointment.

"That's all right. I got twenty hooks tied into the line. You feel anything on there?"

"Yes, sir."

"Okay. Just keep pulling it in. Slow and steady. And be careful for the empty hooks."

The next hook was also vacant, but the third had a small catfish on it, only a pound or two, and as it reached the surface, it started slapping with its tail, causing a violent disturbance over the hush of the placid morning. Clifton got excited and began pulling on the line harder. As soon as he did that, the catfish wriggled off the hook and plopped into the water, its smooth white belly flashing in the sunlight before disappearing.

"Crap. Sorry."

"It's fine," said Swamper. "That was a small one. We'd have let it go anyway. He just saved us the trouble. Just take it slow on the next one. When you pull fast like that, the line gets too taut and that gives them an advantage. Keep it tight, but not so tight that they get leverage. It's a feel thing. You'll get it. Just feel it in your hands."

Clifton nodded again, determined not to lose the next one. Two more empty hooks dangled from clear leader before the next fish nosed the surface.

"Okay," said Swamper, "now that's a nice one. Five or six pounds, looks like. Keep her steady."

The muscles in Clifton's stomach tightened as he methodically went hand over fist against the wetness of the line. His forearms started to sting as he fought against the weight. How could something five pounds be so heavy? The fish fought viciously when it met the cool morning air, splashing so hard that drops of water dappled Clifton's face. But this time he showed patience and eventually lifted the fish to the dock where it flopped on the boards, leaving a film of slime with every convulsion. Its wide mouth repeatedly opened and closed, pulsating for breath.

"Okay, hold what you got."

Clifton's heart thumped in his chest as the long whiskers of the fish twitched against the faded, splintered wood.

Swamper pulled a pair of gloves from his back pocket and put them on. "See those barbs on the side of its head? Right by the gills? Get poked by those little bastards and your hand'll swell up in nothing flat. These gloves are lined with steel mesh. The barbs can't get through. Now watch how I do it and then you can do the rest. Just keep hold of the line."

Swamper pulled out a buck knife from his pocket, opened the blade, and set it on the dock. From his other pocket he retrieved a pair of needle-nose pliers, then grabbed the fish at the back of the head with his other hand. He snapped the pliers onto the shaft of the hook and pulled with a twisting motion; the hook slid out effortlessly. He dropped the pliers, picked up the knife, and, like a skilled surgeon, drew a red line across the throat. A stream of crimson dirtied the blade's silver edge. He set the fish on the dock, where its mouth pulsed slowly before stopping altogether. "Nothing to it. See?"

By the time Clifton had finished, seven catfish lay on the dock, their throats slit and the blue of their bodies already evaporated to a dull gray. None was bigger than the first one Swamper handled, but they were all between three and six pounds. Clifton beamed with pride as he looked over the catch.

"We'll filet this one," said Swamper, pointing with the tip of his knife at the smallest of the group. "We'll fry him up later."

"What about the rest?"

"All we got to do is gut them and remove the heads. Tricky Bob will take care of the rest. Today's Friday, so it's payday."

Clifton had no idea what Swamper was talking about. "Who's Tricky Bob? What do you mean?"

"He buys my cats from me. Colored fella or . . . well . . . black, I guess. Afro-American. Whatever's right to say these days."

Clifton noticed that Swamper seemed uncomfortable as he stumbled for the proper term. And he knew it was because of his own skin color that Swamper felt that way. He'd been called everything in the book, and he didn't take offense, one way or the other, unless the name was spoken with malice. He understood that Swamper was just trying to get it right. "I think you mean *African* American. But black is fine too. Colored is a little out of date though, Swamper. Like, by forty years."

Despite Clifton's attempt to placate Swamper, he still looked ill at ease. "Old habits die hard, but I'm trying. I didn't mean no harm to you. I'm sorry."

Clifton smiled as the warmth of the sunshine now beat down on the two of them. "Listen to you, you old son of a beech. Look who's being polite now."

Swamper's face eased slightly, but he still appeared anxious. "You know what it's like? You ever walk into town, go by the post office, and see the flag at half staff. And as you're looking at it, you've got no idea in the world who the hell died. Must be somebody important, but you ain't got a clue. Looks like everybody around you must know because they don't seem to pay it no mind. But you, you're standing there feeling all ignorant because you got no idea. That's how I feel sometimes when it comes to calling people the right thing. Sometimes I just don't got no idea. Makes me feel stupid."

Clifton could tell by the way Swamper scrunched his eyes, by the softness in them, that it really bothered him. "I promise, it's no big deal. Most black people I know aren't offended by being called black. In fact, most people prefer it. My dad was black," he said, and then paused for a minute. He hadn't really wanted to get into it, but he'd already started. "I remember him telling me when I was little, when the whole African American thing first came around, that he thought it was stupid. He said he wasn't from Africa, he was from America. So were his parents, his grandparents, his great-grandparents. He said he was black, white people were white, and that was that. Really, Swamper, it's no big deal."

"Well, I appreciate it. I didn't mean no harm. I'm just an old fool."

"Forget it." He looked down at the row of fish by his feet. "So what about Tricky Bob? Who's he?"

Swamper gazed out at the river as he nervously tapped the spine of the knife against his palm. "Just one more thing and then I'll tell you about Tricky Bob." He paused for a moment and then turned to look at Clifton. "I knew your daddy.

Just thought you should know. I know what happened to him and all."

Clifton's heart sank a little. A needling heat prickled his chest. He dropped his head toward the fish again, then turned away and looked out at the water. A pair of barn swallows came racing upriver, undulating only feet over the surface. "You did?" A little knot formed in his throat as he watched the birds sweep by. "How'd you know him?"

"Years ago we worked at the pipe shop together. We didn't hardly ever talk much, but I knew him. Like I said, just thought you should know."

Clifton nodded as the movement of the current trickled along. He felt a quick flash of sadness, but it passed as fast as it had come, in the same way a cold chill will sometimes run down the spine for no reason and then disappear. He turned back and said, "How'd you know I was his son?"

Swamper looked out across the river once more, squinting to block out the glare. Or maybe it was for another reason altogether. "Crocket's Mill is a small town."

Clifton nodded again, finding himself squinting in the same way Swamper just had. "Okay, thanks. I appreciate you telling me. So, anyway," he said, wanting to get away from the subject, "who's Tricky Bob?"

Swamper's face finally relaxed; apparently he was happy to get off the subject too. He rubbed a hand through his white hair and said, "Tricky Bob's a fishmonger. He should be coming down the river any minute now. You can set a watch by him. Soon as the seven-twenty coal line comes by, he'll be here directly after. He buys my cats at two dollars a pound, gutted and headless. In fact, why don't you start gutting and I'll tell you about him." Swamper handed the butt of the knife to Clifton. "Stick the point in its ass there, and then rip the belly to the neck. Then turn the knife at an angle and take off the head."

· Clifton sat down on the dock, the warmth of the boards wiggling through his shorts in a pleasant way, and started to grab one of the fish.

"Hold up," said Swamper. "Better use the gloves. They might be dead, but they'll still sting you."

Clifton put on the gloves and took hold of one of the slippery fish, turning it belly up. He stuck the point of the knife into the tiny brown dot of the fish's anus and then sawed a line to the throat, just as Swamper had instructed. The purple-sacked stomach and the beige intestines, which looked like grainy, mashed cornmeal, spilled out.

"Just use your hand and pull that stuff out," said Swamper. "Toss it on the bank if you want to. The coons'll thank you later."

Clifton followed the instructions and was surprised by how easily the viscera pulled away. Immediately, swarms of green-headed flies zipped around him, their metallic bodies glimmering in the sunlight. He put his weight on the butt of the knife to get through the bony spine, which crunched as he worked on the head. As he got into a rhythm, Swamper continued. "Anyway, Tricky Bob works a ten-mile stretch along this part of the New. He comes by every morning and buys the catfish that people catch and then sells them to a few restaurants in Samford. Makes a pretty good living, I reckon, because he's been doing it for years. He gets at least double what he pays me, then the restaurants charge double that, so everybody makes out. It's how I get a little spending money."

When Clifton was on the last of the fish, his gloves now covered in slime, entrails, and blood, he heard the rumble of the next train.

"Hurry up and get that one finished. Tricky Bob'll be here within five minutes—you watch." Swamper took the pile of gutted fish and slid them into the oversize Ziplocs. After Clifton handed over the last fish, he got on his belly and leaned across the edge of the dock. He scrubbed the gloves and then his own hands, creating an oily residue atop the surface. Tiny brass-colored minnows suddenly appeared from all sides, joining in a feeding frenzy as they slurped up pieces of the dead fish that flaked from Clifton's hands.

He tossed the gloves on the dock, and when he felt his hands were reasonably clean, he stood up. He clapped his hands together and put his fingers to his nose. The overpowering smell of fish and guts still lingered like garlic under the fingernails.

Swamper winked at him and said with a sly grin, "Smells just like one of them dirty girls at school, don't it?"

Thankfully, the hum of a little outboard motor coming from upstream saved Clifton the trouble of having to reply. From around the bend, the snub-nosed bow of a flat-bottomed johnboat chugged toward them. Sitting at the stern, with one hand holding the control of the motor, was the darkest man Clifton had ever seen. He wore a white tank top and had a wide-brimmed Bermuda hat sitting low over his eyes. As he approached, he swung the boat around the head of the dock and came in on the downstream side. He brought it in parallel and killed the engine as he slid to a perfect stop only inches from the wooden decking. The bow of his boat barely tapped the stern of Swamper's little skiff, sending off just the slightest *ting* of metal against metal. The tap raised Swamper's eyebrows, but he didn't say anything. A wake rippled downstream in dissipating rings, causing a pair of Canada geese to bob over the little waves like buoys.

Swamper put his foot on the bow to hold the boat in place while reaching down for the rope resting on the metal bench. Like a magician skilled at sleight of hand, he wrapped several figure eights around an iron cleat and had Tricky Bob tied off so quickly that Clifton wasn't sure if he'd actually seen him do it or not.

"Little late today, ain't ya?" said Swamper, tapping at the flannel of his watchless wrist.

"The hell, Swamper. I ain't never been late. Howdy, young'un," said Tricky Bob as he fingered the brim of his hat and nodded.

Clifton gave a tentative wave and said hello in return.

"This here's Clifton. He's thinking of going into business with me. I'm showing him the ropes, so to speak."

"Good, good," said Tricky Bob with a broad smile. His skin was so dark that when he smiled, his white teeth lit up like neon in contrast. He appeared to be about the same age as Swamper, but his arms and shoulders still bristled with taut muscle. A tiny nub of yellow pencil was tucked behind his left ear. "I can always use another fisherman. Cap'n Swamper here's the best in the business. You'll learn good from him."

"Well, he did good today," said Swamper. Clifton noticed that his voice sounded full of pride. "First time hauling a trot line and only lost one."

"Slow and easy," said Tricky Bob. "That's the key. Slow and easy. Just like being with a woman. Get going too fast, you'll blow the whole thing and lose her every time. Ain't that right, Cap'n?"

"Shoot, it's been so long I don't even remember no more. I reckon the thing's broke by now."

"Broke? Shee-it."

"I'm telling you, my swanson's more wrinkled than an old accordion."

The two men got a chuckle out of that, and Clifton laughed despite himself.

"So what you got for me today there, Mr. Swamper? A couple of lunkers?"

"Hell no. Same as usual." He handed the bags over.

"That seems to be the way more and more these days," said Tricky Bob, shaking his head. He got right to work, talking all the while. He held a large scale with an alligator clip hanging off of one end, and he attached each bag to it as he took a reading. He didn't write anything down, keeping the numbers in his head even while talking. "Had Eli from up in McCoy hand over a fifteen-pounder this morning though. They're still out there, but fewer and farther between than it used to be. Don't hardly ever see a forty-pounder come in no more."

After he weighed a bag, he stuck it in one of several ice-filled plastic coolers sitting on the floor. When he was finished with the last bag, he draped a blanket over the coolers and said, "Looks like twenty-eight, even." He pulled a little notebook from the front pocket of his jeans and slipped the pencil from behind his ear. He tapped the point against his pink tongue and then scratched something on the pad. Then he did a little figuring, making notes on the paper. "Comes to one forty-six for the week. That sound about right?"

Swamper looked toward the sky as he added numbers in his head. "It was one twenty-eight before today," he said, mumbling to himself more than he was talking to Tricky Bob. "So that's one fifty-six, ain't it?"

"It was one eighteen before today, you cheap son of a bitch." Tricky Bob smiled and laughed as he looked at Clifton. "I've been dealing with this rascal for the past twenty years and there ain't been one week out of all of 'em that he don't try and cheat me out of ten pounds."

Swamper gave a fox's grin and winked at Clifton. "And there hasn't been one week in twenty years that he hasn't caught me. My mama said you always gotta try."

"Gotta try robbing a poor black man busting his ass to make an honest living? I don't think she had that in mind when she was trying to raise you right." Tricky Bob reached into his other pocket and pulled out a thick roll of cash. He unfolded it, licked his fingers, and peeled off a number of bills. He pinched the money in half and handed it to Swamper. Swamper began counting as Tricky Bob said to Clifton, "You watch him now and make sure he gives you your fair share.

If I know Swamper, he'll have you working like a mule for him in no time while he sits back and sips whiskey on the porch."

Tricky Bob slipped the rope from the cleat and dropped it into the boat. He pulled the string on the motor as if starting a lawnmower and revved it to life. "Y'all be good and I'll see you in the morning." Clifton waved, but Swamper put up his hand to halt him.

"Hold up there. This is only two seventy-two. You owe me another twenty-spot."

This time it was Tricky Bob who winked at Clifton. "You sure?"

"Hell yes, I'm sure."

"Must've miscounted," he said as he peeled another twenty from his roll and handed it over. "Y'all be good." He swung the boat around, and the air clouded with blue exhaust as he chugged away down the river. The two Canada geese honked and frantically scurried toward the bank as he playfully aimed for them.

"Now I guess you see how he got his nickname," said Swamper with a scowl on his face but a smile in his voice.

"Yep, I guess so."

Swamper took the extra twenty and handed it to Clifton. "Here you go. This is for your help this morning."

"I can't take that. I didn't do anything."

"Didn't we agree that you're gonna stop being so damn polite? Take it."

Clifton reached out and received the folded twenty. "Thanks."

"You're welcome. And if you want, you can start helping me every morning to make a little spending money of your own. I'm getting old. Can't rig the line as easily as I used to."

He thought of the possibilities. He'd been considering getting a job bagging groceries at Good Enough's, but what could be better than getting paid to fish? "When do you rig the lines?"

"I usually do it every evening before dark. Beef livers and turkey necks work best. If you want to help, I'll give you half. It's up to you."

"Yeah . . . I mean . . . yeah, I'd love to. You can make a lot of money, can't you?"

"Hell, no. But it helps get some groceries. And it gives me something to do. Season's just starting to pick up now with the warmer weather. Can usually do pretty good until about October. When the cold sets in, that's all she wrote until about April or May."

"Okay," said Clifton, thrilled about the idea of making money while fishing. And he was quickly realizing that spending more time with Swamper wouldn't be so bad either.

"Let's clean this dock and get the guts off. Then we gotta get this little girl in the fridge before the heat spoils her. You come back this evening and we'll fry it up. Then I'll show you how to rig the line. Shoot, you can be running this show on your own in no time. Now grab a bucket and swamp the deck. You gotta earn your keep."

"Yes, sir," said Clifton, trying to stifle the excitement in his voice. But once again he didn't do a very good job. "Swamp the deck?"

"Yeah, swamp it. What—you ain't heard that before? That's how I got my name. In the Navy. I was a cook on a destroyer during the war. Had the cleanest scullery in the United States Navy. My floors shined. My pans sparkled."

Clifton's mind flashed to the orderliness of Swamper's house and kitchen. Of his expertise over the stove. It all made sense. "So what's your real name then?" asked Clifton with a smile.

Swamper's face went rigid and his suddenly harsh tone surprised Clifton. "Swamper's my name. That's all—just Swamper."

Chapter 7

FOR THE NEXT FEW WEEKS, Clifton got up every morning
before daybreak and attended to the trot line, and in the early
evenings he baited the hooks. Sometimes he would go home
during the day, but more often than not, he'd stay around
Swamper's place. He'd help pick weeds in the garden, or he
might go in the skiff to Old Henry's and help carry back a
few groceries. But most of the time they'd sit on the porch
and talk, or if it got too hot, which was happening a lot lately
as July settled in, they'd stay inside by a pair of box fans as
Swamper related stories about his time in the Navy or about
the old days in Crocket's Mill. But the thing they did more
than anything was play chess.

The first time they played, Swamper had noticed Clifton
fingering some of the pieces. He'd said, "You ever play chess
before?"

"Yeah, when I was little. My dad taught me."

"I built that table years ago. A board is nice, but sitting at a table with the board built in is better. Made out of a wild cherry that dropped in the backyard. Had a buddy at the mill over in Samford do some rough cutting for me and then I shaped it up."

Clifton ran his finger along the track of the beveled edge and admired the craftsmanship. Each square had been individually cut and set in place. Half were stained a deep mahogany, the other half red oak. "Did you make the pieces, too? That must've taken forever." He picked up one of the black pawns and fingered it. It was intricately carved to look like a court jester.

"Yeah, they took a while. About a year, all told. Pieces are made from poplar. It's a lot softer and easier to work with. Tommy used to come up here some and play when he was still alive. Lord, I'd beat that man to death."

"I'm impressed."

"You wanna play a game?"

"Sure, I'll play. But it's been a while."

Swamper helped Clifton carry the table away from the corner and set it in the middle of the room, each of them walking carefully to avoid dumping the pieces. Swamper disappeared for a moment and then returned with two folding chairs and a pair of Coca-Colas. He then went to the corner and turned off the radio, which always seemed to be on, and practically skipped back like an excited child. He grabbed one of the pawns, put his hands behind his back, and then held out two closed fists toward Clifton. "Which one?"

Clifton eyed Swamper's hands and couldn't help but think about his father. About the way he'd always played the game. "It's okay. I'll just be black."

Swamper tilted his head and looked at him strangely. "You know that white always goes first, don't you?"

His father's face flashed through his mind. He smiled to himself and said, "Yeah, I know."

Swamper released the pawn from his right hand and set it back on the board. "Suit yourself, boy. That might just be your first mistake."

Swamper clapped his hands together, then blew into his fists like he was about to shoot dice. He moved his queen's pawn two spaces to open the game. Six moves later, Clifton took a sip of his Coca-Cola and said, "Checkmate."

Swamper gritted his teeth and glared at the board as if the pieces were lying. He reached into the pocket of his flannel, tapped a cigarette out from a box of store-boughts, and lit it. He set the box on the side of the table and stacked his lighter neatly on top. The cigarette bounced from the corner of his lips as he said, "One more."

This time, the match was over in twelve moves. "I'll be a son of a bitch. One more."

Over those next three weeks since they'd first met, Swamper didn't win a single game.

IN MID-JULY, on a scorching Friday after Tricky Bob had paid them for their best week so far, Clifton left Swamper to go into town. With his new-found job, he had plenty of cash and was enjoying the freedom that the money gave him. For one thing, he didn't have to steal from his mother's purse as often, though he still checked it from time to time out of habit.

After the walk down the dirt road that led into Crocket's Mill, Clifton was hot, hungry, and thirsty. The first store he came to was Good Enough's Grocery, so he went in and bought a pound of ground beef, not for him but for Bosco. Then he stopped at the Popeyes for a cold drink and something to eat. As he walked through the door, two things instantly hit him: the cool of the air conditioning and the brightness of the restaurant. Everything was bright yellow. Taxi cab yellow. Yellow counters, yellow walls, plastic yellow tables and benches.

He placed an order, and when the food came, he took his

yellow tray to a corner booth. He set the tray and his Good Enough's bag on the table, then sucked down some of his Coke. He was just about to dig in when he felt something slap the back of his head. He spun around quickly to see Colt Jenkins's ugly face staring down at him. A couple of his football buddies were behind him.

"What're you doing, Skunk?" asked Colt, who wore a pair of baggy khaki shorts, flip-flops, and a tight-fitting T-shirt that said CROCKET'S MILL FOOTBALL across the chest. The T-shirt was so snug that it looked like he'd sprouted a little pair of rigid breasts.

"What's it look like I'm doing?" said Clifton as he rubbed the back of his head. "I'm eating. You know, the same thing your mom's doing twenty-four seven?"

Colt's buddies snickered, which only seemed to anger him, judging by the way his face tightened. He rubbed at a light stubble under his chin as he looked down at Clifton's plate. "Imagine that. Fried chicken. Too bad this place don't serve watermelon and greens. Bet you'd have a big plate of them if they had that shit here, huh?"

Clifton's mind whirred into action. He had two options: say nothing, which he had difficulty with, or attack. Attack like an aggressive queen on the chessboard. He chose the latter. "Actually, they do serve it here," said Clifton, "but they're all out. I saw your mom here earlier with three of her favorite bro's from over on the west side of Samford. I overheard her say she had to make sure they were well fed so they'd have energy for the workout she planned to give them later. Not sure what she meant. Does your mom belong to the Y or something?"

Colt's lips puckered and the folds on his face scrunched together like the jowls of a wrinkled dog. He rubbed at his faint beard again. His buddies laughed once more and jeered at him. "Listen, dickface. You're lucky we're in a public place, or I swear to God I'd wear your ass out."

Clifton took a sip from his straw and realized that Colt most likely wouldn't touch him. As always, when it came to dealing with Colt, he knew he should just shut his mouth, but this opportunity was too good to pass up. "That's funny. That's exactly what your mom said to her black posse on the way out the door. And something about loving that dark meat."

Blood filled Colt's cheeks. He turned around quickly and scanned the room, then turned back around and punched Clifton in the arm. The blow sent Clifton to the other end of the booth, where he banged against the wall, knocking his soda over in the process.

"You better watch your back, Skunk-boy. Next time it'll be your head that I come after."

Clifton rubbed his arm as he got back to a sitting position and upturned his cup, salvaging an inch of soda. He thought about using Colt's words for one last perfect mama joke, but decided he'd pushed it as far as he could.

When Colt and his buddies walked to the counter to order, Clifton took a napkin and wiped up the soda and ice cubes on the table. The brown paper bag holding Bosco's hamburger meat was soaked through. He ate his chicken quickly and left while Colt was still in the restaurant. He knew he needed to get a little distance, just in case Colt decided to come after him. Colt might show a little restraint in a restaurant, but if he caught Clifton on the side of the road, it could be a different story. In the parking lot, however, he did manage to hock up a sticky, Coke-laden loogie and deposit it on the windshield of the car that Colt's father had given him for his sixteenth birthday. A Mustang, believe it or not.

He'd gotten only a few blocks down the road and just out of reach of the stores when he heard a car tap its horn and then a crunch of gravel as it slowed behind him.

"Oh, shit," he muttered. "Here we go."

He turned around expecting to see the Mustang, but instead saw a brand-new, bright red Honda Prelude. The glare on the windshield made it difficult to see the driver, but he could make out a waving hand. He stepped off the curb and ducked down to look into the passenger's window as the car sidled up next to him. As the power window slid down, he saw that it was Julie.

"Hey, Clifton," she said. "I thought that was you. Like my new ride?"

Clifton put one hand on the windowsill while gripping his soggy bag of hamburger in the other and poked his head in. A blast of cold air met his face. Julie's blond hair was pulled back into a ponytail. Her tight white miniskirt showed a tremendous amount of her tanned legs, and her tank top looked like it had been painted on by a masterful artist. The seat belt crossed directly between her prominent breasts, which made them stand out even more.

"Wow," he said. He'd meant the car, but he thought it might have sounded like he meant her. Actually, he didn't know what he meant at the moment. "This is yours? I haven't even thought about getting a driver's license yet." And that was true. He'd gotten his permit through driver's ed at school, but his mother had to have the car for work, and anything he ever needed was only a short walk into town anyway. Besides, a car wouldn't do him any good when it came to getting to Swamper's. In the time it would have taken him to maneuver a car down the washboard road, he could have already been there by cutting through the woods of the Killing Pit. And, up until recently, he'd never even had enough money to buy a tank of gas, let alone a car.

"Yeah, my parents bought it for me for my sweet sixteen a few weeks ago. It's so awesome. I love it." She held the steering wheel with her left hand and gripped the knob of the gear shift with her right. "I'm still not too good with the clutch yet, but I'm getting there. You want a ride?"

Clifton squeezed the top of the car tightly, feeling nervous and anxious, thinking about the dirty clothes he had on. Thinking he probably reeked of fish. "That's okay. I don't live too much farther." He couldn't believe what he'd just said, but as he looked at Julie, someone who he'd known his whole life, he suddenly felt intimidated. This wasn't the same little girl who'd once told him his skin looked like melted caramel. *Are you out of your mind? Are you seeing what I'm seeing? I swear to God I'll never forgive you if you don't get your ass in that car. Yeah, but I stink. I'm going to embarrass myself. I don't give a rat's ass in hell if you stink. Get in that goddamned car.*

"Oh, come on," she said with a smile so sweet and pure and luscious that Clifton felt something move. She patted the seat like it was the head of a cute little boy. "Get in."

Are you insane? Get the hell in. Right . . . now.

"Okay, thanks. But I have to warn you. I was fishing this morning, so I might smell."

"I don't care. Hop in."   .

Clifton opened the door and sat down. The seat immediately sucked him in. He didn't think he'd ever felt so comfortable in his life. It was certainly a vast improvement over the vinyl Naugahyde of his mother's beat-up Dodge.

"You have to put your seat belt on. Dad said he'd kill me and snatch the keys if he ever caught me or anyone else without one." As Clifton complied, she continued. "Mom's got me doing all of her errands for her now. She loves it. I dropped my little sister off at her friend's house this morning and then went across the river to the record store in Samford. Check it out—it's even got a CD player." She punched a button and a plastic tray slid out, already holding a silver disk. She giggled and punched it again to make the tray slide back in. "Isn't that so cool? This is like one of the first cars to have a CD player. I'm so psyched."

"Yeah, that's wild," said Clifton. And he really meant it. He wasn't just saying it to get on her good side, though he wasn't above kissing up to her if he had to. He and his mother didn't even have a cassette player at home. All they had was an old turntable that had been his father's and a stack of mostly warped albums.

"Have you ever heard of Guns N' Roses?" she asked as she tapped different buttons on the CD player. "They're this awesome new band from California. They rock."

Before Clifton could answer, the heavy twang of an electric guitar began pounding through the speakers. Little red and green lights pulsed on the equalizer as Julie yelled over the guitars, "You know where you are, Clifton. You're in the jungle, baby." She looked over her shoulder to see if any cars were approaching, and as she did so, Clifton couldn't help but stare at the tightened muscles of her thigh as she engaged the clutch. Her tan legs looked like smooth, shapely sticks of milk chocolate. Maybe even melted caramel. And her breasts jutted out from her chest like a promontory on the edge of a mountain. Like the Palisades. Clifton felt something move again, so he set the bag of hamburger in his lap and prayed she wouldn't notice.

The car bucked slightly and Clifton's head jerked forward as Julie pulled into the road. Once she got going, she turned the music down and said, "See what I mean? I have to keep working on the clutch. Hills are the worst."

"Seems like you already got it. Better than I could do." And now he freely admitted that he was kissing up. And he didn't care. What a day he was having. He'd gotten paid, had messed with Colt with only minor injury, and then found himself being rescued by a fair maiden. Things were going pretty well.

"Thanks. It's so much fun, Clifton. I feel so free. Hurry up and get your license and then I'll let you drive it."

"Yeah, I guess I need to do that soon."

"You still live over in King's Ridge, right?"

"Yeah, just up a little farther," said Clifton as a prickle of heat jabbed at his cheeks. "Right off Kamron. You can just drop me at the corner. That'll work."

He suddenly realized that he didn't want Julie to see where he lived. It was ridiculous, of course, since she already knew the condition of the neighborhood, but he didn't want her to see his house: the sagging carport, the Dodge with rust patches over the wheel wells, the barren yard that struggled to even grow dandelions.

"Don't be silly," she said as she clicked the turn indicator and slowed at his street. "I'll drop you off."

After an oncoming logging truck passed, she pulled onto Clifton's road and then stopped at the corner a second later. Clifton glanced at his house and cringed with embarrassment as he opened the door. "Thanks, Julie. I appreciate it. Believe it or not, you might have saved me."

She turned her head and looked at him quizzically. A yellow strand had slipped from her ponytail and now hung over her cheek. She made a quick sweeping motion with her finger and tucked it behind her ear. For some reason, that single thread of hair nearly melted him. She said, "What do you mean?"

"Just before you picked me up, I had a little run-in with our favorite castrated horse."

She laughed and said, "Colt? He's such an asshole. I can't stand him. Did you hear what he did on the last day of school?"

Clifton shook his head.

"You know that really dorky kid who's into Dungeons and Dragons? A year younger than us. He wears those weird boots?"

"Dweedle?"

"Yeah, exactly. Dweedle. Anyway, on the last day of school, Colt walks up behind him in the hall and for no reason jams a pencil in his ear. Busted his eardrum."

"Get out of here. Are you serious?"

"Dead serious. He lost his hearing in his left ear. Of course Colt didn't get in any trouble. Said it was an accident."

"God, he's a jerk. At least I got a few good shots in on his mother today before he cracked me a good one."

Julie knocked the stick into neutral and ratcheted the emergency brake. "Ooh, tell me."

Clifton shook his head. "No, I better not."

Julie pierced him with those greenish-blue eyes that looked like the gas flames on Swamper's stove. "Just tell me. I'm a big girl."

He knew he didn't have a chance against those eyes, so he told her and she cracked up. "I love it. You know, he's going to kill you one day, but I love it."

Clifton raised his eyebrows and shrugged his shoulders. "If nothing else, he keeps me entertained." He got out and grabbed the door to close it. "Thanks again for the lift. Maybe I'll see you around."

"Anytime. Give me a call if you ever need a ride. Maybe we can hang out or something this summer."

Clifton's heart began racing. Was this actually happening? But for once he played it cool. "Okay, sounds good. I'll see ya." Completely cool.

He closed the door and began walking up the driveway, using every last bit of restraint he could muster not to jump in the air and scream with excitement.

Did she really say "Maybe we can hang out or something?" Yes, my man, she certainly did. I told you to get your ass in that car. I know, you were right. Did you see her? How is it possible that she doesn't have a boyfriend? Jesus, I think I'm in love. You're not in love, dumb-ass, you're in lust. Yeah, whatever, call it what you want, but I've got butterflies swimming around in my gut. Yeah, and jumping beans in your pants. This is true, but I plan to take care of that in just a minute.

When he got inside, he thought he'd take a shower to remove the fish smell and then take a nap in the cool of the air conditioning. One thing his mother didn't skimp on was air conditioning. She hated the heat and liked for the house to be cold. Not cool, but cold.

He found her asleep on the couch with the television on, snoring lightly. The house, however, was spotless. Lately, his mother had been on a neat-freak rampage. He didn't know where she was getting the energy because usually she did nothing but sloth around on the couch. But in the past month or so, the place usually looked pretty good. Still not as neat as Swamper's house, but it was certainly an improvement. *Man, things are looking up all over the place. This might turn out to be the best summer of my life.*

Clifton put the bag of hamburger in the fridge, then went to his room to get changed. He took the money from his pocket and set it on his desk, and then, just as he was about to pull off his shirt, from his window he saw the mailman driving down Kamron. Even though he'd never received a letter from anyone besides Swamper, and he hadn't thrown any more bottles into the river since then, he still got excited about the mail. So before he got out of his dirty clothes, he decided to go check the box. Then he'd shower and settle down for a nap (and a little private date with Julie) before he went back to Swamper's in the evening.

As he walked outside, Bosco barked incessantly when the mailman stopped. *Poor Bosco,* he thought. *The mailman coming is the most exciting part of your day. Actually, for a while, it was the most exciting part of my day too. That reminds me.* He turned around, went inside, and grabbed the hamburger. While walking across Mr. Henderson's yard, he removed the cellophane from the package. "Hey, boy. Brought you a little treat."

The dog sat down and swished his tail in the dirt as if sweeping the floor. His ears perked up when Clifton spoke. "Look what I got you, boy." Clifton turned the Styrofoam plate upside down and had to shake it vigorously a few times before the meat plopped to the ground. Bosco pounced on it and wolfed the pound of hamburger down in a matter of seconds. Clifton rubbed his ears and scratched his snout. "This money's coming in handy, isn't it, Bosco? Maybe I'll get you some stew beef tomorrow." The dog smacked his lips with his long purple tongue and sniffed around in the dirt for any remnants that he might have missed, no longer paying any attention to Clifton. Clifton let him lick the Styrofoam clean before he crushed the package in his hands and walked back to the carport.

He put the trash in the outside garbage can and then went to retrieve the mail. The mailbox didn't offer up anything except a flyer for a car sale in Samford and a bill or two. He was about to go back inside when, from up the side road, he heard the familiar song that always magically turned him back into a six-year-old little boy. The song that always got his heart beating fast with excitement. The song that reminded him of his father and how good things had once been. The tinny melody of Charlie's ice cream truck stirred happy memories—memories that had unfortunately all but faded away as he grew older. He didn't want to forget those times, but, with every passing year since his dad's death, it became harder and harder to remember. But the sound of Charlie's ice cream truck approaching always rekindled the good times.

Clifton found it odd that Charlie would be coming by so early since he didn't usually show up until around six or seven in the evening. But at the moment he didn't care or have time to ask himself questions. He hurriedly scrambled inside and went to his room to grab his money off the desk.

One of the first things Clifton remembered being anxious about was showing up too late for the ice cream man. Even now, at sixteen, he'd never lost that feeling of impending doom, that dread, that unthinkable dismay of running outside in hopeful anticipation, only to find other kids already eating their snow cones and Popsicles. And just as soon as he'd get outside, he'd glimpse the ice cream truck disappearing around the bend.

The screen door leading to the front yard slapped behind him as he took off for the corner where Charlie always stopped. He'd forgotten to close the main door and knew that the cool air was seeping out just as quickly as the hot air seeped in. He also knew his mother would have a fit, but he reasoned he'd be back inside in no time and she'd never know the difference.

He ran across Kamron when there was a break in the traffic and waited at the stop sign. The white truck rolled down the hill, innocently singing its song while the pictures on the side panel—of snow cones, ice cream sandwiches, Chipwiches, and Bomb Pops—reflected off the windows of the neighborhood houses. Surprisingly, Clifton was the only kid waiting to buy something, though probably it was because the hum of the air conditioners in the houses made hearing difficult and also because Charlie had come so early.

The truck rolled to a stop in front of him, and he was immediately surprised. He didn't see the mahogany face of Charlie or the puff of gray hair partially hidden under the spotless white cap. He saw a white man, not dressed in the jumper that Charlie always wore, but instead wearing a pair of jeans and a T-shirt. And he was young. At least compared to Charlie he was young. Probably not even thirty. The man didn't seem to realize that Clifton was waiting to place an order. Instead, he appeared frustrated as he fumbled with different dials above his head. He fidgeted around in the driver's seat and constantly glanced left and right, looking for an opening in the traffic. Kamron Street was busy this close to lunchtime, and today even busier than usual.

The music continued to chime from the bullhorn speaker attached to the top corner of the truck, and the hum of the refrigerator motor snapped out its own rhythm, almost keeping time with the cheerful ice cream melody. The diesel exhaust always reminded him of his father as they would stand on the corner and buy things from Charlie—something for him, something for his father, and something for his mother, which Clifton would give her once they got back inside. She would act surprised and say, "Oh, for me?" as she gave him a big hug.

But those had been happier times. He hadn't willingly hugged his mother in years.

Clifton was just about to say "Excuse me" when the man started smacking the edge of the steering wheel with his palms. "Goddamn son of a bitch. This fucking traffic is killing me."

Clifton was taken aback. It wasn't the language that shocked him so much—he heard that every day at school—but that it had come from the ice cream man. Certainly he'd never heard Charlie say anything like that.

"How do I turn this shit off? I can't even think." He looked at the dashboard and exasperatedly fumbled with switches.

Clifton stepped forward to the opening in the side of the truck and leaned his forearms on the little counter where transactions usually took place. He said, "It's above your head. By the sun visor."

The man turned around quickly, startled, as if he'd just been spooked by a ghost. His eyes weren't kind. They were tight with agitation and annoyance. He locked his gaze on Clifton and said, "What? What did you say? Where the hell did you come from?"

"The music," said Clifton, getting a chill in the brutal heat as he felt the man's gaze upon him. If Clifton had been a dog, the hackle of his neck would have suddenly raised in caution. "There's a switch above your head. If you want to turn it off, you hit that switch. Charlie let me do it once. Turn it on by the radio, turn it off above your head." He forced a little smile, hoping that maybe the new ice cream man would appreciate the help. Instead, the man scowled but still looked above him and did as instructed. The calliope music ceased and now only the rumble of the generator at the rear of the truck could be heard.

"Where's Charlie?" asked Clifton. He was ordinarily rather shy around strangers, but because this man made him nervous, and he didn't quite know how to deal with it, he tried to compensate by being friendly and talkative.

"What?" said the man, now looking again at the lunchtime traffic that flowed by in each direction.

"Charlie. You know—the regular ice cream man?"

The man turned and peered at him, a confused look on his face. Then his expression softened a bit. He acted as if he'd just seen Clifton for the first time. "Oh, he's sick today. I'm the substitute. Just filling in." The man smiled but it chilled Clifton. It wasn't a genuine smile. It was forced. And one of his front teeth was chipped: a tiny triangular flag of space where part of his tooth was supposed to be.

"Oh . . . well . . . tell him I hope he feels better," he said, though something told him Charlie wasn't really sick. Something also told him that this new man wouldn't deliver the get-well wishes anyway. "Can I get a Push-Up?"

The ice cream man still sat in the driver's seat. "I'm off duty. I'm not working right now."

"But you had the music on," he said, surprised by his own persistence. "Besides, it'll only take a second. They're right in that box."

The man sat there for a moment, transfixed, as if thinking deeply about something. As if weighing his options. He got up and walked to the side window where Clifton leaned in. Unlike the diminutive Charlie, who zipped around in the truck like it was his second living room, the man had to hunch a little as he walked. He had solid blue tattoos up and down his wiry arms, and because there were no other colors, and because there were so many of them, Clifton couldn't discern one from the other. "Now what did you say you wanted?" He again showed the broken tooth as he spoke. He moved quickly, with jerky, twitchy motions, and kept ducking down to peer through the windshield as if looking for someone.

"A Push-Up. They're usually in that freezer right there." Clifton tentatively pointed to one of the silver cases in the corner. The man's movements made him uncomfortable.

He slid open the top of the case, and a cold frost seeped out like steam from the spout of a kettle. He reached inside and pulled out a red, white, and blue package. The wrapper crinkled as he held it up. "This?"

"No, that's a Bomb Pop," said Clifton with a nervous chuckle. "You must really be new. Push-Ups are orange. They come in a little tube with a plastic stick at the bottom."

The man slammed the Bomb Pop back into the freezer and quickly rummaged again, muttering something that Clifton couldn't hear. He pulled out a Scooter Crunch sealed in white paper and said, "To hell with it. This is what you're getting. I gotta go."

Suddenly, from just behind the driver's seat, the door to the tiny broom closet flew open with a loud bang. Clifton snapped his attention from the man to the door. A mop handle slipped out and fell to the floor, followed by a young girl, maybe ten or eleven. She rolled out like a barrel of whiskey. Like a bag of spilled groceries. Her feet were bound with duct tape, her hands were bound behind her back—also with duct tape—and her mouth was covered with a fat strip of silver. She writhed on the ground like an inchworm as she tried to break free, her screams muffled by the tape. She looked at Clifton with wide, petrified eyes. He stared back with eyes just as wide, thinking for a moment in his own terror that maybe he knew her.

The man spun around, saw her sprawled on the floor, and immediately eyed Clifton. He sprang toward the window but Clifton quickly pulled his hands away from the tiny stainless steel shelf.

"Come here, you little fucker," said the man.

Clifton backed farther away, his eyes still wide, his heart pounding. He knew he should run, but he felt numb, as if he'd been stuck in one of the ice cream freezers. It took him only a second to realize that if he didn't run now, he might find himself in just such a predicament.

"You say a word and I'll hunt your ass down and kill you." His muscular, tattooed arm reached out toward Clifton. He pointed his finger at him for a second, then grabbed the girl and stuffed her back into the closet before scrambling to the driver's seat.

Clifton took off running. He darted across the busy road without even looking, and before he could think about what he was doing, he found himself in his own yard, almost at his front door. *Oh shit, what are you thinking? Any house but this one.* A car horn honked and he looked back to see the ice cream truck make a dangerous surge across the two lanes of traffic and then slow down in front of Clifton's house. The ice cream man reached out toward the passenger window and pointed again, shaking his finger with angry emphasis. "Now I know where you live," he yelled. Then he smiled an evil grin—the gap in his teeth visible even from that distance— just before he hit the gas and roared off down the road.

Clifton jumped inside and then slammed the front door that he'd previously left open. He locked it, then ran to the side door leading to the carport and locked that one too. Then he sprinted to his bedroom, locked his own door, and jumped in bed, pulling the blankets over him like he used to do when he'd been a little kid, thinking that if the monsters couldn't *see* him then the monsters couldn't *get* him. But unfortunately the grown-up Clifton knew better than that.

He didn't stay under the covers for long, but it was a natural response for him. Hiding under the covers was his coping mechanism.

After Clifton jumped out of bed, realizing he had to do something, his immediate reaction was that he had to get help for the girl. *If I tell Mom, she'll think I'm making it up. She*

can't deal with this kind of shit right now. She's got enough problems. She'll freak out, and as wacked out as she is these days, who
knows what she'll do. And there's no way I'm dealing with the
cops. No way in hell.

Just the thought of having to talk to Scarface made him
jittery. His hands began sweating. His forehead burned. His
heart palpitated. He crawled to his window and poked his
head just above the sill to see if the ice cream truck had come
back. He saw nothing. *Holy shit. What am I going to do? Who
was that girl? What the hell happened? Do I know her? I've got
to get to Swamper's. He'll know what to do. I can't call the cops. I
can't. But you have to. That girl could die! I've got to get to
Swamper's. He'll know. But what if that guy sees you? What if he
comes back? He was big. He'll kill you. Holy shit, holy shit. Tell
Mom. I can't tell Mom. No way. I gotta get to Swamper's. Now I
know where you live. That's what he said. Now I know where you
live. Why are you so stupid? Why'd you run to the house? Anywhere but here. I know. I fucked up big-time. You had to get a
Push-Up. You're too old for the ice cream man. Why did you go out
there? I know, I'm a moron. Shit. What about that girl? She was
freaking. I gotta do something. I gotta get to Swamper's. Then go.
Grab a knife or something and get your ass out of here. Maybe I
should warn Mom. What if he comes back? Just go. He's not after
her. He's after you. I know. I gotta go.*

Clifton ran into the kitchen and pulled a steak knife from the drawer, his mind swimming with ideas as he tried to figure out what to do. He breathed heavily as he checked in on his mother. He peeked into the living room to make sure she was still asleep, though that wasn't really necessary since she now snored even louder than when he'd first walked in. The rhythmic chest rattle was a perfect indicator of how sound she was sleeping. At the moment, according to Clifton's calculations, he was in no danger of waking her up. She didn't look like she'd moved at all, and he wondered how she could be so oblivious to everything going on around her.

He opened the door leading to the carport, the butt of the knife solid in his hand, and locked and closed the door behind him. He lifted the doormat, grabbed the spare key, and stuffed it in his pocket, all the while turning his head from side to side just in case the man tried to sneak up on him. And then he had an idea.

He ran to the shed at the back of the house and found an old jump rope hanging on a nail that his father used to use. Some nights Mr. Carlson would back the car out and skip for close to an hour in the carport. Clifton used to sit on the cool of the concrete, playing with his Tonka trucks, comforted by the whirl of the rope and the *tick, tick, tick* as it grazed the floor, his father keeping time as perfectly as a metronome.

Clifton moved mountains and built cities with those trucks, the black knobby plastic tires rolling over ants, spiders, and pill bugs if they dared get in the way. The bright glow of the overhead light illuminated his world as his dad *ticked, ticked, ticked,* the soles of his sneakers tap-dancing on the permanent oil stains.

But he didn't think about any of that as he grabbed the dry-rotted rope. One of the ends was now frayed like a horse's tail, the other still clinging to its plastic handle. He snapped it off the nail with one hand, still clutching the knife in the other. He looked in all directions again and then took off next door to Mr. Henderson's house. Bosco sat there, brushing his tail in the dust, as unaware as Mrs. Carlson. Bosco seemed to smile at Clifton when he dropped the knife in the dirt and unclipped the chain from the metal loop of the collar. He then laced the jump rope through. "Come on, boy. You're going with me."

Bosco danced in little circles, still not realizing that he was about to leave his confines for the first time in his life. Clifton tugged on the rope but Bosco resisted, not understanding that he could actually go farther than the length of chain he'd gotten accustomed to. Clifton pulled again and this time Bosco followed. And as Clifton began running, it took only a second before Bosco bolted, now pulling Clifton instead of the other way around. He had to pull back hard on the leash to try and keep Bosco somewhat restrained.

His head swiveled from side to side as he and Bosco crossed Kamron Street and headed for Windswept Hills. It was only when they reached the cul-de-sac at the edge of the woods that he realized he'd left the knife sitting in the dirt next to Bosco's doghouse.

Chapter 8

HE HUNCHED OVER AND TRIED TO CATCH his breath before
entering the woods while Bosco pulled at the rope, excited to
keep running. The rope had burned his palm, so he decided to
let Bosco go free, hoping that he wouldn't run off. Even if he
did, Clifton couldn't worry about that right now. Besides, he'd
mainly wanted Bosco's protection while on the road; he wasn't
worried about the ice cream man being in the woods. Not as
much as the road anyway.

Bosco bounded into a stand of poplar, shuffling leaves as
he took off, and Clifton followed, jogging now instead of
sprinting. Bosco stayed ahead of him, but kept his nose to
the trail, stopping every few seconds to raise his leg and
pee on the base of a pine or the slender trunk of a dog-
wood. When Bosco picked up the scent of something and began crisscrossing through the woods like a tacking sailboat,

Clifton yelled for him but kept on jogging. He marveled at Bosco's unabashed fearlessness. The dog didn't seem to have a concern in the world. He had leapt into the woods, scared of nothing. No worries about predators or anything else that might try to hurt him. Clifton wished he could adopt some of Bosco's philosophy, but at the moment, that was impossible.

When Clifton reached the Killing Pit, Bosco was nowhere in sight though Clifton heard the tromping of crisp leaves off to his left. He yelled for the dog again and then headed down the hill toward the road, his face breaking through strands of gossamer far thinner than the lightest fishing line. When he reached the road, he stopped, caught his breath once more, and picked the sticky webs from his face and hair. He yelled for Bosco a third time, figuring he'd probably lost him, when the dog popped out of the tree line right next to a dry creek bed. During the spring, the creek would rush at full capacity after the rains and mountain snowmelt, braiding with similar runoffs as they all raced to join the New River. But at the moment, it was bone dry.

"Come here, Bosco," he said between breaths. The dog rubbed against his bare legs, wagging his tail. "You look like you're having the time of your life." He rubbed Bosco's ears, feeling a little better about things now that he was close to Swamper's house. "Come on, boy."

They crossed the road, Bosco kicking up traces of dust as he located the adjoining trail, acting like he knew where he was going. Then Clifton lost sight of him as the dog got swallowed by a patch of knee-high mountain ferns. An erect tail, slightly curved over, was the only thing visible, parting the plants like a black periscope slicing through a green sea. The fanlike fronds swayed lightly from side to side in Bosco's wake.

When they finished descending the hillside and reached the front steps of the porch, Clifton found Swamper sitting in his rocker, snoozing away. The sight of his friend sent a surge of relief coursing through his body.

Bosco bounded up the steps and nudged Swamper in the crotch with his snout. Swamper snapped to attention and instinctively grabbed at his pants, covering himself with both hands. "What the hell?" he said as he roused from his nap. Bosco set his head on Swamper's leg as a wrinkly hand reached down to pet him. "Who do we have here?"

Clifton climbed the steps and said, "That's Bosco."

"I didn't know you had a mutt. What is he? Got some Lab in him for sure."

"Lab and chow, I think. But he's not mine."

"Whose is he, then?"

Clifton didn't want to bother with explanations. He had more important things to talk about. "Swamper, listen, it's a long story."

Swamper immediately recognized that something was amiss. "What's wrong, boy? You don't look too good."

"I've got a problem," he said. "A big problem."

While Clifton related the events, Swamper sat in his chair, rocking slowly, rubbing Bosco's head, taking it all in. When Clifton finished, Swamper nodded in recognition. He pulled a pouch of tobacco from his pants and quickly rolled a cigarette. He lit it, clicked his Zippo closed, and exhaled a stream of smoke above his head. "I don't blame you one bit for not calling the police. I ain't too fond of the law myself. And after what happened to your daddy, I don't see how anybody could fault you. Not telling your mama? Well, I reckon you know best as far as that's concerned. But we gotta somehow let the law know what's going on. That little girl's in danger. A serious heap. There's a pay phone down at Henry's. We gotta make a call."

Clifton nodded, but still, the thought of talking to the police unnerved him. "But if we call, they're gonna want me to come in and talk to them. I can't, Swamper. I just can't."

"I'll call them. Don't you worry about that. And I'll make it anonymous. I'll just tell them what you seen and give them a description of the fella. We don't have to use no names."

Clifton finally felt a bit of relief. "Okay. I guess we have to. I mean . . . I know we have to. I want to help her—I just don't want to talk to anybody."

Swamper nodded again in that all-understanding way. "Judging by how you described him, sounds like he's a jailbird. You say all his tattoos were blue? No other color?"

"Yes, sir. That's the only color I saw. Just blue."

"Probably means they're prison tattoos. We give the cops that description, they might be familiar with him. Did you recognize one in particular? One that could really give them something to go on? If he's been in the clink before, the cops should have records of all his tattoos."

Clifton thought for a moment as he reflected on the arms that had tried to grab him only an hour before. The arms that had snatched that girl and changed her life forever. "They were pretty much all scrambled together. I think there was one that said 'Mama.'"

"Which arm?"

"His right. No, wait," said Clifton, looking into his mind's eye. "His left. On his forearm. His left forearm."

"Okay," said Swamper as he got up from the rocking chair. "Anything else?"

Clifton thought hard. He tried to visualize that sea of blue India ink. "No, I can't think of anything."

"We better get going. Time's a wasting. You think that dog will ride in the boat?"

"I have no idea. I guess we'll see."

THE PHONE CALL went as planned. Swamper stayed true to his word and kept the call anonymous, despite the efforts of the dispatcher to get him to reveal his name. The police told him they'd already received an earlier call that a girl was missing, and they desperately wanted Swamper to come in to answer questions. But he just gave them the details that Clifton had supplied and then hung up.

By the time they got the skiff back upriver to Swamper's dock, and Bosco had bounded out like he'd been riding in a boat all his life, the sun was getting lower over the mountains. That made Clifton nervous. He felt better now that they'd reported what he'd witnessed, but of all nights, the last thing he wanted to do was walk home in the dark. Actually, maybe that was the second-to-last thing. The last thing in the world he wanted to do was be at home by himself. The thought had been creeping into his mind all afternoon. How could he stay in that house all alone while his mother pulled the night shift? How could he stay there when a psychopath knew where he lived? A psychopath who might want to ensure that Clifton stayed quiet. As he sat on the porch next to Swamper, with Bosco curled between them, he began to feel sick to his stomach. But just as it had happened so often over the last month, it seemed that Swamper had already read his mind.

"Don't you worry. They'll catch that guy soon enough. You know, maybe you should stay here tonight. Only got the one bed, but the sofa makes a pretty good bunk."

Clifton had been thinking the exact same thing, and he felt relieved when Swamper mentioned it. Swamper had brought it up a few times in the past, since they'd become partners in cat fishing, but Clifton had always chosen to go home. But now, things were far different. "Thanks. I think I will."

Swamper filled a cigarette paper, wet the gum with his tongue, and twisted the ends. After he lit the cigarette, he snapped the lighter closed and began twirling it through his fingers like a magician with a silver deck of cards. As he exhaled, he said, "If nothing else, you'll be able to sleep in a little longer before we check the line in the morning. Which reminds me, I guess we oughta get down there pretty soon and bait them hooks."

The nausea that had subsided to some degree suddenly came roaring back when Clifton looked down at Bosco lying on the porch, gnawing at fleas on his hind end. "Swamper, you might have to handle that. I guess I better get Bosco back home before Mr. Henderson realizes he's missing." He'd explained about Bosco on the boat ride back from Henry's, and

Swamper agreed it had been a good idea to steal the dog. "If I run, I can probably get there, drop him off, maybe grab a change of clothes, and get back before it gets too dark."

Swamper looked down at the river where the sycamore shadows were already creeping over the surface. "To hell with Mr. Henderson, boy. From what you told me, he don't give a damn about this dog anyway. I expect he won't lose no sleep over it. I'd be more concerned about getting word to your mama if I was you. Let her know you're okay. We could go back down to Henry's and you could call her."

Clifton knew she'd be worried sick if she came home and he wasn't there. Though she didn't know it, he was aware—because he'd heard her sometimes when he couldn't sleep—that the first thing she did when she got home from work was to crack his bedroom door and check on him. Even before she poured her first glass of wine. "If I call her, she won't go for it. She'll be suspicious unless I explain to her what I saw. And I don't want to tell her. She'll freak out. But if I went home and she saw me grab my sleeping bag or something, I could tell her I was going camping and fishing. She'd buy that."

"You know her better than I do, I reckon."

Clifton thought about his mother's current mental state and knew that he was right; a phone call wouldn't work. As much as he wanted to stay right where he was, he was positive he'd have a much better chance of convincing her if he talked with her in person. He knew the right things to say. The right way to manipulate his expressions to persuade her. In the past, on the very few occasions when he'd been invited to a sleepover party, she had never let him go. Regardless of her problems and disregard for her own well-being, she was still overprotective when it came to him. Though she'd never admitted it, he was pretty sure she was constantly filled with a deep anxiety of losing him. A persistent dread that she couldn't shake. He was all she had. He knew it was because she'd already lost her husband and didn't want to go through that again with her own son. It wasn't necessarily rational, but Clifton understood. He understood that she loved him more than anything else in the world. To the outside observer who didn't know any better, she might have looked like a negligent parent. But Clifton wasn't an outside observer.

"I mean, I'm not exactly itching to go back there, Swamper. But you're right, I have to let her know. A phone call won't cut it with her. Believe me."

Swamper rubbed the bottom of his chin. "I still don't like it. Not one bit. But she needs to know. I'd go with you if I could—you know that." He had a deep look of concern on his face as he gazed at Clifton. "But these old legs can't get me around so good anymore. Can't traipse through the woods the way I used to. I have a helluva time just walking down to Henry's anymore. That's why I usually take the skiff. This is one time when I wished to hell I still had a vehicle."

"I'll be fine. I mean . . . I'm sure I'll be okay." But he wasn't overly convinced. He dreaded the idea of going back, but he tried not to let it show. "Shouldn't take me more than a half-hour at most if I really hustle. Might even make it back before dark. You said the police were aware of the situation before we even called, right?"

"Roger that."

"So every cop on the Crocket's Mill force is probably out there driving around right now. That guy, if he's got any sense at all, is probably holed up somewhere."

Swamper rubbed at his chin again. "Yeah, maybe. But judging by his actions so far, it don't sound like he's got much sense." He stood up from his chair and said, "You sit tight just a minute."

As Swamper walked inside, Clifton scratched the itch that Bosco was still trying to get at. Then he gathered the jump rope and strung it underneath the collar. "You're tired, aren't you, boy? You've never had this much exercise in your life."

A moment later, the screen door slapped shut. In Swamper's flattened palm was a snub-nosed pistol. The short barrel was black, the grip wood-grained. Clifton's heart skipped.

He'd already known the situation was serious, but this seemed to solidify it.

"You know how to use it?" asked Swamper, still holding the gun flat against his palm as he extended his arm in offering.

Clifton tentatively took the weapon and shook his head. He'd never held a gun before, nor had he ever had a desire to do so. He was surprised by how heavy it was, how comfortable the smooth, polished wood felt in his hand. "No, sir. Not really."

"That there is the safety," he said, pointing to a small button near the trigger guard. "Safety's on right now. That's the way you wanna keep it. Go ahead and push it just to see how it works."

Clifton pushed, and the black button clicked and popped out, showing orange around the sides.

"See the orange? That means fire. It's ready to go. Now go ahead and click it back." Clifton snapped the button back to safety. "It's just a little twenty-two. It won't knock you over or nothing if you fire it, but it's still a gun. It can kill. If for some reason you have to use it, it's best to hold it with one hand and have the other underneath the butt for balance. Keep it straight out in front of you. Put your pointer finger on the trigger and pull it slow and steady, just like the trot line. Don't herky-jerk like you see in the movies. Just take a breath, hold it in, and pull slow and steady. Aim for the center of his chest. That'll be the largest target. Hopefully, if the fool has any sense at all, he'll run the other way and you won't have to use it. But it's best you know, just in case. I put a full six-load in it."

Clifton used his finger to wipe away the beads collecting on his brow. Things were getting more and more real with every passing second. "I'll hurry. Maybe I can even help with the trot line if I get back soon enough."

"Don't you worry about no damn trot line right now. Stuff that thing down your britches and get on. And don't shoot your balls off."

"I won't," said Clifton, forcing a smile but suddenly feeling anxious once more.

"And Clifton," said Swamper, his eyes narrowing, "you be careful. I expect the news will be out pretty soon about that little girl. If it ain't already. This town's gonna go apeshit. I reckon your mama ain't gonna be no exception once she hears."

"Yes, sir. I'll be back in just a few."

"All right, get going. And remember, don't shoot your balls off. Ain't nothing more pathetic than a man with no nuts."

Clifton stuffed the gun into the waistline of his shorts where it pressed snuggly against his stomach. The cool of the metal felt surprisingly good against his skin. He grabbed the two ends of the jump rope and snapped them like a pair of reins. Bosco stood up and stretched forward, his hind legs extending out behind him. The toenails of his rear paws scraped against the floorboards as he inched forward. He let out a wide yawn and then they set off.

TRICKLES OF SUNLIGHT seeped through the pine boughs and oak branches, creating bright spots in places on the forest floor as Clifton and Bosco climbed the hillside and reached the plateau near the Killing Pit. Bosco didn't pull on the leash as he had earlier. Instead, he loped ahead of Clifton at an easy pace, his nose to the ground, taking in the earthy smells of the woods. Clifton found it ironic that, for the first time, the woods around the Killing Pit put him at ease instead of frightening him. He was convinced that there was no reason for the man to be in the forest. The guy was probably a hundred miles away by now, maybe in North Carolina or West Virginia, barreling down the road in an ice cream truck. He figured it wouldn't be too hard for the cops to locate a guy making a getaway in a vehicle like that. He hoped so anyway.

But as the woods got darker, as the light seemed to disappear behind the trunks of the trees, as the shadows grew and moved as if they were alive, Clifton realized that he wouldn't be quite so calm if it weren't for Bosco. And also for the gun. He had to admit that it comforted him, but the last thing he wanted was to have to use it. Violence scared him. Sure, he got into fights with Colt, but that was different. That was something that had almost become routine. That was two guys slapping each other around a little, more for the fun of it than anything else. That's just what guys did. But that wasn't violence. Not at all. He'd seen violence; he knew what it was and he wanted no part of it.

By the time he made it out of the woods and set his feet on the asphalt of the cul-de-sac, he had managed to stir himself into another swirl of paranoia. What if the guy was still lurking around? He could be anywhere. What if he was waiting in hiding at the house? What if he'd broken in and done something to his mother? Maybe he should have warned her when he had had the chance.

He began jogging while his mind continued to race through countless scenarios. Bosco stayed ahead of him as they sprinted down the road, now pulling on the rope hard, thinking it was all some sort of fantastic game.

As soon as he crossed Kamron Street and headed for his driveway, he suddenly stopped short, yanking Bosco's leash so hard that the dog hacked like a cat coughing up a fur ball. Sitting in his driveway was a police car, the engine running. The headlights lit up the empty carport, but the blue lights on the roof were dormant. An officer was at the side door, rapping vigorously with his knuckles against a pane of glass as he peered into the house.

What the hell? I heard every word Swamper said on the phone. He never mentioned my name. There's no way they could know. Yeah, well, maybe Mr. Henderson said you stole Bosco. Clifton glanced at Mr. Henderson's house but saw no lights on. *He's not even home from work yet. I can't go up there. I can't speak to a cop. What if it's about your mom? What if that guy . . . Shit, don't say that. You have to go talk to him. You have to. I know, but what the hell does he want? Just remember, you've got a gun stuffed down your pants. Don't let him see it.* He grabbed the end of his shirt with his free hand and stretched it down, making sure it covered his waistline. *I'm going back to Swamper's. Screw this.*

But just as soon as he thought that, the cop turned and began walking toward the squad car, his head pointed at his feet. When Bosco saw him, his hackle raised and he began barking, pulling on the leash. The police officer snapped to attention and immediately saw them standing in the street. Though dusk had settled in and lights were on in some of the neighboring houses, casting little yellow rectangles onto their respective lawns, there was still enough visibility for Clifton to vaguely see the cop's face. And immediately his heart sank. His stomach dropped as if he'd just raced over a bump on a country road. It was Scarface. No question about it. And then he heard the man's voice over Bosco's barking. That evil voice he hadn't heard in eight years, though he'd heard it many times in his nightmares. "Hey, are you Clifton Carlson?"

Clifton jerked on the jump rope and said, "Shut up, Bosco." To Clifton's surprise, he stopped barking, but the fur on his neck still stood erect like the bristles of a stiff hairbrush. "Yes, sir," said Clifton, his voice so meek that it cracked.

"Come up here, son. I gotta talk to you. You got a good hold on that dog?"

Clifton tightened his grip on the rope, wrapping it once more across his knuckles. "Yes, sir."

"Well, come here then," said Scarface, who leaned against the car, resting his backside on the edge of the hood.

Clifton slowly approached as his cheeks flushed. Apprehension overwhelmed him, but as he got closer, he realized he'd been wrong. It wasn't Scarface after all, but some young-looking cop he'd never seen before. *Thank God. It's not him. Yeah, but he's still a cop. And don't forget about the gun.*

Bosco hadn't barked again, but as they got closer, he stiffened and a low growl emitted from deep within his chest like the distant hum of a kid's dirt bike.

"Do me a favor, would you, son, and tie that dog up." There

was something soothing and easy in his voice. It made Clifton relax a little. His heart still thumped a mile a minute, but at least the tension in his body subsided slightly. "Ordinarily, dogs love me. But as soon as I put on the uniform, can't find a one that doesn't want to rip me to shreds."

Clifton relaxed a little more as he walked past the officer and tied Bosco to one of the posts of the carport. The man's voice must have settled Bosco, too, because his hackle had almost completely flattened out. Clifton patted his head and said, "It's okay, boy." Then he turned to face the cop, having absolutely no idea what was going on.

The officer still leaned against the hood of the car, and from inside it, muffled squawks from the scanner seeped out over the idle of the engine. "Son, is your mama's name Sabrina Carlson?"

As rapidly as the tension had eased from Clifton's body, it returned. As was normal with any child who lost a parent, there was always a heightened sense of apprehension over losing the other. It was almost the same fear that his mother had, only in reverse. And with one major difference. What would become of *him*? Where would *he* go? Just after his father had been killed, that was the single greatest worry he'd experienced. It had subsided to some degree over the years, but it always lurked underneath the surface. And now he was faced with a cop in his driveway, asking about his mother. Clifton's mouth had gone dry and he found it hard to swallow. He choked out a feeble response. "Yes, sir. That's her. What's wrong?"

"About two hours ago, we picked your mama up for driving under the influence over in Samford. She's down in lockup right now. I'm sorry to have to be the one to tell you that, but she wanted you to know."

Although the news did hit Clifton like a punch to the stomach, it wasn't as bad as what he'd feared. In fact, after a moment of processing, it sort of relieved him. At least she was alive. And this had nothing to do with the missing girl. And now, as he began to get over the initial shock, he realized that the emblem on the side of the squad car was Samford's. This officer wasn't from Crocket's Mill. "What do you mean, 'she wanted me to know'?"

"She was frantic. Once I got her in a cell, she begged me to get in touch with you. Crying and screaming that you were home all alone with a maniac on the loose. I reckon you're aware of the little girl that's gone missing over here?"

If you only knew, he thought. "Yes, sir."

"Well, your mama heard about it on the television. Said she couldn't find you anywhere. Said she was so upset about everything that she went to a bar before work to calm her nerves. After I arrested her, she begged me to check on you.

Once I settled her down and realized that you were a minor, I called the house a few times but got no answer. Ordinarily, I'd have called a Crocket's Mill officer to deal with it, but they got their hands full right now. So here I am."

Clifton couldn't believe what he was hearing. He'd held only one view of the police for the majority of his life, and that was that they were monsters. Evil, with no compassion. But this cop seemed sincere. He actually seemed human. "So what's going to happen to her? I mean, is she coming home?"

The cop shook his head and looked at Clifton with empathy. "Ordinarily, we'd let her sober up for a few hours and then release her. But after doing standard background checks, I found out this is her third offense. She's gonna be locked up until someone posts bail."

A hard rock formed in the pit of Clifton's stomach. "Did you say third? As in three times?" He couldn't believe it. She'd never told him about any previous convictions. He suddenly felt angry and betrayed. What else had she kept from him?

"I'm afraid so. She actually might be looking at serving a little time. It'll depend on the judge. Again, I'm sorry to have to tell you this, but because you're a minor, I needed to come by. Not to mention your mama was wrecked with worry. It was the least I could do. You got a family member's house you could go to? Otherwise, I'll contact DSS. Department of Social Services. You'd have to sleep at Emergency Care for the night."

"Yes, sir," Clifton lied. "I can go to my grandmother's."

"Well, if you want to get some of your things, I'll take you there."

The rock in his stomach got harder still. "That's okay, I can walk."

"Actually, I'd feel better if I took you. We still got some nutcase running around out here. You don't need to be taking any chances."

Clifton again marveled at the compassion of the cop. The kindness. *If only Scarface had been like this guy, my life could have been so different.* But as quickly as he thought that, he suddenly got nervous again. He'd just lied to the officer. He figured he could have the cop drop him off at any random house, but what if the man wanted to talk to his "grandmother."

"Really, I can walk. It's not that far. I still have to feed my dog, get changed, and—"

Clifton halted when the cop quickly turned his head in the direction of the car's radio, as if looking at it would help him hear better. A static-filled voice crackled over the air. A woman's voice. And whatever it was she said, it sounded urgent. He couldn't make out one word, but the officer seemed to have no trouble. "Shit," he said as he pushed himself off the hood. "Looks like they've found a body. You sure your grandmother's ain't too far?"

"It's right down the road," he said, pointing in the direction of Mr. Henderson's house. "I'll be fine."

The cop started moving toward the car door. As he opened it he said, "Well, you get there and stay put. Tell your granny she can call a bail bondsman in the morning to get your mama out. Shouldn't be more than a few hundred dollars. I'll let your mother know you're okay when I get back to the station."

"Okay. Thanks." He wondered what his mother would say when she heard he was at his grandmother's. But at the moment, that was the least of his worries. *They've found a body.*

"And I'm telling you, get yourself inside. We don't know who this guy is or where he's at, but he's still out there. I gotta go."

The officer hopped in his car, mumbled something into his CB, then turned on the blue lights as he reversed out of the driveway. He punched the accelerator and sped off. Clifton looked at Bosco, who was now lying on the cool of the concrete. "I'll get you home in just a minute, boy. Let me grab my stuff first."

He took the key from his pocket, opened the door, and turned on the kitchen light. But it took him only a second to walk right back outside, untie Bosco, and let him into the house, fleas and all. He wasn't taking any chances. He then locked the door behind him. Bosco began sniffing around the kitchen floor, his tail wagging, excited by yet another new set of surroundings.

Clifton pulled the gun from his shorts, set it on the kitchen table, and sat down. He let out a deep breath as he tried to wrap his mind around everything that was going on. His mother was in jail but at least she was safe. But still, she was locked up behind bars. The thought of her sitting in a cell sent a chill down his arms, but then anger took over as he realized it wasn't her first time. Or even her second.

Even though he was worried about his mother, his thoughts quickly shifted to the little girl. *Jesus, the cop said they found a body.* A surge of guilt overwhelmed him. *Why didn't I call the cops as soon as I saw what happened? That could've made the difference. That little girl might still be alive. I'll tell you why. Because that guy said if you told anybody, you might be next. Don't blame yourself. You had a perfectly good reason. Swamper even said he didn't blame you. And remember, you did call the cops. Yeah, but not right away. She might still be alive. Stop it. Grab your stuff and get to Swamper's. Get there and everything is going to be okay. Yeah, but what about Mom? What the hell's going to happen to her? We don't have any money. How's she gonna get out?*

Shit, what about me? What's going to happen to me? One thing at a time. Get to Swamper's first, then worry about the rest.

He grabbed the gun from the table and held it weakly in his right hand. He called for Bosco to follow him and then turned on every light he could find as he ventured to his bedroom. *If this was a movie, there would be scary music playing right now,* he thought as he slowly crept down the hall. He used the humor to try to keep calm, but in reality he was in a complete panic. What if the guy jumped out at him? Could he actually shoot him? What if he grabbed Clifton from behind? No one except Swamper would know he might be in trouble.

He continued down the hall, the gun unsteady in front of him, and turned his head quickly from side to side and then behind him as he walked. When he got to his bedroom, he flicked the wall switch and then immediately looked behind the door. There was nothing there. But he still had to check the closet. Bosco hadn't acted alarmed in the least, and Clifton knew he was being ridiculous, but he still had to check. He got a hold of Bosco's collar and pulled him toward the closet. He turned on that light with one hand while pointing the gun into the dark maw with the other. Again there was nothing.

With a sigh of relief, he sat down on the edge of the bed

and finally pulled off the stinky clothes that had been encrusted with fish slime all day. Even though he felt better knowing that the man hadn't snuck into the house, he still felt horrible about the little girl. His mind continued to fill with guilty thoughts because he hadn't acted quicker to help her. He considered taking a shower, but for one, he had a feeling Swamper might get worried about him because, thanks to the police officer, he was already running later than planned. And for two, he didn't like the idea of being in the shower under the current circumstances. He'd seen *Psycho* a few years ago, and that shower scene still scared him. So he quickly changed into a clean T-shirt and pair of jeans, then grabbed an extra set of clothes. He stuffed them, along with his toothbrush, into his backpack. As he packed, the framed picture on his bedside table seemed to stare at him. It was a shot of him and his father in the front yard, taken only a few weeks before he died.

He picked up the gun off the bed, shoved it down his pants, and then went back into the kitchen. He thought he was ready to go, but now, like an evening fog dropping over the New River, the paranoia began to settle into his mind once more. He wasn't looking forward to taking Bosco back to Mr. Henderson's and then having to make the journey alone. At night. In the dark.

He scrambled through one of the junk drawers, thinking there might be a flashlight he could use, but when he found it, the batteries were dead. Then he had another idea. Julie. She had said she'd give him a ride anytime he wanted one. If there was ever a perfect time, this seemed like the one.

He pulled out the phone book and found her number but then went back and forth over whether he should call. After everything he'd been through, it seemed silly that he'd be acting nervous over something as trivial as calling her for a ride. But he couldn't help it. What would he say? What if her parents answered? He kept looking at her number, and even grabbed the receiver a couple of times, but he couldn't bring himself to dial. *Just call her. What's your problem? I know, I'm chickenshit. Well, either do it or don't, but you have to get going. The worst that can happen is she'll say she can't. I know. Okay, I'll do it.*

He picked up the phone and dialed, feeling a flutter in his stomach. As the phone began to ring, he paced back and forth in the hallway, going as far as the cord would let him before he turned around and walked the other way. On the third ring, he heard Julie's voice answer.

"Julie? Hey, this is Clifton. I was just—"

Suddenly someone picked up another line and said, "Hello? Hello? Who is this?" It was her father, and his voice was loud, almost frantic.

Clifton began to panic and was about to hang up when he heard Julie say, "Dad, it's for me. I got it."

"You can't be on the phone right now. We have to keep the line open."

"I know. I'll hurry." It sounded like she might be crying, and his instinct again told him to hang up. "I'll be right off."

Her father slammed down the receiver and then Julie said, "Clifton? Sorry about that." She was definitely crying. No question.

"Yeah, it's me. If this is a bad time . . . I mean, I can call back later."

"No, it's okay." Her voice was weak and completely drained. "I mean . . . yeah, it's a bad time. I'm gonna have to get off. It's . . . it's my little sister. She's missing. Nobody knows where she is." And now the sobs really began to echo through the phone. "You probably already heard about it."

Clifton's heart fell into his groin. Could this be possible? All he could think about was the little girl in the ice cream truck, her mouth bound with duct tape, and those panicked eyes looking up at him for help. Now he knew why she'd looked familiar. "Holy shit," said Clifton, his tone subdued and sympathetic. "That's your sister?"

"Yeah . . . we can't find her. After . . . after I dropped her off at her friend's, her friend's mother ran out to the store to grab a few things. Maria was outside playing with her friend in the yard. Her friend went inside to use the bathroom, and when she came back . . . when she came back out . . . Maria was gone. She just vanished."

Clifton was stunned. He had no idea what to say. "Julie, I'm so sorry" was all he could manage.

"Thanks, Clifton. But I gotta go. We're all waiting for any news and I need to get off the phone."

"Yeah, sure, I understand. I'm sure it will be okay," he said, feeling painfully guilty for the lie. The cop had told him just fifteen minutes before that a body had been found. But he wasn't about to mention that. Or the fact that he might have been one of the last people to see her sister alive. "I'm so sorry," he said. And he was sorry, for more reasons than just the obvious.

"I'll talk to you later."

Julie hung up the phone while he just stood there, staring at the receiver in his hand. "Can this day get any more screwed up?" he said aloud. He put the phone back in its cradle and then grabbed his backpack off the kitchen table. "Come on, Bosco. You're officially a stolen dog now. I don't give a damn. You're going back to Swamper's with me."

Bosco looked up with a turn of his head, his tail swishing back and forth. Clifton grabbed the ends of the jump rope and together they walked outside. He locked the door behind him and set off for Swamper's, almost feeling sick. Feeling as disgusted with himself as he ever had. Feeling almost as depressed as when his father had died. He wasn't looking forward to his journey through the creepy blackness, but there was no way he was staying in that house all alone.

Chapter  9

FOR THE THIRD TIME THAT DAY, he walked up the creaking steps leading to Swamper's house. Other than the death of his father, Clifton's life had been rather dull. As mundane as anyone else's. But how things could change in the matter of a few hours. Earlier that morning, as the sun was just raising the crown of its head over the horizon, life had seemed innocent and tranquil. Later that day, when he'd ridden in the car with Julie, he'd been pretty sure life couldn't get any better. But then, in the thick of the heat after he'd witnessed the abduction of the little girl—of Maria—life had seemed anything but peaceful and tranquil. He didn't know how it could get any worse. And now, with the cool of darkness fully encompassing his surroundings, with the crickets chirping, the frogs singing, raccoons invisibly hunting for crawdads by the riverbank, life to Clifton was a confused mix of innocence, peace-fulness, hatred, anger, and death.

Swamper sat outside on his rocker, smoking a cigarette when he arrived. Bosco bounded onto the porch after Clifton let go of the leash, the plastic handle of the jump rope click-ing against the edge of each step as he went. He went directly to the water bowl in the corner, which Swamper had set out earlier, and lapped vigorously, snorting through his nose and grunting but never slowing down to take a breath. When he'd finished, he walked next to Swamper's chair and plopped down on the warped boards of the porch, emitting a deep, content sigh. If Clifton could have seen Swamper's face in the darkness, he would have witnessed worry and strain disappear in the same way a wiper blade clears a fine film of mist from a windshield. One swipe and it's gone. But he couldn't see Swamper's face, nor did the man's voice give any indication of the anxiety he'd been experiencing while waiting for the boy's return.

"Get caught up in traffic or something?" He puffed on his cigarette with one hand and scratched Bosco's snout with the other. "And I thought the whole point was to take this flea-bag home."

And then Clifton broke. Everything that he'd gone through in the last several hours exploded out of him like a violent fit of vomiting. It was as if he had no control. No way of holding anything back. The tears poured like water racing down that dry creek bed in the spring. He explained everything. About the kindly police officer, about his mother's mishap and how he had no idea how she was going to get out of jail or what fate she would face once she did, about a body being found, about how scared he'd been as he'd walked to his room to get his clothes, about how the little girl was Julie's sister. Everything. And the tears ran freely. He sobbed as he relayed the entire story. When he'd finished, he felt exhausted. Like all he wanted to do was fall asleep and forget about everything. Forget about life.

Swamper hadn't said a word during the entirety of Clifton's rant. He had only rocked in his chair, sitting stoically as Clifton unleashed his fears, his confusion, and his anger. And there had been a lot of anger. As he'd spilled his guts, he'd felt an intense, unexpected rage erupt against his mother. Against the man in the ice cream truck. Even against his father, saying that life would be so different if Mr. Carlson had just kept his mouth shut and hadn't ever talked back to Scarface. But mostly what Clifton expressed was his overwhelming guilt for not acting quicker to get help for Julie's sister. "For Maria," he'd said, the name almost painful to utter. That name seemed to split his lips wide open, stinging them as if they'd been exposed to freezing temperatures all day. As if they'd been burned by a brutal winter wind.

"Come on inside," said Swamper after Clifton had finished. "You've had a helluva day. You need to get some shuteye."

Swamper stood up, and Clifton mindlessly followed him into the house like a sleepwalker fumbling down a dark hallway. Bosco got up to follow, but Swamper clamped the screen door closed after nudging the dog away with the toe of his boot. "You got fleas, old buddy. You'll do just fine on the porch tonight."

Bosco let out another little sigh of apparent understanding and curled up on the worn, tattered welcome mat, his back pushing against the mesh of the screen. As if on cue, he twisted his head around and chomped at the base of his tail.

Swamper sat Clifton down on the couch and then went into the kitchen. A floor lamp in the corner sparsely lit the room. Clifton stared straight ahead at the eyes of the buck on the far wall, his mind almost completely free of thought. When Swamper came back a moment later, Clifton honestly couldn't say if he'd been sitting on the couch for a minute or an hour.

"Here," said Swamper, handing over a wide-mouthed Mason jar, a quarter filled with an amber liquid. Clifton reflexively reached out and took the jar, though he was still in an almost hypnotic state. Swamper had an identical jar in his hands, and he sat down on the couch next to Clifton. "Sip on that for a little while. It'll help relax you some. Help you go to sleep."

The sharp smell of the whiskey broke Clifton from his stupor. Unlike most of his peers, he had never had the urge or desire to get drunk. He heard plenty of stories at school about kids going out and getting wasted, but it had never been something that interested him. It certainly would have been easy enough to do since his mother had bottles of wine sitting around the house at all times, but it was for exactly that reason that he'd never wanted to do it. Alcohol was why his mother had more or less dropped out of society. Why she'd also more or less dropped out of motherhood. It was the reason why she was spending the night in jail.

But things were different now. For the first time in his life, Clifton didn't care. For the first time, he felt himself giving up. His father had told him that he always had to fight. But he couldn't fight anymore. He was beaten. He peered down at the surface of the whiskey, the liquor resembling strong tea, and put the rim to his lips as he took a sip. It was warm and burned his throat. "Ugh, it tastes like battery acid."

Swamper showed a slight smile. "You ever tasted battery acid?"

"No, but it couldn't be any worse."

"Just take little sips. You'll get used to it. I ain't saying I

187

want you to become my drinking buddy or nothing, but it'll help loosen you up. Like I said, you'll be asleep in no time." Swamper took a healthy swig and let out an *aah* of satisfaction.

It wasn't long before the whiskey grabbed hold. He had taken only a few small sips, but already his head felt pleasantly lighter. His mood seemed to be improving. At least at first. He felt a rush of happiness as he told Swamper about how Julie had picked him up earlier in the day. But his thoughts of Julie quickly switched to thoughts of her sister. The alcohol was sending his emotions up and down like the undulating lines of a graph.

"Shit, Swamper, if I hadn't been such a pussy, I might have been able to save her. She might not be dead."

Swamper took another drink from his jar. "First off, you don't even know if it was that little girl's body they found. You said the cop was from over in Samford, right?"

"Yes, sir."

"Well, there's plenty of shit going on over there. I'm not saying there's a murder every day or nothing like that, but they got more crime on that side of the river than we got over here, that's for sure. So that little girl could very well still be alive. The cop didn't say they'd found *her* body, did he?"

"No, sir."

"So it could have been anyone. And you did your part. We made a phone call. We did what we could. It ain't your damn fault that some sicko decided to steal her away in that ice cream truck. Hell, if you hadn't seen her fall out of that closet, then those cops might not have nothing to go on. In fact, you've probably done more than anybody else in this world to help that little girl."

Swamper's words, along with a fresh spike of elation on the whiskey graph, made him feel better. But it didn't last long. "I know. But if I'd just called as soon as I saw it, they probably could've chased him down right away."

"That man threatened to kill you. He saw your house. There ain't nobody in this world that would blame you for not calling. You gotta get rid of that guilt because it ain't gonna do no good but to rip you up worse than if you'd swallowed a razor blade."

Clifton swiveled his torso and butt from side to side as he lowered himself deeper into the couch. He held the jar with both hands and rested it on his lap. He took another sip and let the liquid do its magic. "I hear what you're saying, but it wasn't you who saw it. I saw her, Swamper. I saw her all taped up and scared out of her mind. I could've done something and I didn't. And shit, now my mom's locked up. She could go to prison. What the hell am I gonna do?"

"The first damn thing you're gonna do is stop feeling sorry for yourself. Nowhere on your birth certificate does it say that life's gonna be easy. You got me?"

Clifton was a little taken aback, and for a moment he felt hurt. But he also realized that Swamper was right. It was almost as if his father was talking to him. He nodded and said, "Yes, sir."

"Another thing is, you gotta get over this guilt. Like I said, it ain't gonna do nobody no good. It ain't gonna bring that little girl home. It's the same thing as worrying. It don't do a damn bit of good."

Clifton nodded again. His head was swimming now, and he suddenly felt emotions bombarding him from all sides, bouncing around in his head like Ping-Pong balls. He didn't know if it was the whiskey or not, but one thing he recognized for sure was that as harsh as Swamper's words were, he had said them because he cared. And again, maybe it was the whiskey, but he realized that he cared about Swamper too. He recognized how much the man's friendship meant to him. They'd spent every day of the last month together, and though it wasn't a tremendous amount of time in the whole scheme of things, he felt like he'd known him his whole life. "Yes, sir, I got you."

"I'm gonna tell you a little story. It's something I haven't told nobody in a helluva long time. But I'm gonna tell you because I think it's important. There's a point to it, is what I'm saying." Swamper quickly rolled a cigarette and scooted an ashtray on the end table closer to him. "When I was a little boy, probably a little younger than you, a circus came to town. Back then, and remember I'm talking about fifty years ago, every spring a traveling circus would come to the school. They'd set up their tents, their games, their freak shows, set them up all over the ball fields behind the school. My mama would squirrel away money for months in advance so I'd have enough to be able to go and maybe get a cotton candy and play a game or two. You can imagine what a big time it was. If you think there ain't much to do in Crocket's Mill these days, just imagine what it was like back then."

Swamper stopped and took a sip of whiskey and a pull from his cigarette. Clifton felt himself drifting away on a cloud of alcohol as he imagined the circus scene. It sounded so innocent. A different time when the only worry was scraping up some change to go see the circus. He slumped further into the couch as Swamper continued.

"They had two shows back then, for one day only. There was an afternoon show, and then later was the big one, with all the lights and everything. Pretty girls dressed up in sparkly outfits, walking on high wires, acrobats on the trapeze, elephants, tigers, clowns. They had it all. And sideshows too, where all the geeks were. A man who'd bite the head off a rattlesnake, a bearded lady. You name it, they had it. In fact, that's where I saw my first set of bare titties."

"At the circus?"

"Yep. Three of 'em."

"How'd you see three of them?"

"Well, this isn't the story I had in mind, but I'll tell it to you first. One of the freak shows had this lady they called the Trilogy. There was a painted sign outside of her tent that showed this beautiful woman. She was painted up like an Arab. You know, with silk and lace and one of those mask things hiding her mouth. In the painting, she had three arms and three legs. Well, me and my buddies had to see that, so we paid a dime apiece to go in. There was a fat man inside, dressed in white robes and had one of those little red hats on his head that looked like a little box. Like the Shriners wear. You know the ones?"

"Yeah. It's called a fez, I think."

"Right, a fez." He dragged on his cigarette and continued. "So he starts talking to us about the amazing Trilogy and all that. Getting us excited. Anyway, she finally comes out from behind the curtain and starts dancing around to this Arab-sounding music. Strange horns blowing and all that. At first she's only got two regular arms, and we thought we'd been had, but then she starts peeling off some of her silks and there's the third one. It was miniature. Almost like a kid's arm, and it stuck out from her side. Like the kid had been swallowed and was trying to bust free through the woman's ribs."

Clifton took a sip of the whiskey. "That's weird. What about her legs?"

"Well, we were waiting for that next, but then the fat man says, 'You know what else she's got three of?' He said it slyly, and kind of raised his eyebrows at us as he talked. Now we were young boys, but we knew what he was getting at. He said, 'For an extra dime, she'll show them to you.' We reached in our pockets and pulled those dimes out faster than you can say lickety-split. We couldn't believe it. We kept glancing behind us to see if any adults were coming, but it was just us boys. Well, she shakes around a little more, teasing us like she's a burlesque dancer or something, and then she drops her bra. Sure enough, there's three of 'em lined up in a perfect row. Except the middle one didn't have no nipple."

Clifton laughed. "Get out of here. You're messing with me."

"I shit you not, sitting there like a string of mountains."

Clifton laughed again. "Was she pretty?"

"Hell no. Had a face like the ass-end of a whipped mule. It was bad. Actually, if you want to know, I felt a little sorry for her."

"I don't know if I buy it."

"That's the God's honest truth," he said, holding his hand up in oath, the cigarette squeezed between his fingers. "If I happened to own a Bible, I'd swear on it right now. But that's not the story I wanted to tell you," he said, taking a draw and then ashing it with a flick of his thumb. "That was the year before. Before the time I'm about to tell you about. So my buddies and me would go to both shows. After the first show, we'd hide away behind the folds of one of the canvas tents and try to sneak into the second show. Some years we got away with it, some years we didn't. This particular year, we managed to get away with it, so we had seats right up close—on one of the bleachers in the front row, right in front of the ring where the tigers were."

Swamper took another draw off his cigarette and exhaled a stream of smoke that gravitated toward the top of the floor lamp in the corner. Then he extinguished it.

At this point, Clifton had stretched himself out on the couch, and before he realized it, his head was resting on Swamper's shoulder. The whiskey was making him sleepy, and he closed his eyes so he could see the circus in his mind's eye. The earlier horrors of the day had all but disappeared.

"Now back in those days, they didn't have no fences or gates to block the audience off from the actual circus. There were several rows of bleachers underneath the canopy of the tent, and in front of them there was a little area for people to walk as they made their way to their seats, and then just on the other side was the rings where the circus people and animals performed. The rings were sectioned off with wooden posts lying on the ground—I guess they call them landscaping timbers today—but that was it. I could have run into the middle of the ring if I'd wanted to without nothing there to stop me.

"Anyway, the first part of the show was where they brought out the tigers. They had heavy steel collars around their necks and chains that was fastened to the collars on one end, and to metal spikes driven into the ground on the other end. The spikes were actually set into what was the infield of the baseball diamond. There were three tigers, and they were beautiful. Scary, to be sure, since they were only sitting about twenty feet away from me and my buddies in the front row, but they were beautiful. The three of them each had their own pedestal, and I'll never forget how their muscles pumped out of their fur when they leapt up on them. They were a sight to behold.

"Since they were the first act, a lot of latecomers were still straggling in, which made me mad because as they walked by, they were blocking our view. But we were so filled with excitement that it didn't matter all that much. Anyway, I was staring at the tiger that was closest to me, admiring it, when this little boy, probably no older than eight or nine, started screaming. He was standing just to the right of me, with a Coca-Cola bottle in his hand, and appeared to have gotten lost from his parents. It was loud in there, with all of the excited chatter from the crowd and the ringmaster yelling through his bullhorn. But because the boy was so close to me, I couldn't help but notice him. He was still screaming and looked scared as he started walking in front of me. He was looking up into the crowd, searching for his parents, and wasn't paying no attention to where he was walking. He stumbled over one of the timbers that formed the ring, and the next thing you know, he was actually on the other side, still looking up toward the crowd. He hadn't fallen, but I remember watching some of the Coke foam up over the mouth of the bottle. It's funny how sometimes the strangest little details stick with you.

"But what happened next, I'll never forget. It was like the whole thing happened in slow motion, and it was like I was the only one who seen what was unfolding. That tiger that was closest to me eyed that lost, screaming boy, and I saw the muscles of its back tense. And then it pounced. Because the boy was so close, and there was some play in the chain—not much but a little—the tiger had enough room. He jumped off the pedestal and clamped on to the boy's neck in less than a second. And remember, this happened right in front of me. I'd seen it coming but there was nothing I could do. In a matter of seconds, that boy was flat on the ground, no longer screaming, and the muscles of his neck was spread out all over the grass. Have you ever cleaned a pregnant bass before?"

It took a second before Clifton realized Swamper had asked him a question. He stirred, turning his head from side to side, and said, "What? Are you asking *me?*"

"Yes, I'm asking you. Who else would I be asking? You ever cleaned a pregnant bass?"

"Yeah, sure. A couple of times I guess."

"Well, you know what it's like then. That stomach is all bulging and nearly busting like a full balloon. And then when you stick the knife in and slit the belly, all the eggs and everything else comes spilling out. That's what that boy's neck looked like. Except this was much bloodier. Blood all over the place. There was goopy strings of it hanging from the tiger's jaws, and immediately there were trainers with whips coming after the animal. I remember it was the school janitor, Mr. Vansulk, who was one of the first to jump in and help pull the tiger off the boy. I remember the rage on his face as he grabbed the nape of the tiger's neck and tried pulling it away. His arm muscles rippled like waves. The tiger turned on him and took out a small chunk of Mr. Vansulk's forearm with his claws before the trainers with the whips got the tiger under control.

"At first, the crowd was silent. I think people thought it was part of the show, but I knew for sure that it wasn't. But then the crowd started to erupt. Again, it was like slow motion. It was like the sound of one of those fighter jets that sometimes fly over. You know, you see the jet first, and then the thing is almost out of sight before the sound of the engines comes roaring overhead. And then there was complete panic. People began rushing for the exits, me and my buddies included. It was pandemonium as we all rustled out of there, like cattle getting herded through a gate.

"Now shortly after it all happened, I was in a state of shock. But as the days rolled on, I felt nothing but guilt. And this is my whole point. The boy died. They rushed him to the hospital in Roanoke, but he was DOA. And what I felt was probably the same as what you're feeling right now. Why didn't I do something? I was right there. I saw what was going to happen even before it actually did. I saw the boy stumble. I saw the tiger tense up and stare at its prey. If I'd just jumped up and grabbed the boy, I might've been able to save him. It took me a long time to get over that. It took me a long time to realize that, realistically, there was nothing I could've done.

"But that guilt stuck with me. And it didn't do no good but to just make me feel miserable. It's the same with that little girl. Maria, you called her. You saw her in that truck, but there wasn't nothing you could do except tell the cops, which is exactly what you did. Unlike me and that little boy, at least what you did might help save her. For that boy, there was nothing I could've done. At least you tried. That's more than I can say."

Clifton's mind continued to swim as he now lay completely

horizontal, his head on the couch, his hair brushing the side of Swamper's leg. He looked up at the bottom of the old man's chin and throat, crinkled like a turkey's neck and covered with a light stubble of gray beard. As Clifton began to speak, he had trouble enunciating his words, as if his tongue had been coated in concrete. "But just like you said, there was nothing you could've done. I mean, you were a kid. You couldn't go up against a tiger."

Swamper gave a soft smile, as if to say that Clifton had understood his point whether he realized it or not. "Exactly right. And neither could you. You're just a kid too. Okay, maybe a young man, but it doesn't matter. You were going up against a tiger. That man, whoever he is, is just as much a predator as that tiger was. At least with the tiger, he was just following his instincts. That man, he's going against nature. He has chosen to do wrong. Has chosen evil. What the tiger did wasn't evil. It wasn't unnatural. So if you think about it, what you faced was far more dangerous than what I did when I was a little boy. That's why you got no reason to feel guilty, son. You should be proud you had the gumption, the balls, to call the police. Especially when you consider what those very same police once did to your father."

"How do you know what happened to my father?" asked Clifton. Swamper had alluded to it before, but Clifton had never had the courage to say anything. But the whiskey had made him braver. "I mean . . . the police, the papers, they all said it was an accident. There was never a trial. Not really even an investigation."

"Like I told you before, it's a small town. People know. People ain't stupid."

Swamper set his arm across Clifton's chest and gently patted his shoulder. Clifton grabbed Swamper's forearm and gave it a gentle squeeze, as if saying *thanks for understanding* without using any words. The flannel of the sleeve was smooth in his hand, but he felt something underneath the material that intrigued him. The pads of his fingers probed at several bumps of tight, muscular tissue. As he pressed on the mysterious lesions, he sensed Swamper trying to pull away.

In his now drunken state, Clifton didn't even think about what might be considered proper etiquette. "What are those bumps, Swamper? They feel like tumors or something." Clifton continued to probe at the growths, trying to imagine what they looked like. If he pushed hard on one side, it was as if the whole mass of tissue would slip to the other side like a marble rolling beneath the skin.

"Those are just scars," he said, patting Clifton's shoulder again. "It's a long story and ain't nothing for you to be worried about."

But Clifton wasn't to be deterred. The alcohol had given

him a newfound determination and confidence. "Well what happened? I got plenty of time."

Clifton, still lying down and looking up, saw the dewlaps of Swamper's throat quiver as he swallowed. "That's a story for another night. You need to get some sleep right now. You've had a long day." He tried to remove his arm and squirmed a little as if trying to get up, but Clifton wouldn't let him go.

"Come on, Swamper. Just tell me. You already told me about a kid getting eaten by a tiger. How much worse could it be?"

Swamper cleared his throat and forced a faint chuckle. "Well, I don't know if it's worse, necessarily. I guess that all depends on how you look at it. But it brings back painful memories, which ain't all that fun to dig up sometimes."

Even with the cloud of alcohol lurking in his brain and affecting his judgment, Clifton could still recognize that Swamper was uncomfortable. "That's okay. I understand. Sorry I brought it up."

"No, it's all right. You'll hear it sooner or later anyway, I reckon. Sometimes it's good for memories, painful or not, to occasionally be unearthed. These here scars," he said, now un- buttoning his cuff, folding it back, and scrunching it up to his elbow, "is from an accident that happened years ago while I was on the job."

Clifton didn't sit up. Instead he gently grabbed Swamper's arm at the wrist and elbow and lifted it a little above his face in order to get a better view. "This happened at the pipe shop? Where my father used to work?" The knotty growths, about four or five in all, were hard in some places, mushy in others. The varying consistency and bruised purple color of the welts reminded Clifton of a basket of priced-to-go plums at the grocery store. Each blemish was about five inches long and was raised a good half inch in relief over Swamper's forearm. They looked like a band of giant crawling beetles.

"Yep, at the pipe shop. Long story short, there was an explosion and my arm got ripped up pretty good."

Clifton yawned and felt his eyelids getting heavy. "But what happened?" he asked, stretching his legs over the end of the couch arm. He felt fully relaxed. In the last hour, he hadn't once thought about his mother's predicament or the craziness of the day. "You gotta give me a little more than that."

"Well, what can I say? It was an evening shift and a lot of us were working overtime because we had a big order of drain pipe that was past due for a company over in West Virginia. They were building a mall over there and we were already two weeks late on filling the order. Anyway, I always worked with the same fella. A guy by the name of Bill Epperly, but everybody called him Sweets. Don't even know where the name came from, but I'd known him since we was in school together. Since the thirties I reckon, and we'd always called him Sweets. Me and Sweets worked for close to twenty-five years together. And I don't mean in the same building, I mean we was partners. We worked as a team. Usually had teams of two and we'd been together longer than anybody. Poured enough pipe to get from here to California and back, I reckon. Sweets and Swamper. Swamper and Sweets. We were like M&M's. Or salt and pepper.

"You work with somebody that long, you get to know him better than your own family. Hell, it got so when he went to the bathroom and came out, I could tell you what he ate for dinner the night before." Swamper gave a little laugh and then he got quiet, as if his mind had gone to a distant place. He pulled a ready-rolled cigarette from a box on the end table and lit it with his Zippo. He fingered the lighter for a moment, then set it on top of the pack.

"So that night, we were hustling because our foreman was on everybody. The foreman's boss was on his ass, so of course he was on ours. That pipe had to get poured. Now the whole process isn't that complicated, but you gotta be careful. Patience is the important thing. Just like pulling in those trot lines, it's something that takes practice and patience. Plus, you're working with extreme temperatures. Over a thousand degrees. So there's not a lot of room for screwing up. Anyway, me and Sweets was manning the mold and this . . . this other guy was going to pour with his partner. Well these particular casts were cold, so it was vital that they pour the ore extra slow, and me and Sweets would monitor it, making sure it was smooth and was setting up right.

"At first, things was going fine, but then they started pouring too fast. Me and Sweets both started screaming for them to stop, but it was too loud or too steamy, or I don't know what, and they kept right on going. Well, the combination of the fast pour and the cold mold caused the ore to start bubbling over. Some of it spilled over on to a gas main, and before any of us knew what happened, there was a huge explosion. I got thrown clear across the room. Got knocked out instantly. I don't remember nothing for three full days after that. The last thing I remember was yelling at them two guys to stop pouring and then *boom*. Next thing I know I'm in the hospital. And I got lucky. Only thing wrong with me was these scars, a few broken ribs, and a busted shoulder from when I got shot across the room. The explosion leveled the whole side of the building. I mean leveled it. It rattled the windows in houses up to a mile away. Sent a fireball hurling into the air a hundred feet high. Of course, that's just what I've been told. I was out like a light.

"Anyway, long story short. Sweets and one of the pourers was killed instantly. Me and the other pourer survived with not much more than a few scars. Fire marshal said that me and that guy just happened to be on the lucky side. Sweets and the other pourer were on the side where the gas main decided to blow out. Only good thing is that they didn't have no time to suffer none."

Swamper went off to that distant place again, staring at the front door but not seeing it at all. His mind was elsewhere. But then he came back. He looked down at Clifton who was already asleep. Swamper had no way of knowing that Clifton had barely even heard him mention the name *Sweets* before he passed out.

Swamper mumbled something, halfway to himself and halfway to Clifton. "Well, it's better this way, I reckon. Because that man who survived with me, that man who poured too fast and killed Sweets, that man was your daddy. And I ain't never forgiven him until right this very second."

Chapter 10

WHEN CLIFTON AWOKE, sunlight already streamed through the front windows. It felt like a stack of knitting needles was piercing the hazy film of his eyes. As he lay on the couch, he couldn't seem to lift his head. And he was thirsty. His tongue felt like coarse sandpaper and all he could think about was a glass of water. When he raised himself to a sitting position on the edge of the couch, his head began to throb. If he moved too quickly, he swore he could feel his brain sloshing around, ricocheting off the inner walls of his cranium.

He rested his elbows on his knees and dropped his chin into his open palms. He let the tips of his fingers massage his temples and upper jaw as he tried to piece everything back together. *Well, Swamper was right about one thing. I sure slept. And I never once thought about Maria or Mom or anything else.* And that was true. But the problem was that now everything came flooding back to him two-fold. The fear and anxiety that he'd felt the day before, combined with the remnants of last night's alcohol, instantly made him queasy. Rolls of sweat beaded on his forehead and pangs of hunger gnawed at his gut.

He stood up and tried to make his way to the kitchen, but he found it difficult to keep his balance. He had to put his arms out in front of him and grab on to the back of the couch in order not to fall. *God, why would Mom do this to herself every day on purpose? I'll never drink again. Never.*

Clifton filled a glass from the spigot, trying to recall his conversation with Swamper. He remembered the story about the three-titted woman—that he remembered for sure. And the tiger. But then what? He vaguely remembered touching the scars on Swamper's arm. Or was that a dream? A work accident? He remembered Swamper talking about one of his friends at the pipe shop, but he couldn't recall his name. And then everything had gone fuzzy. He remembered looking up at Swamper's face as he spoke, but then his world began to spin. He'd closed his eyes to stop the spinning and then things began whirling around the inside of his head instead. And that was it. The next thing he knew, he'd woken up on the couch.

Now, as he drank the water, it felt like liquid gold sliding down his throat. He drank several glasses and got a little relief, though now the water slopped around in his hollow belly, making him feel nauseated. He went out to the porch and was surprised to see Bosco; he'd all but forgotten about him.

He patted Bosco on the head as the dog strained to greet him, but the jump rope around his collar had been tied to one of the vertical posts. Clifton definitely didn't remember doing that, so he assumed Swamper must have. He also assumed, judging by the tied-up dog and how quiet it was in the house, that Swamper wasn't there. He'd had a feeling that Swamper was gone when he'd first woken up, just like some people could sense being watched while they slept. He called out for the old man several times but was answered at first by silence and then by the horn of a morning train. When he looked down at the dock, he saw that the skiff was missing. A moment later, when the train rolled by and the wheels screeched along the rails, he thought his head might split in half. He pushed the heels of his hands into his temples and felt the blood pulsate through them. *Never again.*

When the train disappeared, he stretched his arms above him and breathed in the moist air coming off the river. The sunlight that had stung his eyes earlier had slipped behind a gray cloud, and as Clifton looked behind him, he saw a whole troop of similar clouds slowly rolling in from the west. Barn swallows swooped by in opposite directions as they searched out places of refuge, and the ovals of yellowed beech leaves fluttered by as the breeze gradually increased. *It's gonna storm soon. If I leave right now, I might be able to beat it.*

Five minutes later he had his shoes on—which he didn't remember removing—and had the jump rope in his hands. "Let's go, Bosco," he said as he looked up at the ever-darkening clouds roiling like wisps of black smoke. There was something about an approaching storm that had always thrilled him. Like life was put on hold for a few minutes. If nothing else, he was thankful for the storm because it was blocking out the unbearable July sun that would have played hell with his hangover.

The breeze, which continued to strengthen as he walked up the path toward the road, at least provided some relief from the humidity. And as miserable as he was, in a way he felt as if he'd earned a small badge of honor. His first hangover. It was like he could now shelve that one away and mark it off his list. Not that he actually had a list, and even if he did, he didn't think getting a hangover would have been on it, but he still felt a small twinge of pride that he'd done it.

If he had had a list, one of the things on it would have been to see all fifty states. As it was, he'd seen only two: Virginia, of course, and West Virginia, where his parents had taken him to the state fair when he'd been little. He barely remembered it, but he still counted it. Another thing on the list would have been to catch a citation catfish. Not necessarily a state record, but just a fish big enough to earn him a certificate and get his name in the paper. He wanted to swim in the ocean. He didn't care which one, but he wanted to see the waves and bodysurf them. He wanted to snow ski. The mountains generally got a fair amount of snow in the winter, but there was nowhere to go skiing. He'd decided that once he saved up enough money, he was going to try to buy a car so he could go. And also to the beach. Yesterday, he'd even entertained— just for that brief window of time when everything was going so well—that maybe he and Julie could go together. But the shutters on that window had closed quickly.

Those daydreams were extinguished once he reached the road. A heavy dose of reality hit. He realized he wouldn't be going near a beach, or anywhere else with Julie, anytime soon. Her sister was most likely dead. All at once he realized that he really needed to get home. Really needed to find out what was happening in Crocket's Mill. Had to find out if the man had been caught. Had to find out about Maria. Had to find out what he was going to do about getting his mother out of jail. Had to feed Bosco. Had to *return* Bosco.

Just as he crossed the road and got ready to jump on the trail toward the Killing Pit, an old pickup truck crested the hill. It was a two-tone beige Ford and looked like it had come off the assembly line in the fifties. An older gentleman with shoulder-length graying hair was driving. He was a diminutive man, and his eyes barely made it over the crest of the large steering wheel. He stopped the truck in the middle of the road, and Clifton made a halfhearted wave. The man hand-cranked the window and said, "Hello there, Buster Brown. You and your dog need a ride to town? Looks like a storm's coming round." He poked his head out the window and glanced through his thick glasses up toward the sky.

It was only when Clifton heard the voice that he realized that the driver wasn't a man at all, but actually a woman. She had a baseball cap tucked down tightly on her head, she wore a baggy shirt that revealed no chest as far as Clifton could tell, and her face was plain with no makeup. A dream-catcher hung from the rearview mirror, the web and feathers swaying back and forth like a miniature pendulum. Clifton had a feeling she might be one of the Hell's Hill Hippies who lived in the mountains on the fringes of Crocket's Mill. He'd heard about them, and had occasionally seen them in town, but those sightings were rare. It was widely known that a troupe of six or seven women—though some said up to a dozen—lived together on a sixty-acre plot up on Hell's Hill. They ran an organic farm and were more or less self-sufficient. Rumors had been flying around forever that they grew marijuana up in the hills, but since different groups had been living there, off and on, for the past twenty years without incident, Clifton kind of doubted it.

But what wasn't rumor at all was that the Hell's Hill Hippies had one rule that they strictly enforced: No men allowed. They believed strongly, and took pride in the fact, that they could survive just fine without a man's help. But apparently, judging by the current offer of a ride, they had no problem helping a man if the situation presented itself. Clifton's mind, which he could tell was running a little slower than usual, processed the different possibilities. He could almost feel the rusty gearwheels trying to turn in his head, the teeth grinding without proper lubrication. If he took the shortcut, it would probably take about the same amount of time as it would if the woman drove him in to town. And with the way he was feeling at the moment, the less walking he had to do, the better. Besides, he sort of wanted to see what was going on in Crocket's Mill. Was the town in a frenzy? Had they boarded up all the windows because there was a monster on the prowl?

"Okay, thanks," said Clifton. "A ride would be great."

The woman motioned with her thumb toward the bed. "Just drop the gate and your dog can ride in back. Then hop on in."

Clifton did as instructed and with only a little prodding,

just like when they'd taken the skiff, Bosco jumped in. When Clifton sat down and closed the heavy door behind him, it let out a shrill squeak, causing more pain to shoot through his head. Between him and the woman was a cardboard beer box filled with egg cartons. The woman saw Clifton eyeing them. She put the truck into gear and said, "I'm taking the eggs into Samford. We sell them to a whole food place over there. You ever had a fresh egg? I mean one that was just laid?"

Clifton shook his head.

"There's not much on this earth that's better than that. The yolks come out a rich gold, almost orange like a sunrise. Not yellow like the eggs you get from the store. I'd offer you a couple but I can't break up the dozens."

Clifton looked at the stacks of cartons sitting in the beer box. "That's okay, I'm not really hungry for a raw egg at the moment anyway." In fact, just the thought of it, along with the jostling of his body as the truck hit the ruts, made him feel sick. "You must have a lot of chickens."

The woman carefully set a hand on the edge of the box to steady it as the rough road caused the Styrofoam cartons to squeak. "We do. Got a whole coop full of them. This box here has eighteen dozen eggs in it. Right now we're getting that much about every two or three days. They're laying real good lately."

Clifton leaned his forehead against the side window and

watched as the clouds spit little drops of water against the glass. He again wondered why in the world anybody would willingly subject themselves to alcohol. It had tasted horrible, and other than a brief period when he had felt happy and downright silly, he didn't see what the attraction was. And certainly, with the way the aftereffects were treating him, he promised himself once more that he would never drink again. He closed his eyes and thought about getting home. He would make some phone calls to the police station in Samford and then hopefully take a nap.

"You heard about what's been going on in town? Crazy stuff."

Clifton opened his eyes and sprang to attention. He tried to produce a little saliva from the layer of cotton in his mouth, but it was impossible. He swallowed and said, "I heard a girl got kidnapped."

The woman kept her eyes on the road while talking out the side of her mouth, just like Popeye had done in the old cartoons. For some reason, this intrigued Clifton though he couldn't say why. "Yeah, the little girl's still missing. No trace of her so far. But they did find a body."

Clifton again tried to produce some saliva so he could speak. He felt blood pulsing in his ears, felt the lobes getting itchy and hot. But he also felt relief. "What do you mean they found a body? It wasn't the little girl's?"

"No, like I told you, they haven't found her yet. Least that's what they're saying so far. But this morning the radio said that yesterday the police got an anonymous tip to go check out Charlie Day's place. You probably know him. The ice cream man? A black fella? Sweet as pie."

Clifton nodded, but the apprehension filling his body made it almost impossible to speak. "Yeah, I know him."

The rubber of the windshield wipers made an annoying bumping sound as the woman tried to clear the few freckles of rain dotting the dry windshield. "So they go out there last night and find Charlie dead in his living room. The radio didn't say what happened, but they did say it wasn't from natural causes. Said it was being investigated as a homicide. They did say they thought it was linked to the little girl's disappearance. Said the ice cream truck was in the driveway but that his car was missing. So be on the lookout for a yellow Lincoln. Don't really see how anybody could miss it."

The relief of a moment ago instantly disappeared. He felt worse than he had when he'd first woken up. But not because Charlie was dead. Of course he felt bad about that, but what struck him more than anything was something else she'd told him. *The radio said that yesterday the police got an anonymous tip to go check out Charlie Day's place.* Assuming the kidnapper guy was still in the vicinity, and assuming he was most likely watching the television or listening to the radio, then he wouldn't have to be a rocket scientist to figure out who gave the anonymous tip. And if that was the case, then Clifton could be in even more danger than he'd ever imagined possible.

"What about a suspect? Do they know who did it?"

"They didn't give any names, but they did give a description of a guy they're looking for. White male, six foot, late twenties. Got a lot of tattoos. So be on the lookout for him too. The whole thing's crazy. I've been living in these hills for years and never heard of anything like it. You hear about stuff like this in the big cities, but I never thought it would happen in Crocket's Mill. Never."

As he listened to her describe the man, the image of Maria being stuffed into the broom closet haunted him. Those wiry arms lifting her, the look in her eyes, the silver tape across her mouth. It all haunted him. For a moment, Clifton thought he might be sick.

"You know what's funny?" said the woman as she looked into her rearview mirror.

"What's that?"

"Look at your dog back there." Her eyes were switching back and forth between the mirror and the road. "See what he's doing?"

Clifton turned to look at Bosco. His front legs were perched on the bubble of the wheel well, his snout pointing directly into the breeze. His mouth was open and he looked like he was smiling as the wind pushed the black fur away from his face. Little sprinkles of water beaded on his coat like raindrops on the hood of a freshly waxed car.

"Isn't it funny how dogs love to stick their heads out a window and let the wind rush over them? You can be going sixty-five down the highway and it won't bother them at all. They're happy as can be. Like they think they're the Red Baron or something. But then if you're sitting at home and you grab the scruff of their neck and blow in their face, they go crazy. They hate it. They'll freak out like they think you're torturing them."

Clifton turned back around and gave a halfhearted smile. "Yeah, I guess you're right."

"I don't know—it's just one of those things I think about sometimes."

When she got to the end of the road and nosed the front of the truck to the stop sign, she clicked her turn indicator. "Like I said, I'm heading over the bridge into Samford. Which way you going?"

"I'm going that way," said Clifton, pointing toward Crocket's Mill. "Thanks for the lift."

The woman looked over the tops of her glasses toward the dark clouds. They spat flecks of rain with more frequency now, but it still wasn't out-and-out raining yet. "I hate leaving you out here when the sky's about to open up. It won't take me any time to run you into town."

"That's okay. I don't live far from here." He cocked his head and looked out the windshield as he grabbed the door handle. "Looks like I've got just enough time to make it. Thanks again."

"You be careful."

Clifton closed the door and had turned to head toward town, his mind now chock-full of fear, when the truck's horn sounded. When he looked back, he couldn't hear what she was saying, but he did see her gesturing toward the bed of the truck. *Bosco. Jesus, I forgot Bosco.* He shook the alcohol-soaked cobwebs from his head, gave the woman a little wave and smile as if to say, *Oops, stupid me,* and then let the gate down. Bosco stood on the end, his tail wagging, but hesitated like a puppy at the edge of a boat dock. Clifton grabbed the ends of the jump rope, gave a little tug, and Bosco leapt onto the gravel.

As the truck pulled out, Clifton got a lungful of exhaust. Perhaps, he thought, as punishment for forgetting Bosco. "Let's get home," he said. "You must be starved. Hopefully, Mr. Henderson left you out some food."

Maybe it was the increasing wind, maybe it was the dark clouds overhead, or more likely it was because the little town of Crocket's Mill was dealing with a murder and a kidnapping, but whatever it was, there was a gloomy, ominous feel in the air. For one thing, even though it was late morning, traffic was almost nonexistent on Kamron. And as he got into the center of town, he saw almost no one on the sidewalks. But at the police station, there was a flurry of activity. Cop cars were parked all over the place. There were Crocket's Mill squad cars, Samford cars like the one he'd seen the night before, silver and blue state police cars, and several unmarked ones too. There was even a television van from Roanoke parked on the corner. A cameraman and a perfectly made-up woman holding a microphone stood on the sidewalk. She held a card over her hairsprayed head, apparently not too happy about the wind and drizzle.

Clifton stayed on the opposite sidewalk when he passed the police station, trying to avert his eyes from everything going on. But it was hard to do. He also kept looking around for any sign of the ice cream man. He was sure the guy was waiting around every corner, ready to jump from an alley and grab him.

Just past the station, the first rolls of thunder echoed off the surrounding mountains. White needles of lightning zigzagged over the ridges. Telephone wires began swaying gently above the sidewalk as the breeze picked up. Bits of paper, a

Popeyes wrapper, and small leaves and pine needles whipped at Clifton's feet. A plastic Coke bottle clattered and rolled toward Bosco's paws, but he didn't seem to notice. Instead, he stuck his snout directly into the wind, his moist black nose twitching as he tried to decipher the overload of information blowing at him.

When Clifton looked up at the mountain ridge in the distance—which he actually couldn't see anymore because a bruised purple cloud enveloped the peak—something on a telephone pole caught his eye. And then as he glanced behind him, he realized that every telephone pole lining the street looked the same way. Someone had already put up signs asking for information about the disappearance of Maria O'Kane. If Clifton had been paying attention when he had walked through town, he would have noticed that there were signs on the doors of every store, too.

He approached the piece of paper that was stapled on to the pole closest to him, staring at the picture as the corners flapped in the wind. It was her all right. A miniature version of Julie. The girl he'd seen come crashing out of that broom closet. The fear in her eyes. The muffled screams behind the duct tape.

The photo was already beginning to smudge as a fine spray of rain fell over it. And then, just as Clifton was turning away, a larger drop hit the picture, just below the little girl's eye.

Clifton turned away and felt sick once more, the irony not escaping him as that tear dripped down her face, smearing the ink and partially erasing her.

As if it was meant to be, as if Mother Nature had held out for as long as she could, the rain didn't let loose until Clifton reached his corner. So he and Bosco had only a quick sprint until they were underneath the shelter of the carport. But they weren't alone. As Bosco shook his body to dry out, some of the water flew against the metal quarter panel of the Dodge. *What the heck is she doing home? How'd she get out?*

Like a giant flashbulb, a blue curtain of light suddenly covered the neighborhood, instantly followed by a booming clap of thunder. It cracked so loudly that the tin roof above his head rattled. Bosco immediately hunched down and alligator-crawled underneath the chassis of the car, disappearing from view. The rain was now coming down in translucent sheets. It fell so hard that only the outline of Mr. Henderson's house could be seen across the way. The trunks of the trees were bent nearly parallel to the ground, and now, even under the protection of the carport, Clifton was getting soaked. A grayish spray enveloped the neighborhood, and a rush of whitewater poured from all of the downspouts like raging waterfalls. He figured Bosco would be fine for the time being, so he opened the side door and walked inside.

His mother sat at the kitchen table, her elbows resting on the edge, her face smothered by her hands. Clifton shook his head in the same way Bosco had just done, then rubbed a hand over his coarse bush of hair to remove any excess. If nothing else, the cold rain had woken him up a little. "What're you doing here?" he asked, his voice flat and without any hint of compassion. "Thought you'd still be locked up."

A few gasps of breath managed to filter through the cracks of her fingers as she said something inaudible.

"I can't understand you, Mom."

Clifton stood next to the table, looking down at her. His body gave a quick shudder, maybe from a chill when his wet skin met the cool of the air conditioning, maybe from just being disgusted with her. When she removed her hands, a set of goosebumps erupted along his neck and arms. Long strands of ratty, greasy hair partially veiled her sunken face. Her complexion was haggard, pale, almost green. Dark half-moons of fatigue were smudged beneath her eyes, and her hands noticeably shook as she reached for her box of cigarettes. She lit up and then thumbed the lighter, rotating it several times in her hand before methodically setting it on top of the box just so, which he'd seen her do a thousand times before, but for some reason this time it struck him as strange. He'd watched Swamper do it in the same exact manner the night before. She took a drag and then pressed the heels of her hands into her eye-sockets to stanch the tears. "I said, I got bailed out." She sniffled and seemed to calm a bit.

As much as Clifton wanted to be angry with her, wanted to be disgusted by her, wanted to make her feel horrible for what she'd done, instead, now as he saw how pathetic and defenseless she was, saw her hands tucked to her chest as a billow of smoke rose from them, saw her frail body huddled in the chair and trembling like a rat riddled with poison, he couldn't muster the energy. She was his mother after all. He loved her regardless of everything. And besides, it didn't look like there was any way to make her feel lower or more ashamed than she already was. There was no way to make her hurt worse. So instead of beating a dead horse, he walked next to her, put his arm around her shoulders, and gently squeezed. She vigorously stubbed the cigarette into the ashtray as if it had tried to cause her harm, as if she had a vendetta against it, and then tilted her head into Clifton's chest and began sobbing. Between breaths she said several times over, "Thank you, baby."

Clifton held her for a few minutes, staring out the window as the rain continued to pound, as a pool of chocolate water formed in front of Bosco's doghouse. When she calmed, he let go of her and took a seat in one of the straight-back chairs. "So what happens now?" he asked. "The cop that came over here last night said this wasn't the first time. You never told me about getting arrested before."

His mother's already anguished face twisted into a look of even deeper pain. "Those other times were fluke things, Clifton. I hadn't even had that much to—"

"Stop it, Mom," said Clifton. He didn't yell or get angry. He kept his voice calm and even. "No excuses, okay? I don't want to hear that crap right now. You lied to me. Or at least you kept the truth from me. You've been depressed for years. I know. I get it. But I don't want to hear excuses right now. I just want to know what happens from here. More importantly, what's going to happen to *me?*"

Mrs. Carlson nodded. She reached for the box of tissues on the table, wiped her eyes, and blew her nose. She set the spent tissue on a growing mound that had already formed next to her. "What's going to happen? Well, I talked to a public defender this morning before I got bailed out. He said that if I voluntarily commit myself to the rehab center—the one over in Samford—for thirty days and get myself cleaned up and dried out, then most likely the judge will show leniency. He won't . . . he won't take you away from me." She broke down again into painful sobs.

Anger arose in Clifton just as quickly as the compassion had a moment before. "What do you mean, 'take me away'? Where the hell would I go? And what will happen to you?"

"I want to get better. I'm tired of it. Tired of the drinking, tired of the hangovers, tired of feeling like shit all the time. Tired of neglecting you. I'm sorry, baby. I'm so sorry. I don't even know how all this happened. Don't know where I've been for the last few years. I look at you and realize that you're all grown up. My baby has grown up right in front of my eyes, and I was too messed up to watch it happen. Too messed up to experience my little boy grow into a man. God, you look like your daddy."

Clifton's jaw tightened and his teeth, beyond his control, grated against one another. "But what happens to ME?" he shouted as the all-too-familiar anxiety churned in his gut. "Do I get locked up at the juvie or something while you get yourself sober? Do I get punished because you're an alcoholic? A drunk? Why should the rest of my summer get ruined because you have to get fucked up all the time?"

He'd wanted the words to sting and they probably had, but Mrs. Carlson's expression didn't change. The pain in her eyes had reached its limit, and there was no way for them to reveal anymore anguish than they already showed. She sniffled and gasped a couple of times before she spoke. "Because you're a minor, the court would order you to a state home if you couldn't stay with family. So you're exactly right. But you can stay with your grandfather. It's already been worked out."

"My grandfather? I don't even know my grandfather. So I get shipped off somewhere for the last month of my summer with some racist old man that I've never even met? That's what I get? Thanks, Mom. Thanks a whole bunch."

Mrs. Carlson's eyes had gone dry, as if she had simply run out. Her voice was flat and calm. "You do know him, Cliffy. He's the one who bailed me out this morning. From what he told me, I guess you know him as Swamper." She tried to force a little smile. It was an unsure smile, one that said *I have no idea how you're going to take this.*

And that was exactly how Clifton felt. He wasn't at all sure how to take the news. Swamper was his grandfather? One part of him wanted to be elated, but another part of him was angry. *What the hell did I do to deserve this? All this shit that's happened to me in the last twenty-four hours? Stop your whining. That's what Swamper would tell you. He'd tell you to stop your bellyaching. Your father would say the same thing.* He looked at the lighter on her pack of cigarettes and couldn't believe he'd never realized it before now. The clues had been in front of him the whole time. *I knew your daddy. I know what happened to him.*

"Swamper's my grandfather?"

"Yes, baby," said Mrs. Carlson. Tears welled in her eyes once more, but for the first time, those tears seemed to have a hint of happiness in them. "I had no idea the two of you had been spending time together. He told me everything this morning. How he wrote you a note. How you started fishing with him. He said that every day he wanted to tell you, said it was killing him, but he didn't know how I'd react. How you'd react." She took a couple of quick gasps of air and grabbed another tissue. "He loves you, Cliffy. He told me as much this morning. Believe it or not, maybe this whole thing—this arrest—is a godsend.

"Today was the first time I talked to my daddy face-to-face in nearly seventeen years. After he refused to come to my wedding way back when, I made a vow that I never wanted anything to do with him again. And as hard as that was, I stuck to it. I felt abandoned by him. Betrayed. You have to understand, I was close to Daddy when I was young. I loved him very much. And I'd never really known him to be a racist when I was growing up. Well, maybe he was a little, but he wasn't a bad man. He wasn't evil or anything. He would never have done anything to harm a person just because of their race. Nothing like that. So when I got pregnant and your father asked me to marry him, I had no idea my own daddy would react the way he did."

Clifton looked at his mother in disbelief. "Wait, so you're

telling me I was an accident? That you and Dad had a shot-gun wedding? Jesus, what else haven't I been told?"

"You weren't an accident, Clifton. Don't put it that way." She dabbed at the corners of her eyes with the wadded tissue. "You're the best thing that ever happened to me. But, yes, I got pregnant before I was married. Your father and I had only known each other for a few months. But we loved each other. We truly did. And you have to understand, it was a very diffi-cult time for me. It was the early seventies. There weren't too many white women marrying black men at that time. Cer-tainly not around here. But I never imagined that I couldn't count on my daddy for support. So you have to understand how hurt I was when he refused to come to his own daugh-ter's wedding, even if it was sudden and not under ideal cir-cumstances. I assumed his refusal to be there was because I was marrying a black man. After talking with him today, though, I now realize that race was only a small part of it. A very small part. It was much more complicated than that. We weren't very good at communicating back then. He was stubborn and so was I. But we had a heavy talk today, Cliffy. I mean, we both got seventeen years worth of stuff off our chests.

"And it was good. I mean, as good as it could be under the circumstances. I don't know why things happen sometimes. I

don't know what God's plan is or what He intends, but some-times things happen for a reason. I truly believe that. I think that all of this happened so we—the three of us—could finally be together. I'm going to get better, Cliffy. I swear. I promise. It's not gonna be easy, but I'm checking myself in right away. Today in fact. You need to get some things together. I'm going to pack and then I'll take you by Daddy's. By Swamper's. I mean, I assume that's what you want to do. It's either that or temporary foster care at the Children's Home in Salem."

Clifton sat in the chair, his mouth agape, as he took in everything his mother had just told him. He didn't know what to do or say. He nodded and said, "Okay."

"Okay, what? You'll go to Daddy's?"

Clifton stared at his mother, still as stunned as if she'd smacked him in the face with a cast-iron skillet. "Yeah," he said.

"Well, let's get ourselves some showers, get cleaned up, and put some things together." She paused for a moment, then stood up and gave Clifton a hug as the tears started once more. "I'm scared, baby. And I'm sorry. I'm so sorry. There's nothing worse in this world than realizing that you've failed as a mother. That you're a bad parent. That's what I realized last night while I was sitting in that jail cell."

Clifton gently grabbed his mother's arm and stroked it. He patted her hand. "You didn't fail, Mom. You did fine."

"You have no idea what that means to me. Thank you, Cliffy. But I'm gonna do better. I promise. They say that what doesn't kill you only makes you stronger."

Clifton smiled and squeezed her hand. "Then you must be pretty damn strong I guess."

She let out a surprised laugh and squeezed him hard around the shoulders before heading to her bedroom. He didn't know what to think. He was a wayward balloon inflated with mixed emotions that seemed to rise and fall with no warning. He wanted his mother to get better and was happy she was about to receive help, but he was angry that she'd let it come to this in the first place. He couldn't believe or grasp that Swamper was his grandfather. That they shared the same blood. But he was angry because he felt like he'd been duped. Like he'd been left out of the big secret in town that everyone else had been whispering about behind his back for years. What was it going to be like when he saw Swamper? Would things be awkward and uncomfortable? His feelings undulated like that balloon in a sporadic wind. Up and down. Up and down.

With everything that had transpired in the last few minutes, he had completely forgotten about the other things going on. The fact that a girl had been kidnapped, that Charlie had been murdered, that a psychopath was possibly looking for him. He'd also forgotten about his hangover, which finally seemed to have subsided. The irony that both he and his mother currently had hangovers, and that they had both vowed to never let it happen again, didn't escape him. He even managed a slight smile.

When he heard his mother get into the shower, he turned on the television to see what the latest news was in Crocket's Mill. *One thing's for sure,* he thought as he sank into the couch, *I can't handle many more days like the ones I've had lately.*

Chapter 11

THE DRIVE TO SWAMPER'S was one of the strangest trips he'd ever experienced. It was only a few miles from his house, but it seemed like he and his mother were going on a road trip to a foreign country. To a new, unexplored land on the other side of a mountain, which in a way, he decided, was exactly what he was doing. For one thing, despite the relationship he and his mother had had over the last few years, when he really thought about it, he'd never been away from her for more than twenty-four hours. Never. Not once in his life. For another, he'd never known any other blood relatives other than his parents. Or at least, he'd never been aware that he knew them. Swamper was his grandfather. His mother's father. He still couldn't get a firm handle on that. And how was it possible that his true grandfather, his own flesh and blood, had happened to be the only person in the world who'd ever found one of his messages in a bottle. Coincidence? To Clifton, that seemed highly unlikely. He had so many questions he wanted to ask. So many things to clear up and get straight. He felt nervous. Instead of butterflies, a nest of angry hornets swarmed in his stomach as he drove through town.

And that was another reason why the trip was strange. Because *he* was driving. He didn't have a license nor had he ever been behind the wheel before except for a couple of days of practice during a driver's ed class at school. As they'd gotten ready to leave, and just after he'd taken Bosco over to Mr. Henderson's, his mother had said, "Would you mind driving? I want to finish putting on my makeup."

Ever since his mother had spilled her guts to him and apologized for everything, she seemed to be in a remarkably good mood, all things considered. It was as if her admission of guilt and her remorse had had a cathartic effect on her. As if she'd purged her soul of her sins and was now ready to seek redemption and forgiveness at the rehab center. She genuinely seemed excited to get there. To get her life back on track. She seemed to have already accepted her problems and was now ready to start anew.

"Mom, just in case you forgot, I don't have a license," he

said as they were about to leave. "I barely passed the test to get my permit."

"Oh, who cares. It's only a few miles. And after last night, I don't think I'm going to have a license for a while either. You might as well start learning. Looks like you're going to be the driver in this household for the next few months."

"But—"

"Just drive," she said, handing him the keys. "There's only one way to learn. Besides, I want to at least look presentable when I show up at the center."

Clifton chuckled despite himself. "Mom, I really don't think you have anything to worry about. It's a place for drug addicts and alcoholics. They don't exactly expect you to look your best when you get there. Maybe when you leave, but not when you show up." Clifton found it humorous—and so very much like her—that she wanted to look nice when she arrived at the rehab. Up until lately, when things had begun to get really bad, she'd always taken special care with the way she looked when she went out in public. Not as much when she went to work, but anywhere else, she always had her hair fixed right and her makeup on. And Clifton had to admit, as bad as she'd looked earlier when he'd first arrived home, she now looked like her old self again. Her eyes were a bit swollen and puffy where she'd been crying, but she looked revitalized ever since she'd gotten everything off her chest and admitted that she needed help. As Clifton pulled out of the driveway, applying the brakes a little too hard at first, he took all of his mother's actions as a good sign that her time in rehab might be successful.

"All the same," she said as she looked at a small pocket mirror and began applying lipstick, "I don't want to look like a slob."

When they got into town, Clifton stared straight ahead as they approached the police station. Cop cars lined both sides of the street, and uniformed officers—as well as plainclothes detectives—scurried in and out of the building like ants traveling back and forth to their lair. Many of them hunched under umbrellas even though the rain had all but subsided. The news van was still there, but the reporter and cameraman were no longer in sight. While Clifton drove, Mrs. Carlson applied mascara to her lashes. She didn't look at anything but the mirror in her lap as she worked.

A fine mist tickled the windshield, and the sky was the gray of an abandoned wasps' nest, but the pounding rain had stopped. The sound of rushing water filled his ears as the tires rotated over the wet road. An oncoming car went through a large puddle and a whitewash of spray rose from the ground as if the car were fording a river. Clifton squeezed the top of the steering wheel and held a deep breath as he drove past the police station, praying that he wouldn't make a mistake and run into a parked police car.

After they got through town, Clifton took a left onto the road that would lead him toward Old Henry's and then to Swamper's. "You know," said Mrs. Carlson as she screwed the mascara dipstick back into its container, "as much as I despise the police, that cop last night was awfully nice. I mean, I guess he didn't have to check on you, but he did. I still hate them all, but he at least showed some humanity."

The hardtop quickly gave way to the dirt road, and suddenly Clifton felt a whole new dynamic as the tires sloshed in the wet mud, attempting to gain purchase. It was like trying to run in sneakers over a frozen pond. "Yeah, he was pretty nice," said Clifton, who eased his grip on the wheel and let his foot off the accelerator a touch. "But he had to come check on me as part of his job. Because I was underage and all."

"Yeah, well that might be what the law states, but it didn't mean he had to do it. He could've just said he did it. I guess with this crazy nut on the loose, they're not taking any chances."

"He offered to take me to my grandmother's house. Said he didn't want me out on the streets alone."

"Yeah, I know. He told me."

"I had to tell him something. I guess if I'd known about Swamper, I could've said my grand*father's*."

Mrs. Carlson stared out the passenger window as clear beads rolled along the glass. "Lord, I haven't been out this way in years. Look, that's the road down to Old Henry's," she said, a happy calmness in her voice as they passed the turnoff to his place.

"So you've been to Swamper's place before?" he asked, finding it hard to believe—despite everything he now knew—that his mother had actually set foot on that property.

"Yes, I've been there. A long time ago. Mama and Daddy moved out this way just after I finished high school. Daddy wanted to be on the river. He wanted to get away from town. He thought the fresh air and the peaceful surroundings might do Mama some good. The cancer was just starting to get to her then. Anyway, I was renting an apartment in Samford with a girlfriend and taking classes at Virginia Tech. This was just before I met your daddy. So I'd get out and visit them every once in a while."

Clifton was once again overwhelmed. His sanctuary, his little secret place on the river where he liked to escape. What he'd thought of as his and Swamper's clandestine shack in the woods actually wasn't a secret at all. His own mother had been there many times before. Years ago, before he was even born. And more surprises seemed to be around every corner. "You went to college?"

"Yep, for a little while. I was taking classes and thinking

about getting a degree in education. Then I met your daddy in the spring, got pregnant, and I never went back. Always planned to but never did. That's the way it goes sometimes."

When Clifton got to the trail crossroads that led down to Swamper's place in one direction and up to the Killing Pit in the other, he brought the car to a stop. "Well, here it is," he said.

"This is it?" she said with surprise. "There used to be a driveway. It wasn't much of one, but you could at least drive down to the back of the house."

"I guess it's gotten grown-over since he stopped driving."

"I reckon so," she said as she looked out the window, trying to locate her father's house through the verdant canopy of leaves.

"Are you gonna come down?" he asked, suddenly feeling extremely nervous, realizing he wasn't going to see his mother for a while. Realizing that he was about to face his grandfather for the first time, or at least for the first time since he knew him as such.

"Clifton, I think I better move on. I don't want to get all wet and muddy. Like I told you, Daddy and I talked this morning for the first time in forever. I don't think I better overdo it." She forced a little smile. "We better take things slow. I've had a lot of anger toward him that I've let build up over the years. Some of it was his fault, some of it mine. Let me go get myself straightened out, then I'll try to fix things with Daddy."

Clifton saw tears begin forming like the swollen raindrops on the windows. "Don't start crying, Mom. You'll smudge your makeup."

She nervously chuckled and stoppered her tears. She smoothed the fabric of her pants, running her palms against the pleats, and then did the same with her sleeves. "How do I look?"

"You look fine, Mom," he said. And he meant it. Despite the hell she'd been through in the past twenty-four hours, she really didn't look too bad. He couldn't believe she was the same woman he'd seen at the kitchen table earlier. There was a shine in her cheeks that he hadn't seen in years. There was optimism in her eyes.

"Thank you, sweetie. You gonna be okay?"

"I'll be fine. I mean, I'll get to fish every day with Swamper. It's not like you're dropping me off at a stranger's house. You just . . ." and then he was at a loss for words. What should he say? "You just get sober"? "Get straight"? "Get your shit together"? He finally decided on, "You just get well. That's the most important thing."

The tears began to form once more. "I will, honey. And

I'm sorry. I'm so sorry for everything." Black streaks trickled down her rouged cheeks. She used her finger to try to stop the flow but it was no use.

Clifton leaned over and hugged her. Then he opened the driver's-side door, reached in the back for the backpack he'd hastily stuffed with a few changes of clothes, and then exited. Mrs. Carlson slid over into the driver's seat and rolled down the window. "I love you, baby. They said I'll be in for thirty days minimum. No visitors allowed, but you can write me. Please do that, okay?"

"I will," he said. He poked his arms through the straps of his pack and hoisted it onto his back. "Good luck."

"Thanks, Cliffy. I'm going to miss you. But when I get out, things are going to be different. I promise. I'm ready for a change. I love you, baby. Love you more than you'll ever know."

"I love you too, Mom."

"Come here," she said.

He leaned over and ducked his head into the open window. She placed her hands on his cheeks and kissed his forehead. "You sure I look okay?" she said as she again pushed away trails of mascara with her pointer finger.

"You look beautiful. I'll see you in a month."

"Okay. Oh, and make sure to get our mail. I left the checkbook in the junk bowl on the counter. There's a little money in the account. Can you take care of paying any bills that are due?"

"Yeah, sure, I guess."

"I'll just send my letters to the house since you'll be checking the mail anyway. Oh, and what about money?" she said as she reached over and fumbled with her purse. "I need to give you a little cash."

"I'm fine, Mom. I grabbed my money before I left." He tapped the front pocket of his shorts.

"Be careful, Cliffy. I can't believe I'm leaving you when there's a crazy man on the loose. God, I'm so sorry."

When she started to cry again, he decided it was time to go. He slogged through the slick mud of the road and around the back of the car before dropping down onto the trail. As he descended, the ferns dried their fronds on the cuffs of his jeans. He noticed that the woods smelled fresh and that the storm had wiped out the humidity. One of the normally dry runoff creeks now flowed down the mountainside like quicksilver. When he got to the bottom of the hill next to the back of Swamper's house, he saw steam rising off the New and drifting downstream like a band of runaway ghosts. The river smoked as if it had been set on fire days before and now only smoldered.

He took a deep breath. *Guess it's time to go meet Grandpa.*

HE TAPPED LIGHTLY on the wooden border of the screen door and then let himself in. He slid his arms out of the straps of the backpack and dropped it on the couch. A strong smell of gasoline filled the room. It wasn't unpleasant, but it was strange. "Swamper?" he said as he looked around, locking eyes with the buck on the wall.

"Back here. In my room."

Over the past month, one place Clifton had never gone was Swamper's bedroom. He'd seen it, of course, mainly in passing while heading to the bathroom, but he'd never actually stepped foot inside. There had never been a reason to.

Clifton walked down the corridor, almost cautiously, as if stalking something in the woods. The pungent odor of fuel got stronger with every step he took. The hornets in his stomach began to buzz once more. *You're being ridiculous. Everything's still the same as it was before. Yeah right. This is my grandfather.* He stopped at the threshold and looked in to see Swamper on his knees, bent over near the bedposts, a steel gasoline container in his hand. "Hey," said Clifton. "What're you doing?"

Swamper looked back over his shoulder and nodded but

didn't make eye contact. He turned around and went back to work. "Hey, boy. I'm pouring kerosene."

Clifton took a few steps into the room to get a better view and immediately noticed something strange. Each of the iron feet of Swamper's bed was resting in an empty tuna fish can. Swamper had the yellow nozzle of the gasoline container placed in one of the cans and was filling it with kerosene. Clifton was puzzled, but at the same time he was thankful for the distraction. Avoiding the obvious topic of conversation relieved him to some degree. "What the heck're you doing?"

Swamper finished pouring and wiped the nozzle with a rag before setting the gas can on the worn pine slats of the floor. "Pouring kerosene. Put it at the feet of your bed and it keeps the bedbugs away. They can't get into your covers that way. Don't you do this at your house?"

Clifton wrinkled his face. "No, I can honestly say we don't do that. I've heard that expression before, about not letting the bedbugs bite, but I didn't think...I mean...I didn't think bedbugs actually existed."

"Hell, yeah, they exist. At least they used to when I was little. Mama always poured kerosene and we never had no problems. Reckon I've always done it since then."

"Whatever works, I guess."

Swamper stood up and lifted the gas can to his chest. "Let

me go put this away. You hungry? You need something to eat?" He still didn't make eye contact with Clifton.

Clifton realized for the first time that he actually was hungry. The last thing he'd put in his stomach was whiskey from the night before. He'd been feeding off of adrenaline ever since. He also couldn't help but notice that Swamper seemed to be avoiding the subject just as much as he was. "Yeah, I could eat something if you're making it."

On the bedside table, Clifton saw a black-and-white photo of what must've been his grandmother when she'd been young. Her hair was short and bobbed, and Clifton imagined it was exactly how his mother would have looked if she'd grown up in the late thirties. Swamper saw him looking at the picture and said with a smile, "That was my Millie." Then he walked out.

Clifton followed him down the hall and through the living room toward the front door. Swamper turned his head and glanced at the backpack on the couch as he passed. Outside, he placed the can of kerosene by the top step of the porch stairs. "Would you mind taking that to the storage shack in a little while?" He looked over to the wood line where a small structure stood, resembling, more than anything else, an old outhouse. The branches of a beech tree hung over the shed, its ridged leaves tapping drops of rainwater onto the roof.

"Yeah, sure. I'll do it right now." Clifton leaned over to grasp the handle.

"Not just yet," said Swamper, who wiped his hands on the rag and then dropped it on top of the can. "Maybe we should sit and talk for a spell first. What do you say?" He nodded toward the chairs.

Clifton took a seat as the knots in his stomach tightened. He felt nervous in the same way that he did when waiting for the principal to call him into his office. And though he'd never experienced it, he imagined it was the same feeling that a boy felt when his father was about to have the birds-and-the-bees talk with him. The boy knew it was coming, and each party, both the father and son, dreaded the conversation, yet they knew that it was inevitable and had to be done.

"Okay," said Clifton.

Swamper sat down in his rocker. "I see you brought a knapsack with you. Guess that means you're gonna stay a while?"

"Yeah, I guess," said Clifton, who stared straight ahead at the view he'd grown to love so much. The gray sky had broken, and puzzle pieces of turquoise were starting to filter through. The vapor trail from a jet slowly dissipated, blending like fresh paint with the wispy cirrus clouds. The river still burned, but the smoke was lifting as it drifted downstream in the light breeze.

"I reckon your mama already told you everything?"

"Yeah, most of it, I guess. But I still have some questions." Clifton's stomach tightened another turn, but just as quickly as it did so, some of the tension began to subside. He began to feel better. Relieved. It was time to get everything out in the open. He imagined it being similar to the way his mother had felt, how she had suddenly seemed happy despite the dour circumstances, once she spilled her soul. "I don't understand a few things."

Swamper faced straight ahead too, rocking slowly as he took in the same view as Clifton. Drops of water fell from the corner of the porch roof and dripped, dripped, dripped into a puddle next to the foundation of the house. "Sure. Go ahead and shoot."

Clifton took a deep breath and then let loose. He wasn't sure where to begin, so he just let the words fly out as they came to him. "So you're my grandfather? Okay, I'm starting to understand that. But how come you never said anything to me? I mean, you knew, right? And how come I never knew you before? Mama once told me, a long time ago, that it's because you were racist. Because you didn't like my daddy. Because you didn't want her to marry a black man. And how did you find my bottle in the river? That seems a little too coincidental. What's going on? Do you hate black people? I've never heard you say anything about it before. But maybe that's because I'm half black. Maybe you were just being careful. The only thing worse than a racist is someone who is a closet racist. Someone who is too scared to say it to my face. Someone who pretends to be your friend but then says things behind your back. How'd you get my bottle with the note in it? How? What the hell's going on?"

Swamper continued to rock as he pulled his pouch of tobacco from the pocket of his overalls. He rolled a cigarette and lit one of the twisted ends. "Whoa there, horsey. Now that's a lot of questions." He blew a puff of gray smoke into the air that drifted away like the fog over the river. The sun now poked out from behind a cloud, and the temperature on the porch instantly went up by a good five degrees. The birds in the surrounding woods began twittering, acting as the final proof that the storm had indeed passed. "But I think I can answer 'em all. Let me explain myself the best that I can. Okay?"

"Yeah, okay," said Clifton, who felt guilty for laying it all on Swamper in one fell swoop. But again, he also felt relieved that it was all out in the open.

"First off, I ain't a racist. I don't know what all your mama told you, but the reason me and her hasn't talked in all these years doesn't have nothing to do with your daddy being black—if that's what you're thinking. Well, maybe it did to some degree. At least back then it did. Things have changed,

Clifton. I ain't perfect. Never claimed to be. When I was young and growing up around here, the attitude toward black folks was different than it is today. I ain't proud of it, but that's just the way it was. Anyway, I'd be lying if I said I was thrilled when your mama told me she wanted to marry a black man. I guess I was embarrassed and worried about what other folks would say more than it bothered me that he was black."

Swamper took a long draw off his cigarette and exhaled deeply. His face relaxed a little. Just like Clifton and his mother, his admission seemed to be doing him some good. "The reason I was against them marrying had to do with *who* he was, not *what* he was."

"What do you mean? I don't get that."

"Because of what I told you last night. About my buddy getting killed. But I think you missed it. I reckon I gave you a little more whiskey than I should've. You'd already fallen asleep."

Swamper then repeated the story he'd told the night before. When he'd finished, he said, "So I blamed your daddy for Sweets's death. Then not too long after that, I find out your mama is dating a black man. Never met the fellow, I just heard it from gossiping friends. She never told me herself. She hid it from me. Then I find out she's pregnant and marrying this fellow. Well, I wasn't at all too happy. But then when I found out *who* it was, well, that's when I lost it. That's when me and your mama fell out of sorts with each other. I felt like she was marrying him just to defy me. Just to make me mad because we didn't always see things eye to eye. But it wasn't about your daddy being black. Mostly it wasn't, anyway. And now, all these years later, I can finally admit that it wasn't your daddy's fault that Sweets died. It was an accident. Just one of those things. You're the one that helped me realize that. And just by listening to the things you've said about him, about the way I see how he raised you for the little time he was around, he must've been one helluva good man."

Clifton tried to absorb everything. He kept his eyes focused on a set of turkey vultures circling high in the now completely blue sky. He appreciated Swamper's candor, but he wasn't quite ready to let him off the hook just yet. "You know, I don't think of myself as black. Or white. I'm just me. If I was walking down the road and saw you, I wouldn't think to myself, 'Here comes a white man.' Same if I saw a black man. But I know most people do. I've seen the way people look at me if I'm out with my mom. I've seen the way they look at her too. So does the fact that I'm half black bother you? Are you embarrassed to be with me? I don't mean to be nasty, but I want to know. Being prejudiced doesn't seem like something that can just change overnight."

Swamper sucked the cigarette down to the nub, nearly burning his fingers in the process. His eyes narrowed as he looked over at Clifton. His face was stern and serious. "To answer your question, no, it doesn't bother me at all. More than anything, *you're* what helped me change. *You're* what made me realize that skin color doesn't mean a damn thing."

"Me? What'd I do?"

"It's not what you did. It's who you are. You're a good kid. You're smart. You're funny. I was thinking about all this last night after you fell asleep, and I came up with an example. You wanna hear it?"

Clifton nodded.

"It's like this house. It's the things on the inside that matter. I don't give a damn what the outside looks like. A sagging porch. Peeling paint. A tree leaning against the roof that I probably should've cut down years ago. That don't make a damn bit of difference to me. It's what's on the inside that matters. So like I said, I don't think I was ever really a racist. I was just acting according to how I was raised. You can believe that or not, but I know it's true." He paused for a moment as he took a last drag off his cigarette and then flicked it over the porch. "Except maybe toward the Nips. But that's a different story. They bombed our ships. Attacked this country. I knew men that were killed at Pearl Harbor. Some from boot camp when I was up in Michigan. I don't think a lot of you young folks quite understand what men of my generation sacrificed for America. For your freedom. But anyway, I'm just an old fool of a man."

Clifton didn't like what he'd just heard—about Swamper's views toward the Japanese—but in a way he also understood. Not the racism, he didn't understand that, but at least he understood where Swamper was coming from. It was just like he'd said earlier: People can't simply change overnight. He also realized that adults weren't always right. He felt like he'd always been trained to believe that adults knew best—in school from teachers, from people on the news, from the president in speeches—but he'd witnessed over and over how wrong they often were, Swamper included. He looked at Swamper as an ideal, he put him on a pedestal, but he also realized that the old man was only human. He wasn't perfect. Clifton shook his head, almost ashamed. "No, you're not. You're not an old fool."

"One last thing and then I'll shut up. But I want you to know. I did a lot of thinking between last night and today after I saw your mama. Life's about change, and I've changed. And you've helped me with that, so I thank you. I've realized that no matter what color a person's skin is on the outside, everyone's blood is the same color on the inside. You and me have the same blood. Same blood, same color. You're my grandson, and I couldn't be prouder."

Clifton was suddenly a little embarrassed. He didn't feel like he'd done anything to deserve the praise he was receiving. "I'm not really sure what to say. But thanks. I mean,

I'm glad I've met you. I'm glad you're . . . I'm glad you're my grandfather."

"Well, I'm glad too. And by the way, don't think you can start calling me grandpa. That'll make me feel old."

They both chuckled for a moment and then things went quiet. There was a lull as they both looked out over the New, absorbing everything that had been said. Clifton watched a cow feeding in the field across the water. He heard its faint low as it communicated with the others around it. After a minute or two of silence, Clifton spoke again.

"So how the heck did you happen to find my bottle? I don't get it."

Swamper smiled and pointed upstream. "You can't see it now because of all the leaves, but in the winter and spring when the trees are still bare, you can see the Palisades from here."

Clifton strained his eyes and moved his head from side to side to try to locate the cliffs, but he saw nothing.

"Well, take my word for it. Right here from this porch I've got a perfect view. So I was sitting here one day when I saw you tossing things into the water. Or at least I thought it was you, but from this distance I couldn't be sure. Either way, I wanted to see what *somebody* was throwing into the river. But I was pretty sure it was you. You have to remember, you might not have known that I existed, but I've always known that you did. You might say I've kept tabs on you over the years. When your daddy died, I was this close," he said, pinching his finger and thumb together, "to introducing myself to you. It wasn't right the way your daddy got killed. I wanted to reach out to you. Wanted you to know that I was hurting for you. I even called your mama to talk with her about it, but she didn't want nothing to do with me. Anyway, when I saw you throwing things into the water, I decided to go down to the dock to see what it was all about. When I saw several bottles floating on the water like fishing bobbers, I used my long-handled net and scooped one out. By the way, it took me forever to get the note out of that damn bottle. I ended up having to smash it against a rock.

"But anyway, after I read your note, I knew that it was time. It was a sign that you and me finally needed to get acquainted. I realized that you needed me. And that maybe I needed you. I realized I needed to finally reach out to you, and I prayed that it wasn't too late. So that's how it happened. You have no idea how difficult it's been for me to not be able to talk to my own grandson. Especially when he's only lived a few miles away for the past sixteen years. Millie died shortly after you were born, and with Sabrina refusing to talk to me, it was a horrible time. Ever since I finally met you, I've been busting at the seams to say something, Clifton. But I was scared. Afraid that if your mother found out then she might prevent us from seeing each other anymore. I've wanted nothing more than to be able to talk with you. To spend time with you. To go fishing together. This last month has been the best month of my life."

"Wow," said Clifton, trying to fathom what Swamper had gone through. "But now it looks like things are going to be okay. Mom's getting help and I'm staying here. We had a good talk on the way over. She had only good things to say about you."

Swamper turned his head and looked sideways at Clifton as if he didn't believe him.

"I'm serious. She said you were a good man. She said you and her had had your differences over the years, but she thought things were going to be okay now."

Swamper rocked slowly as he seemed to weigh Clifton's words. "You know what it's been like for me not being able to talk with you? You know what it's been like to see you as a little boy in town and not even be able to say hello? I'll tell you what it's been like. Let me give you another one of my famous examples," he said, smiling. "Like I told you, I've been doing a lot of thinking since last night."

Clifton recognized the sly grin on Swamper's face. The playful glimmer in his eye. He was about to go in some crazy direction to make his point.

"You ever been in a restaurant or some other public place

and had to hit the head really bad? I'm not talking about taking a piss. Which, by the way, never did make no sense to me. Why would anyone wanna *take* a piss? But anyway, I'm talking about having to take a smash so powerful that it could crack the hull of a battleship. Where your gut is boiling and if you don't go right then, it might end up in your shorts. I'm talking about the way your stomach gets after eating a couple dozen fried oysters. You know what I mean?"

Clifton smiled and nodded despite having no idea where Swamper was going. He replied, "*That's* what it felt like not being able to talk with me?"

"No, not that. Hold on, I'm getting there. What it was like is this. So after you go and do your business, then you have to wipe. And this is what I'm getting to. This is my point right here. After taking a crap like that, then you realize that there's no toilet paper in the bathroom. No paper towels. No napkins. No nothing. The feeling that I got from not being able to talk to you was just like that. It was horrible."

Clifton could tell that Swamper, in his own unique way, was actually being serious, but he couldn't help himself. He started cracking up. "You've got to be kidding me. That's the weirdest, strangest, most disgusting analogy I've ever heard. So you're saying that not being able to talk to your grandson was the same thing as not being able to wipe your ass?"

"Yep. Identical."

"Well, here I am. You're talking to me now, so what does that mean?"

Swamper rubbed the scruff over his Adam's apple as he contemplated his answer. After a moment of thought he said, "Well, I reckon you're like the lost roll of toilet paper."

"I'm the toilet paper?" said Clifton. "How do you figure?"

"You search every cabinet, every drawer in the bathroom. Behind the mirror of the medicine cabinet if there is one. Every nook and cranny as you shuffle around with your pants and shorts bunched at your ankles, trying not to trip. After you've searched everywhere for something to wipe with, you start to get panicky. You start to sweat. You don't know what you're going to do. And then, hidden behind the toilet, sitting on the tile of the floor, you catch a glimpse of something. It's a half-used roll that someone stashed away in case of an emergency. Imagine the feeling you have at that very instant. Right when you thought your life couldn't get any worse, suddenly you realize everything is going to be okay. Go ahead and get that picture in your head for a second. You got it?"

Clifton chuckled as he closed his eyes and imagined the ridiculous scene in his mind. "Yeah, okay I got it."

"That feeling, that amazing sense of relief, that's the feeling I had when I saw you show up on the railroad tracks that day. Standing there with your fishing rod and bucket. I knew right then and there that everything was going to be okay. You were the toilet paper."

Clifton opened his eyes and got ready to make a wisecrack, but he saw that Swamper's face was taut and serious as he looked straight ahead. It almost seemed like he might cry. Clifton quickly closed his eyes again so Swamper wouldn't know he'd seen him, letting the silence of the afternoon do the rest of the talking instead.

Chapter 12

OVER THE COURSE OF THE NEXT WEEK, things between Clifton and Swamper returned to the way they had been before. There was nothing awkward or uneasy about their relationship. But in the town of Crocket's Mill, things were far from normal. Neither Maria nor the yellow Lincoln had been found. The newscasters reported that the police had several leads and were looking for a "person of interest" but they wouldn't release a name. All they gave was the description of the man. Rumors were flying around town that the "person of interest" was the same man who'd been released from prison on that first day when Clifton had met Swamper. The same man Old Henry had complained about in the store. Since that man had originally been from Alabama, there was a lot of speculation that he had probably left town already, with or without Maria, and was long gone. But whether he was still around or not didn't make most of the people in Crocket's Mill feel any better.

It didn't make Clifton feel any better either. But as every day passed, his anxiety about the ice cream man dissipated a little more. That guy was on the run. He had to have more important things to worry about than coming after Clifton. He rationalized, and Swamper had concurred, that the man had simply made an empty threat that day to scare him. At this point, there was no reason for him to search out Clifton unless he was totally crazy.

Nevertheless, since Clifton had arrived for good at Swamper's, he'd left the premises only a handful of times. Mostly he'd stayed close to home, checking and baiting trot lines, doing chores around the house, helping Swamper clean, and he even went swimming a couple of times. They'd become roommates of sorts, sharing in the responsibilities. He took the skiff down to Old Henry's one day for a few groceries, and he made two trips to his house to get the mail, but other than that, he'd mostly stayed close by. They'd also played a lot of chess, and so far, much to Swamper's chagrin, Clifton was still undefeated.

After his second trip back from getting the mail, Clifton had returned with Bosco. This time for good. He and Swamper had discussed it and decided that Bosco was their dog now. That he wouldn't be going back. They joked that they hadn't stolen him, they were just borrowing him permanently. Swamper even conceded to let the dog come into the house after Clifton spent a full day giving him a dozen flea baths. Overall, considering the circumstances, things had been going pretty well.

During that first week after Maria disappeared, there had been two things that Clifton had wanted to do that he didn't end up doing. For one, he'd entertained the idea of going to Charlie's funeral out at the black Baptist church, which was located about five miles from Swamper's place. Or as Swamper said, "About five miles as the fly crows." But since the kidnapper was still on the loose, and Clifton would have had to walk, they decided it might not be such a good idea. Secretly, he wasn't overly disappointed anyway, since the road to get there would have taken him directly past the spot where his father had been killed.

The other thing he'd thought about doing was volunteering to be a part of one of the search teams that had been organized to scour the rural outlying areas of Crocket's Mill. The police were welcoming any and all volunteers to walk certain sections of the surrounding hillside. In fact, one morning while Clifton and Swamper sat on the porch finishing their breakfast, they saw a team down below working each side of the railroad tracks. One part of Clifton had wanted to help, mainly for Julie's sake, but another part of him said,

You were probably the last person to see Maria alive. You sure you want to take a chance on being the first person to find her dead? In the end, he decided against it.

The day after he'd seen the search team, three days since Maria had been abducted, he was sitting on the dock in the early morning sunshine cleaning a couple of catfish when a boat came chugging from upstream. It was a larger boat than he was used to seeing on the river, and it created a large wake as it motored along. The wake wasn't created because the boat was going too fast, but more because the stern seemed to be weighted down—as if it was dragging something. But when the boat passed, Clifton didn't observe anything being pulled behind it. He waved to the several men onboard, but none of them waved back. They seemed serious about whatever it was they were doing, and he got the impression that they didn't have time to bother waving to some kid on a dock.

When the waves rolled up a minute later, with some of the water spilling onto the deck and wetting his bare feet, he noticed that the water was muddy. He also saw a dirty trail following behind the boat, as if chocolate milk were leaking from the stern.

He gathered his gutted fish, dropped them into Ziplocs, and then crossed the train tracks since he wasn't expecting Tricky Bob for another twenty minutes. When he got to the porch, he asked Swamper what the boat was for. Swamper sat in his rocking chair, smoking a hand-rolled. "That's a dredge boat. It's looking for the little girl."

Clifton was confused, and it must've shown on his face because Swamper continued. "It's dragging a set of grappling hooks behind it. Those hooks'll grab just about anything that's sitting around on the bottom."

The thought that conjured in Clifton's mind unnerved him. To think of that cute little girl's body rolling around on the bottom of the river, as aimless as the dregs in a cup of tea, was bad enough to imagine. But then to think that she might get impaled on a cold, unforgiving dredge hook, well, that only darkened the picture.

But as it turned out, the dredge boat came up empty, which was both a good and bad thing. It was good because it gave hope to the town, and most important to Julie and her parents, that Maria might still be alive. At the same time, it was bad because that feeling of the unknown still hovered above the town like a heavy cloud of poisonous gas. Like a noxious miasma that made everyone sick. They wanted answers. They wanted the girl to be found safe and sound. They wanted Charlie's murderer to be caught. Whether he was found dead or alive, no one seemed to care.

But after a week, there hadn't been any significant break. The news reports and articles in the paper used all of the same clichés that cropped up anytime there was a missing persons case. *The police are staying tight-lipped because they don't want to hamper the investigation . . . The most critical window is within the first twenty-four hours of the disappearance . . . It is still being treated as a search and rescue at this time. It is not a recovery mission as of yet . . . The police are asking anyone who might have seen anything—anything at all—to please come forward. Sometimes what you might consider insignificant can be extremely valuable to detectives . . . The tiniest strand of evidence could break this case . . . If you see anyone acting suspicious, do not approach them. Instead, please contact the authorities immediately . . . Investigators say they've had a lot of promising leads, but so far they've been unable to apprehend a suspect.*

EXACTLY A WEEK after Maria disappeared, Clifton went down extra early to check the trot line while Swamper stayed inside to cook breakfast. Tricky Bob would be coming by in the next hour to pay them. It had been a slow week—at least a slow week as far as catfishing was concerned—and they hadn't caught much.

It was still dark as Clifton began pulling in the line. On the black surface of the water, a faint sprinkling of stars bounced along in a condensed cluster. Behind him, a rooster crowed from some distant farm nestled in a mountain hollow. Far across the river, on the horizon over Samford, the sun had barely started to show. The antennas on the tallest buildings still slowly flashed their red lights, warning low-flying planes to beware. But from where Clifton now stood, he could hardly see his hands as they worked the wet, weightless line; he suspected he hadn't caught a thing.

Since his first experience with the trot line, he'd rapidly become something of an expert. He now played a game with himself every morning, trying to predict how many pounds of fish were on the line just by giving it an initial tug. He could usually guess correctly within four or five pounds. This morning, unfortunately, his guess was zero and he was just about right. Out of the twenty hooks on the line, there was only one fish, and he wasn't even two pounds. Clifton backed out the barbed hook from the fish's lip with exasperation and dropped him into the water.

Since he didn't have any fish to clean, he decided he'd grab a quick bite of breakfast and then get an early start over to the house. He hadn't checked the mail in a couple of days, and also he wanted to drop off his most recent letter to his mother.

"I'm gonna head over to the house," said Clifton as he shoveled the last bite of scrambled eggs into his mouth. "Unless you want me to wait until after Tricky Bob comes by."

"No, go ahead. I'll deal with him."

"You want me to get anything at the store? I can come back through town if we need something."

Swamper stood at the sink, scrubbing a dish in soapy water. "We're low on milk. Could use some bacon too, I reckon."

"Okay, I won't be gone long." Clifton got up and set his dish on the counter next to the sink. Swamper grabbed it and let it disappear into the suds.

"You got the twenty-two?"

Clifton hesitated. "I don't like carrying that thing. Makes me feel uncomfortable."

"You'll find out what uncomfortable is if you run into that fella and don't have nothing to protect yourself. You know Bosco can't go, so take the damn gun. I ain't generally like this, but right now I'm not asking you. I'm telling you."

Clifton nodded as he left the kitchen. He stuffed the letter into the front pocket of his cutoffs and grabbed the gun from the lockbox by Swamper's desk. He stuck the gun in his waistband and then pulled down on his shirt to make sure it was concealed.

From the kitchen, Swamper yelled, "You need a flashlight?"

"No, sun'll be up in a few minutes."

Clifton opened the screen door quickly and then shut it behind him, preventing Bosco from escaping. The dog wagged his tail, eager to follow. A moist imprint formed in the dusty mesh where his nose had pushed against it. "You can't come, boy. Unless you want to take a chance on going back to prison."

The morning was still and the temperature perfect. Cardinals twittered back and forth to one another in the branches overhead as Clifton left the house, and behind him, the *caw caw* of a crow sounded near the river. When he got to the dirt road, the sky had lightened enough to where he could vaguely see, but as soon as he stepped over the barbed wire and entered the woods again, the darkness closed in once more.

He'd walked only fifty feet and was just getting ready to make the ascent toward the Killing Pit when he heard something coming toward him. Far up the hill, a branch snapped and some leaves shuffled around. His first instinct was that it was a rummaging squirrel. He'd always been amazed by how much noise one little squirrel could make on a quiet morning in the woods. But squirrels didn't snap branches. Deer? Maybe, but despite their size compared to a squirrel, they were generally far quieter in the woods. And Clifton also noticed that the birds had quit singing ahead of him. Since he hadn't yet made a sound on the beaten trail, he figured the sudden silence of the birds meant that whatever he'd heard up ahead was probably another human. That familiar panic started beating in his chest as he halted his steps and fine-tuned his ear. He didn't have to listen very hard. More branches popped, more leaves shuffled, as whatever it was got closer.

With every passing second the sky reddened, and he could now see the faint outline of the trail. Like a difficult chess match, his mind whirled as he tried to figure out his next move. Stand there? Walk forward? Turn and run? In the half a second it took to process all of that, a dark figure appeared at the top of the hill, coming down the trail at a brisk pace. Clifton finally made a decision and turned to run. As he did so, the figure apparently saw him because a distant voice said, "Hey, come here."

But Clifton wasn't about to stop. All he had to do was get across the road and he'd be back at Swamper's in no time. The paranoia and panic ate at him. *Aren't you being a little ridiculous? It's probably nothing to worry about. Yeah, but what if it is? He's right behind me.* He couldn't be sure if the man was running after him or not—his hearing was a bit muffled as the wind from his own strides filled his ears. The stubby nose of the gun barrel dug into his pelvis with every step he took. He knew he shouldn't turn his head, but he couldn't help it. He had to look. So when the gray of the road appeared before him at the end of the wooded gauntlet, he turned to see. Sure enough, the figure was still behind him and appeared to be gaining. He nearly choked on his own heart as he widened his strides and gave it everything he had.

Just before he reached the road, something grabbed at his ankles. A second later he found himself hurtling through the air as a sinking feeling squeezed the hollow of his stomach. It was the same feeling he'd once had when he'd lost control of a bicycle on a steep hill and knew there was nothing he could do about it. He was about to slam hard. As he made contact with the road, he ducked his head and crossed his right arm against his chest. Small rocks and pieces of gravel tore into his shoulder and then his back as he log-rolled twice across the hardpack. The tip of the gun's barrel had scraped away a layer of skin near his crotch. But he didn't even feel it. He popped up as quickly as he could, his knees bleeding and his T-shirt ripped, mentally cursing the rusty barbed wire that had tripped him.

He now saw the vague form of a car parked off the side of the road about forty feet from the trailhead—which he swore hadn't been there earlier—its right tires in the weeds, its left ones on the gravel. It looked like a yellow Lincoln. Clifton's chest heaved, and adrenaline pumped through his body. A prickling fear ran across his skin like the soft furry legs of a scurrying spider. Through an opening in the trees, a beam of sunlight popped out and shined directly on the man as he exited the woods. It was like some sort of weird religious phenomenon. The beam seemed to track his movements, as if God was spotlighting him. Clifton didn't know what was happening, but the man was well lit as he slowly walked across the road, now taking his time, a maniacal smile on his face. He opened and closed his hand like he was trying to squeeze juice from a lemon, causing the blue tattoos on his right arm to dance. Clifton discerned one that said WES in block letters across his biceps, but everything else was a blur.

"I remember you," said the man. The gap in his teeth stared at Clifton like a dark eye from the hollow of a tree. "You remember me?"

Clifton's mind raced, but unfortunately he couldn't get his feet to do the same. He was frozen. The whole thing reminded him of one of those showdowns on a TV Western, where each cowboy walks toward the other in the center of town, their guns at the ready. Except this was real. Clifton felt a throbbing in his shoulder. He felt blood pulsing from a wound on his knee. But he didn't feel any pain. For some reason, as desperate as the situation was, he couldn't erase the high-noon shootout scenario that kept flashing across the screen of his mind. But suddenly it all made sense. He reached into the front of his shorts and pulled out the gun. His hand shook badly, but despite the shaking, the ice cream man halted in the middle of the road. He put his hands up and out in front of him as if pushing against an imaginary wall. "Whoa, take it easy," he said.

"I'll shoot you. I swear to God I will." Clifton's eye was

trained on the beaded sight at the tip of the barrel. The bead was focused directly between the man's two upraised hands and pointing at the center of his chest like a football through a set of goalposts.

"Hey, just take it easy. I'm going to go back to my car over there," he said, motioning with his head toward the vehicle. "And you can go on to wherever it was you were going." He took a slow and careful step backwards, as if trying to avoid the strike of a rattlesnake he'd nearly stepped on.

Clifton put his other hand on the butt of the gun, just as Swamper had instructed, and tried to stanch the shaking. It didn't do much good. "Where's Maria?" he said. His voice sounded weak and scared to him, which is exactly what it was. "What did you do with her?"

The man took another step backwards, his hands still up in the air at shoulder-height. "Hey, dude, I don't have any idea what you're talking about. I don't know any Maria."

"That's the girl you—"

But he didn't have time to finish because the man wheeled and made a break for the car, weaving a bit as he went. Clifton followed the man's broad back with the tip of the barrel, but he couldn't bring himself to fire. The man opened the heavy door of the Lincoln and quickly slipped inside. A second later the taillights sent a red glow through the dawn as the engine revved to life. *Shoot him, goddamnit. Pull the trigger. I can't. Do it. Hurry up. But she might be in the car. I might hit her. Aim at a tire. Do something.*

The rear-wheel drive spun the tires into motion, sending a spray of gravel across the road. A few pebbles landed at Clifton's feet as the blood-red of the taillights disappeared in a heavy cloud of dust and blue exhaust. The lights zigzagged as the hind end fishtailed before righting itself and speeding off down the lane toward Crocket's Mill.

Clifton jumped on to the trail and ran down the hill, both of his hands still white-knuckling the cross-grid of the grip. He bolted up the steps two at a time and pulled the screen door open so hard that he nearly ripped it off its hinges.

Swamper was in the kitchen wiping down the counters when the door slapped against the side of the house and then against the jamb. "Clifton, that you?"

"Yeah," he said as he approached the entryway.

"What're you doing back so soon? Get lost or something?" Swamper smiled as he looked up from the counter, holding a moist rag in his hands. His eyes immediately went from Clifton's panicked face to the gun hanging loosely at his side. His smile evaporated. "What the hell?"

"Come on. We gotta make another phone call."

271

CLIFTON PULLED FURIOUSLY on the starter string as he stood in the back of the skiff, his torn shoulder now throbbing with pain. The aluminum hull rocked back and forth with his jerky movements and clanged against one of the dock's posts. Clumps of green slime peeled away from the wood like smeared paint each time the skiff smacked against it. "Come on, you piece of shit," he yelled. "Start already."

Swamper sat in the front of the skiff facing Clifton. He was quietly smoking a cigarette. "Did you remember to pull out the choke?"

"Yes!" he snapped as he looked at the choke button. Then he realized that in fact he hadn't. He pulled the knob out but made no attempt to apologize. He grabbed the starter handle again and this time the engine coughed to life. A blue smoke enveloped him as he revved the throttle with a turn of his wrist as if gassing a motorcycle. When he set her in motion, a muddy layer of tepid water sloshed along the flat bottom of the skiff, sending old cigarette butts and plastic cracker wrappers toward the soles of Swamper's boots.

He opened up the engine full bore as he raced toward Old Henry's. He kept his head on a swivel and his eyes at full attention as he peeked over Swamper's shoulders, on the lookout for the tips of rocks or submerged logs.

"You might want to slow her a notch or two," said Swamper as he continued to smoke, the smell of the tobacco hitting

Clifton in the face as it traveled downwind. Swamper had to yell to be heard over the motor, the breeze, and the sound of the prow slapping against the surface. "Water's down a bit. The grass is nearly all the way to the top."

Clifton didn't pay any attention. *I know what I'm doing. I gotta get to a phone.* He continued to race down the channel, sending a flock of green-headed wood ducks scurrying for cover as he did so, the tips of their wings nipping the water as they hastily struggled to take flight. Only a minute after Swamper had spoken, the engine began to whine and labor. Clifton let off the accelerator and said, "What the hell? Shit. We gotta call the cops." He looked to Swamper for help, his eyes seeking advice though his stubborn mouth refused to ask for any. A moment later the only sound was water lapping off the aluminum hull as the boat sluiced through the river and slowed to an almost complete stop. "Why'd the engine die? What's going on?"

Swamper took a final drag and then flicked the dog-end into the water where it extinguished itself with a hiss and a trailing signal of smoke. "You're gonna need to pull the tail out. The prop's most likely bound up with weeds and grass. Bogged the engine down."

"Shit," said Clifton. Panic overwhelmed him. The quicker he got to a phone, the quicker the cops might be able to track the man down. And find Maria. The guy was close. He hadn't left town as most had suspected. *Maybe he'd been hiding out in those woods somewhere. But somebody probably would've seen the car and reported it. Hell,* I'd have probably seen it.

Clifton leaned on the handle with all of his weight until the propeller of the small outboard engine broke the surface. A throng of lily pads, watercress, and grass, like a knot of thick, uncombed hair, had wrapped around it. The weeds covered the shaft's cowling and dripped like the strands of a wet mop.

"I got a square of two-by-four tied to a string sitting down by your feet. Jam that underneath the pivot and it'll keep the engine up out of the water."

Clifton located the piece of wood and did as instructed. Then he got to work unraveling the mess as the boat drifted aimlessly. It reminded him of having to clean out the roller of his mother's vacuum after he'd inadvertently sucked up rug tassels, broom straws, and anything else that wasn't supposed to go up there. He found a flathead screwdriver rolling about on the bottom of the skiff, and he used that as a pry bar to help loosen the weeds.

Meanwhile, Swamper had grabbed a spare paddle and was using it as a keel to keep them pointed downriver. An oncoming train whistled as it approached along the bank, and a snapping turtle, its black carapace as big around as a hubcap, was already sunning itself on an exposed rock in the early morning sunshine. But Clifton paid no attention to either as he worked. All told, it took about five minutes to clear the debris, but to Clifton if felt like five hours. When he finished, he dropped the prop back into the water and restarted the warm engine, not needing to pull the choke this time.

"Might wanna take it a little slower," said Swamper.

Clifton tensed his jaw and grated his teeth as he tried to refrain from replying. He cranked down on the throttle to get moving, but once in motion, he eased off a bit.

Old Henry's dock was void of people when they approached. Clifton slid the skiff next to it, and Swamper reached up and tied off to a rusty cleat. Clifton immediately jumped out and ran to the telephone booth at the far end of the gravel parking lot. It took Swamper a bit longer. He hobbled up the metal pool ladder and then slowly walked toward the phone where Clifton waited impatiently, tapping his foot like a spoiled little girl exasperated with her mother.

He had already dug a handful of change out of his pocket and now held it loosely in his palm. When Swamper got there, Clifton extended his arm and said, "Come on, Swamper. Hurry up. We're wasting time."

Swamper eyed the money and then looked at Clifton. "Reckon you might oughta make the call this time. You saw everything, not me."

Clifton felt a heavy ball of lead sink into his stomach. He

looked at Swamper in wide-eyed disbelief. "Me? You know how I get when it comes to the police."

"Well, you know what? It's time you got over it. There's a little girl's life at stake. The quicker you call, the quicker they might be able to find her. And you don't need no money, just hit nine-one-one."

Clifton held the change out stupidly for another moment. With a cruel snap to his voice he said, "So now that you're officially my grandfather, you think you need to start teaching me all of life's lessons or something? Trying to help me become a *man?*"

Swamper looked directly at Clifton and locked eyes with him. "In a lot of ways, I think you're already a man well beyond your years. At the moment, though, you're acting like a selfish little brat. A little mama's boy. Now hop to it and make that call. I'm going inside to get a drink."

Clifton mumbled something inaudible under his breath as Swamper headed toward the steps. *What an asshole. Does he know what I just went through? Face-to-face with a murderer.*

A thin stream of smoke chugged from the stovepipe poking out of Old Henry's tin roof, and the rich odor of fried pork filled the morning air. Clifton punched the buttons and stuck the receiver to his ear. His heart still raced as he finally began thinking about everything that had just happened. He'd been so filled with adrenaline and in such a hurry to get to a phone that he hadn't had time to actually stop and realize how close he'd just been to being killed. *I could've died. Jesus, I was this close. Thank God Swamper made me take that gun.* As he waited for a dispatcher to answer, he saw a wrinkled flyer taped to the inside glass of the phone booth. Maria stared straight back at him.

The call didn't take long. All he told the woman was that he'd run into the man. He explained where it had happened and gave a description of what the man looked like. Most important, he told her about the yellow Lincoln and which way it had been heading. When she urged him to come down to the station, he refused. When she asked for his name, he hung up, forgetting to mention the new tattoo he'd seen.

Five minutes later, as he stood on the dock watching blue-gills investigate his dissipating drops of spit, Old Henry's screen door creaked. When Swamper approached, he had two bottles of Coke and a greasy brown paper bag in his hands. He handed one of the Cokes to Clifton. "Here ya go," he said.

Clifton took the bottle. "I'm sorry, Swamper. It's just—"

"You don't need to explain nothing. I gotcha. You wanna eat here or wait until we get back home?"

"How about here?"

Swamper sat down on the end of the dock, letting his long legs dangle over the edge. Clifton sat down next to him and reached into the bag.

"Careful, they're still piping hot."

He took a handful and popped them into his mouth. Then he heard the distant chug of a motor from far upstream. Tricky Bob was sitting in his boat, the brim of his Bermuda hat hanging low over his head. "Look who's coming."

Swamper glanced upriver at Tricky Bob, who continued to roll along. As Swamper chewed on a mouthful of cracklin, he said, "Oh, hell. He's probably giddy with excitement right about now. In the twenty years I've been doing business with him, there ain't been one Friday out of all of 'em that I haven't been out on that dock waiting for him to pay me. The whole way down the river I bet that old son of a bitch has been smiling to himself, thinking that I died or something. Probably thought he was gonna get a free week out of me."

He spat a piece of fat into the water while Clifton shook his head, unable to contain his laughter.

Chapter 13

THE FOLLOWING MORNING, Clifton woke up sore and achy. His shoulder was swollen, but his knee was fine after he'd cleaned it the night before. He'd had to use some of Swamper's whiskey to dab at the cuts since that was the only thing he had. The smell of it had almost made him gag and brought back memories of how horrible he'd felt the day of his hangover.

As he lay in bed, trying to wake up, he told himself that he really wanted to go by the house and check the mail, mainly because he wanted to see if he'd received a letter from his mother. But he quickly talked himself out of that. After his terrifying confrontation with the man the day before, he told himself he wasn't going to go anywhere until the guy had been caught. However, after he got up and was eating breakfast, Swamper gave him some news that changed his mind.

"They found the Lincoln abandoned in Roanoke late last night." Swamper stood at the stove, cooking his own eggs after he'd already given Clifton a plate. He reached for a can of pepper on the shelf and tapped some into the pan. "On a side street only three blocks from the Greyhound station. Apparently, most likely after you called, they had every officer in Crocket's Mill and Samford staked out along the roads. Every damn road leading in and out of the county. But he still managed to slip through. They got a huge manhunt going on over there right now."

Clifton chewed a mouthful of eggs as he took the information in. "Wow, maybe they're gonna get him. If I'd just called quicker and hadn't been such a baby about it, maybe they would've gotten him."

"Cut that crap out," he said, shaking the end of his spatula at Clifton with rebuke. "No more guilt trips for you. They're gonna get him. It's just a matter of time."

"But nothing about Maria?"

"Nope, nothing about her. But I'll tell you this, those descriptions you gave the police are still exactly what they're telling people to be on the lookout for. So you should be proud of what you've done. They still aren't releasing a name, but they sure are describing just like you said."

Swamper's report gave Clifton the confidence he needed to go ahead home. If the car had been found all the way over in Roanoke, more than forty miles away, then he felt pretty sure that the man was nowhere near the Crocket's Mill area any longer.

However, he did take the gun with him. As much as he hadn't liked carrying it before yesterday, he now admitted that it had helped save his life. And he chose to take Bosco, too. The more protection the better, he decided. If Mr. Henderson happened to see them, then he'd deal with it. But Bosco was going.

HE TOOK the long way into town because he wanted to see if anything interesting was happening. In a way, he also hoped he might see Julie, though he kind of doubted it. He'd thought about her a lot over the last week, trying to imagine what she and her family must be going through. He even thought about calling her, but he didn't have any idea what he would say.

But as he'd suspected, he didn't see Julie. When he passed the police station, he slowed for a moment, thinking about the dispatcher he'd hung up on. She had practically begged him to come down there. He looked at the glass door, which almost beckoned him, and he immediately started sweating. His hands got so wet that he had trouble holding the end of the jump rope. He turned his head away and went on. *I can't do it.*

When he got to his mailbox, he emptied it and then reached into his pocket for the letter that he'd planned on sending yesterday. It was wrinkled and had smudges of dirt on the outside, but he put it in the box anyway. *If she only knew what that letter's been through.* He raised the flag on the side of the box and then headed up the driveway toward the house, shuffling through all of the mail. Mostly it was flyers and junk mail, which he promptly deposited into the empty trash can in the carport. But there was one addressed to him from his mother, which he planned to open as soon as he entered the house.

But opening the door wasn't quite as easy as that. He had the key in his pocket, but that wasn't the problem. What if the man had somehow gotten back to Crocket's Mill? *I remember you. Do you remember me?* A chill ran up his arms, and it took him a moment to shake the thought. *Stop it. The car was found in Roanoke. That's an hour away. He's on a bus by now.*

Regardless, he made sure that Bosco entered the house first. He watched the dog closely to see if he acted concerned, but all he did was sniff around the legs of the table, licking the floor for crumbs. The air in the kitchen was hot and stale, and Clifton raised a few windows and left the front door open in order to get some air circulating. He filled a water bowl for Bosco and set it on the linoleum, then sat down at the table to read his mother's letter. He split the envelope apart with his index finger and unfolded the pages. A warm feeling went through him when he saw her neat handwriting.

July 24, 1988

Dear Clifton,

Thank you for the letters you've written me so far. I'm sorry for the delay in responding to you, but things have been a bit tougher than I thought they were going to be. But don't worry, I'm good. I mean it. I'm really good. I didn't have any idea what kind of sorry shape I was in until I got here and started talking with the doctors, the counselors, and the other patients. And I'll tell you what, if you thought our life has been crazy, you should hear some of the stories I've heard in here. Unbelievable. But I'll save those for when I get out.

There's one counselor here who has been really great to me. Her name's Laura. She's about my age, and just like me, she lost her husband when she was young. Except she lost him to an overdose of heroin. She was pregnant at the time, so she has raised her daughter by herself, just like I raised you. So we have a lot in common and she's made my experience a little more bearable. By the way, her daughter is the same age as you and she's a real cutie! Wink, wink. Maybe I can set you two up after I leave.

But enough about me. How's my baby? Are you getting along okay with Daddy? I miss you so much I can't even tell you. I'm so sorry for how neglectful I've been over the years. I don't know what was wrong with me. The doctors say

I've been in a prolonged state of depression ever since your daddy died, and I've been numbing myself to the pain ever since with alcohol. Using it to try and help forget my pain and anguish. But all I was doing was hiding and not facing reality. And in the process, I let you down. You can probably see where some of the ink is getting smudged now. That's from the tears that I can't seem to stop. I've never cried so much in my life as I have since I've been in here. Not even after your daddy died. Laura says that if they collected all the tears that are shed in this place in a year, they could probably start up their own ocean. I think I've probably cried at least a small sea's worth on my own. But believe it or not, the crying is good. It helps. I'm getting rid of the pain. I'm getting rid of the anger.

Laura says that it would probably be a good idea for both you and me to go to some counseling together once I get out. I know we've never really talked about what happened to your daddy, but maybe it's about time that we started. Believe it or not, I think I'm even willing to forgive those police officers for what they did. It wasn't right and there was no excuse, but I'm finding compassion in my heart that I never knew I had before. For so long I hated them. Wanted them dead. Wanted to kill them myself. But I don't feel that way any longer. I know it's only been about a week since I got sober, but I'm telling you, Cliffy, I'm not going back. It sickens me when I think about what I've let myself become. How I didn't take care of you. Here come the tears again! I wouldn't blame you if you never wanted to speak to me again. I wouldn't blame you at all if you hated me.

You've always been such a sweet boy, Clifton. You've always stuck by me when you had no reason to do so. I guess what I'm trying to say is that I love you and I'm sorry. Things are going to be different once I get out. I promise. I'm ready to start over again. As crazy as it sounds, I think getting arrested was the best thing that ever happened to me. It probably saved my life. More importantly, it probably saved our relationship.

Well, I guess that's about all I have to say right now. If I keep writing, all these tears are going to mess it up so bad that you won't be able to read any of it! Please keep writing to me as often as you can. You have no idea what it means to me. I wait eagerly for the mail every day in hopes there is something from you. Only three weeks to go and then it'll be time to start over. I was thinking that it might be nice to go to the beach for a few days before school starts. You and I haven't gone anywhere together in forever and, horrible mom that I am, I realize you've never even seen the ocean! Might be nice to sit in the sand for a few days, don't you think? We don't have much money, but we could probably scrape up enough to go for a few days. Maybe Daddy would even want to come along. Do you think he'd like to do that? He always loved the ocean. He used to take me all the time when I was little. Anyway, that's another story altogether.

Oh, and don't worry, I still have a job when I get back. As much as I've complained about that place in the past, they've been wonderful through all of this. I guess there's something to be said for working for a big company. They have a program for employees who get into trouble like I've gotten into, and it is paying for my treatment here. I'm also getting a partial paycheck and will continue to draw one for up to three months before I have to go back to work. It's kind of like disability.

So I've got a lot to be thankful for. But mostly I'm thankful for you, Cliffy. I love you more than you can imagine. Please keep Daddy out of trouble and tell him hello for me. Life is good, my baby. Keep writing and I'll see you soon.

I miss you tons and love you more,

Mom

As Clifton refolded the letter, one of his own tears fell on the paper, combining with all of his mother's old ones. He put the letter back in the envelope and stuffed it into his pocket. He thought her words already sounded like the mother he'd remembered having years ago.

Bosco PULLED HARD on the leash as he directed Clifton toward Windswept Hills and the woods, almost as if he wanted to get away from Mr. Henderson's house as quickly as possible. Clifton didn't protest or really care, again feeling confident that if the Lincoln was found all the way in Roanoke, then he didn't really have anything to worry about. But regardless, he tapped the bottom of his shirt to reassure himself that the gun was still there.

As he walked down the road, he didn't really pay much attention. Instead, he reflected on his mother's letter and how good she had sounded. He also replayed the conversation that he and Swamper had had on the end of Old Henry's dock after Tricky Bob stopped by and gave them their pay.

"Swamper, I should've shot him. He was standing right there. I had the gun pointed right at his chest."

Swamper's jaws worked a piece of crispy pork as he said, "Well, that might've done more harm than good anyway."

"How? I mean, if I'd shot him, the police would probably already have him in custody. Then they could find Maria. The only *harm* it would've done is that maybe I would've wounded him. Or maybe killed him. And I don't see that as really doing harm anyway. Who cares about him?"

Swamper continued working his jaws and then spat a fatty bolus into the water. A swarm of minnows instantly converged on it as it bobbed on the surface, sending out grease rings in tiny concentric circles. The bravest few of the school began nipping at the clump of fat, and then more followed in turn, feeding like miniature piranhas on the leg of a wild goat. "I don't mean harm to him. I mean harm to you. If you'd shot him, and whether he lived or not, you'd have had to live with that for the rest of your life. I don't think that would've settled too well with you."

"What do you mean? You saying I can't handle it?"

"Well," said Swamper. He licked the tips of his fingers and took a sip of Coke. "I guess, in not so many words, that's exactly what I'm saying. And don't get me wrong, that ain't a bad thing. In fact, it's a good thing. I think you got a lot of your mama inside you, which is also a good thing. Your mama had a lot of her mama inside of her too. Neither one of them had a bad bone in their body. They always looked for the good in people, never the bad. Me, on the other hand, I never trusted nobody. I rarely forgave a man, even if he just looked at me funny. Sometimes I wish I'd taken a page from their book. Probably saved me a lot of hassle over the years."

Clifton looked at Swamper with a sideways glance. "What's that got to do with me not shooting the guy?"

"I guess I'm trying to say that it's best that you didn't. I think in the long run you'd have felt bad about it. Probably regretted it, especially if he died. No matter what kind of a son of a bitch he is, I don't think you'd want the weight of a dead man on your conscience. The cops'll get him. Hell, they might have him already. You did the right thing by getting down here and calling. Once again, you did your part."

"Yeah, maybe. But a big part of me keeps saying I'm nothing but chickenshit. Nothing but a big pussy."

"The hell with that. I'd say it takes more of a man *not* to shoot a gun than to actually shoot one. Like you told me earlier, you weren't sure if that little girl was in the car. What if you'd missed? What if you'd sent a hunk of lead into the car? What if you'd accidentally shot her? Then how would you feel? No, sir, I'd say you showed what kind of a man you are by *not* shooting. By being able to think that quickly on your toes. A lesser man would've just started blasting away. A chickenshit man, as you say, would've been the one to start pulling the trigger without no regard for anyone else. A chickenshit man would've only been interested in saving himself. You were more interested in protecting someone else. That's a real man, Clifton. I swear, sometimes I think I've learned more from you in a month and a half than I did in the last sixty-five years combined."

Clifton looked down between his feet as they swung over the water, feeling slightly embarrassed. He'd noticed that Swamper had a knack for making him feel that way. "Yeah, but what about hanging up on the dispatcher a few minutes ago? She wants me to go down there. Said if I looked at mug shots and could positively identify the guy, it would be a huge help. Could break the case, she said. But I don't want to do it. I don't want to go down there. How's that not chickenshit?"

Swamper finished the last of his Coke and set the empty bottle on the dock's edge. He swept his hands against one another to remove the crumbs, then fumbled in his pocket for his pouch of tobacco and began rolling a cigarette. "Well, that's a tough one. I can see where they're coming from. But I can see where you're coming from too. That's a decision you're gonna have to make on your own. But I ain't gonna judge you either way." He paused for a moment while he pushed the roller of the Zippo down the leg of his jeans and lit his cigarette. "My daddy always told me to never judge a man until you've walked a mile in his shoes. That way, if you find out he's an asshole, you're already a whole mile away and you got yourself a brand-new pair."

As CLIFTON STEPPED over the curb at the end of the cul-de-sac and entered the woods, his mind kept repeating that conversation. He couldn't help but smile as he thought about Swamper's joke, but then he thought about everything else. Had he really not shot at the man because he was worried about missing? About possibly hitting Maria if she was in the car? Or was that bullshit? Was he just fooling himself? Fooling Swamper? Trying to convince himself that he'd done the right thing. Maybe he'd just been chickenshit, plain and simple. And what about going to the police station? He'd been right across the street just a little while before. But he hadn't done it. He *couldn't* do it. Ever since he'd hung up on the dispatcher, that was the thing that kept gnawing at him more than anything else. That he couldn't do it. *Maybe tomorrow.*

Bosco tugged so hard on the leash when they got to the edge of the woods that he started hacking. His tail stood erect, the tip curling over toward his back. Clifton reached down and removed the jump rope. He'd barely gotten it free when Bosco took off. Clifton heard something dart through the leaves ahead of Bosco, and immediately his heart jumped. But he saw a flash of tan and the white of an alert tail zip through the straight-standing poplars before it disappeared, with Bosco hot on its tracks. Clifton smiled, feeling the happiness and excitement that Bosco was experiencing at the moment.

When Clifton entered the woods and began following the trail, he walked only twenty feet or so before he saw something out of place lying on the side of the path. He stopped and looked for a moment before approaching, trying to figure out what it was. In a way, it looked like a brown snake stretched out on the ground, but part of it was hung up on some scrubby pines, giving the appearance that its hind end was floating in midair. And it didn't move. Clifton took a step forward to see if the thing would try to get away, but once again it didn't move. He took another step forward. And then another. Once he realized that whatever it was wasn't alive, he took a few more steps until he stood over the top of it. In the distance he heard Bosco shuffling through the leaves. It sounded like he was on his way back. "Come on, Bosco," he yelled as he bent down and picked the thing up.

It was the velvet of deer antlers, and it was the softest thing Clifton had ever remembered touching. He wondered if it could be from that same deer he'd seen weeks before. The one that almost got killed. He rubbed it through his hands, then touched it to his face and smoothed it against his cheek. There was a gamey, musty smell to the velvet, but it wasn't unpleasant. It just smelled like the woods. Clifton held it against his cheek until Bosco walked up, panting and almost smiling. The dog's nose twitched as he carefully sniffed the tip of the hanging velvet. "What do you think, Bosco? Do I look like a movie star?" He tossed the strand behind his neck and then wrapped it once around his throat like a woman might do with a scarf or mink stole. "Come on, boy. I'll bring it home and let Swamper take a look at it." Bosco wagged his tail as if saying he thought that was a good idea.

When the trail forked, Bosco took the right branch toward

the Killing Pit. For a minute, Clifton thought about staying left and going down and taking a swim at the Palisades. He didn't really have anything else to do. But he figured that with everything that had been going on lately, he should get back so Swamper didn't worry. He could always jump off the end of the dock and take a swim there if he wanted to.

The rocky outline of the Killing Pit had just come into view between the leaves of the rhododendron grove when the hair on Bosco's neck bristled. He halted, leaving one paw curled and suspended in midair. His ears perked to attention and his snout pointed toward the sky, the tip of his moist nose wrinkling as he tried to interpret the information on the faint breeze. Clifton stood frozen behind him, trying to ascertain anything that he could, but he came up empty. He didn't see, hear, or smell anything out of the ordinary. At least not at first.

As he stood motionless at Bosco's right flank, trying to hone all of his senses, he thought he might have heard a voice. Maybe even a pleading voice. But he also thought he might be going crazy with paranoia once more. Then the next time he thought he heard it, he happened to be watching Bosco; the dog's ears had twitched. "What is it, boy? What do you hear?"

Bosco took a few silent steps forward, his attention now completely locked in on the direction of the pit. Clifton stayed right behind him, his heart fluttering, his right hand now on the butt of the gun tucked in his shorts. Then he heard a voice again, slightly louder than before. He remembered back to when he'd first passed the Killing Pit on his own, well before any of the recent craziness had even taken place, and he'd been so scared that he had convinced himself he'd heard voices. Maybe even his father's voice. But this was real. He was sure of it. Even if he wasn't sure, watching Bosco's reaction convinced him. Somebody was in the Killing Pit. And then all of the pieces began to fit together as he and the dog slowly marched forward.

That's why the guy was on the trail that morning. Why else would he have been there? Maybe I can save her after all.

Bosco picked up his pace as they got closer, and Clifton stayed right behind him. He thought about pulling the gun from his waistband, but with every step he took, he was convinced that he wouldn't need it. Bosco reached the edge of the pit first. His hair still stood on end, but his tail dropped between his legs. Instead of barking, he began whining. It was a pitiful whine that told Clifton something was wrong. Terribly wrong.

Clifton slowly made his way to the edge. He cautiously peered over, scared that something might jump out at him from the depths. Like a jack-in-the-box or a can of snakes. A sharp stench from the bottom instantly slid into his nostrils.

It took a moment for his eyes to adjust to the deep blackness filling the hole, but then he saw something. There was a figure lying in the murky water. He couldn't see a face. Only shadows. Only vague forms. And then a voice rattled weakly as if gargling sand. But it wasn't a girl's voice as he had expected. It was a man's. A voice that was hollow as it echoed and bounced off the old stone and rose from the bowels of the pit. The voice was frail. Almost sickly. "You gotta go get help. I think I'm bleeding internally. I don't have much time. Both my legs are busted for sure. Don't get too close or you might slip too."

As Clifton's eyes slowly adjusted, he suddenly realized that there was a second person at the bottom of the pit. The first man's body, the man who had spoken, was twisted and lay unnaturally like the branches of a weathered, windblown tree. But underneath those gnarled legs was a second body. A much smaller one. A body without life or color. Clifton could see a set of naked legs and naked arms. The torso seemed to be submerged, but it was too dark to make out a head or face. "Is that the missing girl? Is that Maria?"

The voice returned. "Yeah, it's her."

"Is she . . . is she alive?"

The man immediately replied, his voice a little louder now, but the answer seemed to come to Clifton in slow motion. He heard what he said, but he had trouble comprehending it. Or maybe he didn't want to comprehend it. "Hell no. She's dead as a doornail. And stinks like shit. Go get me some help before I end up the same way."

Clifton stared into the darkness in disbelief at what he'd just heard.

As the man continued, his voice grew stronger, the same way a candle burns brighter just before it goes out. "We got a tip that the kidnapper had been seen in this area yesterday. This morning I had an idea after his car was found. Sure enough, I was right. He dumped her in here. But as I was looking down, my shoe slipped on one of those goddamned mossy rocks. My feet shot out from underneath me. It's a wonder I didn't break my neck. Busted my radio all to hell. I've been down here for probably six hours or more. Now go get me some help. My squad car's parked down on the road by the trailhead. Use the CB and tell dispatch what happened."

Clifton now understood. But he hated what he was understanding. "Your squad car?"

"Yeah, I'm a cop. What the hell you think this uniform's for?"

Clifton suddenly felt terrified as memories rushed back to him. His voice was meek and unsure as he replied, "I can't really see."

"Well do me a fucking favor, if it's not too much to ask,

and go get some help. Before I drown in my own stinking blood."

Clifton felt sure he knew the answer to the next question, but he asked it anyway. "What's your name—so I can tell them at the station?"

"Brader. Sergeant Randall Brader. Now get your ass in gear, boy."

Clifton bent over and tried to force his eyes to cut through the darkness. He felt the cold of the gun barrel dig into his stomach. He stared as hard as he could into the abyss, trying to make out the features on the man's face, but all he saw was a blank grayness. Gray legs, gray arms, a gray face. A gray man with no identifiable marks. With no scars. But Clifton knew the scars were there. Pocked all over. Even though he couldn't see the man's face, he still knew exactly what it looked like.

"And you're sure she's dead?"

"Goddamn, son, can't you smell her? It's like being stuck at the bottom of a cesspool. She's been dead for at least a day. Probably more. Now go on. What're you waiting on?"

Clifton pulled back from the opening of the pit with a faraway look in his eyes. He mumbled to himself in a voice that was almost confident, like a chess player saying *check* but knowing that *mate* was only a move away. "I was just making sure."

As he stood up, the boa of velvet around his neck slid off

his shoulders. He made a hurried grab for it, but it was too late. The velvet dropped into the hole, floating like a leaf separated from its branch. Clifton heard frantic splashing as Scarface slapped at it. "Goddamn, what the hell's that?"

Clifton didn't bother to respond. Instead he took off down the trail. When he got to the road, the squad car was parked in the exact same spot as the Lincoln had been, the tall weeds brushing against the quarter panel and passenger door. He stopped in the road, looked at the car, and saw that the driver's side window was down. Muffled squawks came from the radio, but he didn't bother to go toward it. Bosco, however, walked over and investigated. His first order of business was to raise his leg and pee on the rubber of both rear tires.

Drown in my own stinking blood reverberated through Clifton's head. *Yeah, well maybe that would be the best thing for you.*

"Come on Bosco. Let's go." Clifton dropped off the road and on to the trail. A second later, Bosco caught up and whipped past his legs, disappearing into the ferns.

"It's your decision, is all I'm saying. Whatever you do is between me and you and nobody else. I ain't gonna blame you, no matter what you decide." As Swamper spoke, he patiently sprinkled a fine line of dry tobacco down the folds of a rolling paper, licked the gummy edge, and twisted it up. He brushed the remnants off his pants and onto the porch. The lighter shuffled through his fingers a few times after he lit the cigarette, and then he set it on the flat arm of the rocker.

Clifton bounced his leg nervously as he sat in the other chair, shaking the planks of the porch just enough to jostle Bosco's head ever so slightly. The dog kept his chin resting on the floor between his front paws and didn't seem to notice. "I don't know what to do, Swamper. I swear to God, I can't take much more of this. I think I'm going crazy. What do I do?"

"I already told you—you're the one's gotta make that decision. But I understand no matter which way you go. Can't blame you either way."

Clifton continued to bounce his leg. He nervously turned his head behind him every so often, as if he expected to see the cop coming down the trail at any minute. *The longer you wait, the longer he suffers. Yeah, but the longer I wait, the longer Julie and her family suffer. That's true, but what's another hour or two in the whole scheme of things? It's another hour or two of their family not knowing, that's what. It's another hour or two that could be the difference between that cop living or dying. Exactly right. He didn't care about your father's life, why should you care about his?*

Suddenly Clifton stopped bouncing and stood up. He was

tired of arguing with himself. "Guess I'll take the skiff if that's okay."

"You know it is. You want me to come along?"

"I guess I can do it."

"What about just walking up to the squad car and using the CB like he said?"

Clifton shook his head as he looked up through the woods. "I think I'd rather use the phone."

Swamper nodded in understanding. He carelessly ashed his cigarette over the arm of the chair, and a few stray flakes snowed down on Bosco's head. "For what it's worth, I think you're doing the right thing. Not because I give a damn about that son of a bitch up there. He can rot in his own stink for all I care. I just think you'll live easier. It's the right thing for *you*."

"Yes, sir. I guess so."

Chapter

THE DAY AFTER CLIFTON FOUND SCARFACE, he walked into town and through the doors of the police station. He identified himself and was immediately ushered to a back office where he sat down with a detective. The detective spread a handful of mug shots over the table, and Clifton picked out the man in less than a minute. As it turned out, the people of Crocket's Mill had been right: He was the same guy who'd been released from the penitentiary in Samford. Clifton then told the detective everything he knew, everything that had happened, and then he walked out. He didn't know how much good it would do, but at least he'd cleared his conscience. It was too late to save Charlie. Too late for Maria. But maybe it would save someone else.

By early April of the following year, the man still hadn't been caught. There were rumors that he'd been spotted in

Virginia, as well as other states across the country, but nothing ever materialized. He'd gotten away with murder, plain and simple. As for Sergeant Brader, he survived his injuries but was laid up in the hospital for weeks. The newspaper said he probably wouldn't have survived if his fellow officers hadn't found him when they did. He was praised for his excellent police work, won several awards and honors for locating Maria, and was overall regarded as a local hero.

Although Clifton hadn't expected to see Julie back at school when classes began a few weeks after her sister's death, she was there. He never said a word to her about how he'd seen Maria that day in the ice cream truck, nor did he say anything about being the one to find her and Sergeant Brader at the bottom of the Killing Pit. What would the point have been in that? He didn't see how it would do anything but upset her unnecessarily. So he'd kept his mouth shut.

But as the school year went on, their friendship grew stronger. Mostly because he still acted the same way toward her as he always had. He'd noticed that even though most of the kids at school had shared their condolences and shown sympathy for Julie, they also treated her like a bit of a pariah. It was almost like she was contagious. As if they believed that since her sister had been abducted and murdered, if they got too close to her then they might be next.

He also noticed how a lot of the kids snuck glances at her

in the hallways and then whispered to one another as they passed. Even though it didn't seem to bother her, it certainly bothered Clifton. Because of it, he made an even more concerted effort to act normally around her. In fact, it was similar to the way she'd acted toward him so many years before when Mr. Carlson had been killed. The connections, the ironies, the odd coincidences that now bound the two of them together didn't go unrecognized by Clifton. In a way, he thought that maybe it was a sign. *Maybe it's fate or something. Twisted fate, to be sure, but still, maybe it's fate.*

At least that's what he thought as he stood on the football field on a cold, blustery April afternoon. The winter had been extra long, and spring still hadn't really arrived yet. In fact, patches of snow still clung to life on the north faces of the surrounding mountains. He stood next to Julie, his coat zipped up to his neck, shivering as he held the strings of his two balloons. She was also shivering, and strands of her hair flew over her face like blond tassels. He had decided the night before that today was the day that he'd talk with her.

As they waited for Mr. Longsworth to give the word over the bullhorn, Clifton suddenly felt someone smack the back of his head. Before he even turned around, he knew who it was.

"Hey, Skunk, what're you doing here?" asked Colt as he looked over at Julie and smiled.

"I'm just standing here, freezing my ass off. Minding my own business. I'm not in the mood today, Colt. It's too damn cold."

"Hey, you know what I heard?" he said, apparently sensing weakness. "I heard a while back that your mom got busted and went to jail. Heard she was a booze hound. A complete wino. Heard she likes to get drunk as a *Skunk*." He laughed and flashed another smile.

Despite the cold, a warm heat prickled Clifton's skin. He had no idea where Colt had gotten his information, but he was suddenly very angry. And embarrassed. His mother's arrest was something he didn't want anybody to know about. Especially not Julie. But he refused to be beaten, so he quickly dug deep into his archives.

"Yeah, well, I heard something about your mom too. Heard she got fired. That's too bad. I'm really sorry."

Just like a slow, dim-witted cow who still hasn't figured out an electric fence, Colt didn't seem to realize he was being set up once again. "What're you talking about? She didn't get fired."

"That's not what I heard. Rumor has it she doesn't work at the sperm bank anymore. Got fired for drinking on the job."

The punch hit his shoulder so hard that he nearly let go of his balloons. Before he even had a chance to retaliate, Colt scurried away like an overweight rat, disappearing into the thick crowd. But as usual, it had been worth it because Julie was laughing.

"Where do you come up with that stuff?"

Clifton had his hands tucked into fists in the pockets of his coat. He shrugged and said, "I don't know. It's a gift. What can I say?"

"You okay?" she asked.

"Of course. The jacket gives some extra padding." He didn't even bother to rub his shoulder. "I almost feel guilty. Like I'm picking on the mentally challenged or something. God, he's an idiot."

A few minutes later, after Principal Longsworth's voice rattled through the bullhorn, the blue and gold balloons shot toward the sky like a flock of spooked doves. They didn't soar peacefully as they had the year before, but instead whipped horizontally across the field on a strong draft before rising skyward. But despite their rapid departure, Clifton had managed to keep watch of both his and Julie's balloons. At least for the first twenty seconds or so. He wondered if she'd noticed that as soon as they had released them, the string of his blue balloon had wrapped itself around her gold one like the tendrils of an aggressive vine.

As the crowd began to disperse after Principal Longsworth made the announcement—much to the dismay of the students—that classes would resume in ten minutes, Clifton walked back to the building with Julie at his side. He was nervous and thought of a hundred different reasons why he shouldn't say anything. But finally he just stopped dead in his tracks and said, "Could I ask you something?"

Julie halted and turned to face him, almost as if she'd been expecting it. She smiled and said, "Sure. What's up?" She used several of her fingers to pull the hair back from her face, but the wind was so unrelenting that she finally gave up.

Clifton stared at the ruddiness of her cheeks as he began to talk. Each side of her face looked like the bright skin of a ripened tomato. Because of her hair flying around, he couldn't make eye contact, which he was actually thankful for. He swallowed and said, "I was wondering if maybe you'd ... maybe ... want to go to the junior prom with me. If you're going with somebody else, that's cool. I understand. I just thought I'd ask."

Julie pulled the hair away from her face once more. This time the strands managed to stay tucked behind her ears long enough for Clifton to see her green eyes. The tomatoes of her cheeks seemed to ripen slightly. She smiled. "That's really sweet of you, Cliffy. But I'm afraid somebody just asked me yesterday."

Clifton felt his heart drop, but he did his best not to let her notice. "That's cool. I kind of figured somebody probably had. Just thought I'd ask." He paused for a moment and looked over the top of her shoulder. Far away and barely noticeable, a spattering of balloons floated in front of the backdrop of the snowcapped mountains. "Who're you going with?"

Julie glanced away for a moment, toward the front doors of the school, and then back at him. She almost looked embarrassed. "You're not going to like it."

"What do you mean? Who is it?"

"Colt asked me."

Clifton's eyes widened despite his best efforts to prevent them from doing so. A high-pitched ringing buzzed in his ears. "Colt *Jenkins?* Are you serious? You're going with Colt?"

"Well, nobody else had asked me. It's only three weeks away you know."

"Yeah, but Colt? I mean, I thought you couldn't stand him."

Julie glanced down at her feet and then looked up with a catlike grin. "Oh, yeah, you're right. I *can't* stand him. He's an asshole. I was just kidding, Cliffy. I'd love to go with you."

Clifton felt his heart stop. He wasn't sure if he'd heard her correctly. "What?"

"I was just messing with you," she said, and laughed. She playfully slapped him in the shoulder with her gloved hand. "What took you so long? I've been waiting for a month. I was starting to think I really *might* have to go with Colt."

Clifton still stared at her, nearly dumbstruck. "So you'll go with me?"

Julie made a fist and knocked it in the air as if tapping on an invisible door. "Hello? Clifton? You there? Yes, I'll go with you. I'd love to."

He tried to pull himself together and regain his composure, but he wasn't sure how good of a job he was doing. Inside he was busting. "Okay, cool. It should be fun. And, man, you're evil. You had me going."

Julie shrugged in the same way Clifton had earlier. "What can I say? It's a gift."

On a Friday afternoon and with exactly one week to go until the prom, Clifton got off the school bus feeling good about everything. About life. About Julie. About everything. He and his mother had already gone into Samford to have him fitted for a tuxedo, and he was pretty sure his mother was more excited about the prom than he was. After the New Year, she'd gotten a promotion and had been moved to the dayshift. She now worked from eight to five each day, which gave them more time in the evenings to spend together. She was even taking a couple of night classes at the community college, thinking she might try to get her nursing degree.

Most important, she'd managed to stay sober since she'd returned from rehab, and Clifton felt like he had his old mother back. The mother he remembered before his father died. She'd turned into a completely different person. Or maybe not a different person but the person she'd once been. The kind, sweet mother who Clifton had been missing for years. The medication she was on for her depression was doing wonders. She finally seemed happy, and she and Swamper were actually talking on a regular basis now. He'd even come over for dinner a few times.

As Clifton stepped off the bus, the sunshine warmed his body. It was one of the first really warm days of spring and he felt excited. He felt happy to be alive. The pinkish-red flowers of the redbuds were finally blooming around the neighborhood, and an earthy smell of rejuvenation filled the air after the long, icy winter. In the distance, the tops of the mountains were still gray and leafless, but along the foothills, things were beginning to green up with the pastel colors of spring. *Man, this feels like fishing weather. I'm gonna see what Swamper's up to.*

He still tried to see Swamper and Bosco as much as he could, but with school, homework, and everything else, he usually got over there only on the weekends. But with the coming of the warmer weather and school ending in another month, he planned to be there every day starting soon.

When he arrived, he found Swamper in his usual spot, rocking slowly, a light haze of smoke around his head. Bosco lay next to him but didn't even bother to get up. Instead, he just thumped his tail lazily against the porch. As Clifton hopped the steps, he was surprised to see a glass of whiskey in Swamper's hand. In all the time he'd been around Swamper, he'd seen him drink only on a couple of occasions, and never during the middle of the day.

"Hey, boy," said Swamper. "What're you doing here?"

"Just wanted to see what you were up to. And wanted to ask you something," he said, but he was confused by Swamper's demeanor. "What're you up to?"

"I'm just setting here, having a few drinks." He looked off into the distance, blinking hard as if trying with all his might to prevent tears from flowing. "Feeling a little down for some reason today." He took a drag from his cigarette and then a sip of whiskey. A solitary ice cube clinked against the glass. When Bosco got up and tried to nudge his head between Swamper's knees to get a scratch, and Swamper rebuffed him by locking them together, Clifton knew something was wrong.

"Swamper, what the heck is going on?"

"You know, I don't really have no idea," he said as he continued to train his eyes toward the river. The sycamores, walnuts, and oaks lining the water were beginning to green, taking away some of the gray drabness of winter, but he could still see the rounded clumps of squirrels' nests tucked into the V's of the branches. In another week or so, as the leaves took life and spring gained control, the nests would completely disappear from view. "Actually, believe it or not, I'm happier than I've been in years."

"Well you got a funny way of showing it."

"I know. I guess I've just been sitting here thinking about how lucky I am. This time last year, I was pretty sure I was going to end up dying out here one day, not knowing if anybody'd ever even find me. And I was pretty positive I'd never get to talk to your mama again. Never had no idea I'd get to meet you. My only grandson. Now, a year later, you and your mama are the two most important things to me in this world. I can't tell you how lucky I feel. How fortunate I am to have you in my life, Clifton. I know I've told you before, but you've taught me all kinds of things. Made me a better man."

"Then why the heck are you so sad? Seems like you should be happy."

"I don't know. That's just it. I reckon when you get older, sometimes things just hit you a certain way. Sitting out here by myself so much, sometimes I do a lot of thinking. Too much thinking, maybe. Anyway, I'm all right. What is it you wanted to ask me?"

"I just wanted to know when you thought the fish would start biting. I think this might be the year we catch a lunker."

That seemed to be just the right medicine that the doctor had ordered for Swamper. His eyes brightened, and where he'd been slumped in his rocker before, he had now readjusted and sat up straight. "This warm weather'll give you the itch, won't it? I expect we can start running a line in the next week or two if the weather holds. Spring's come later this year than I can ever remember. Have to get the last of the snow melted off the peaks and let it run on through. Once it clears, we oughta be able to get a line out."

"That sounds good to me." Clifton clapped his hands together with a sharp smack and then sat down in the other chair. "Man, I can't wait."

When Bosco heard the clap, his tail made a hollow *thump thump* against the porch floor. He then began pawing at the top of his muzzle. They both watched with amusement as the dog, almost in comical fashion, tried getting at an itch that he just couldn't reach. "You know," said Clifton as he watched Bosco struggle to alleviate his discomfort, "I never thought about it before, and I have no idea why I'm thinking it now, but it's impossible for a dog to pick its nose."

Swamper took a heavy draw from his cigarette and pondered that for a second. "Yeah, that might be so," he said, nodding his head. "But who cares? He might not be able to pick his nose, but a dog can lick his own wanker. There ain't no man on earth who can do that, no matter how hard he tries or how bad he wants to get it done."

Clifton cracked up. One thing that he had really learned to appreciate about Swamper was that he had always, even from the very first day, talked to him like an adult. So often, Clifton thought, other adults, teachers, whoever, always seemed to talk to teenagers like they were trying to protect them from something. Like they didn't think kids knew what was going on in the world. And he hated that. But Swamper never held back just because Clifton was younger. "Yeah, well, speak for yourself, old man. Maybe you just never tried hard enough."

"Oh, trust me. I've tried." He grinned now as he took a final draw from his cigarette and flicked it over the railing. Whatever melancholia he'd been experiencing earlier had vanished. "It's downright impossible. Don't matter how you do it—it ain't happening. You can bend over like you're touching your toes, roll on your backside in the middle of the floor, twist your body this way or that, but it can't be done. It's God's cruelest trick against man, if you ask me. I think it proves that God is actually a woman."

Clifton shook his head as he continued to laugh. "You think so?"

"Maybe," said Swamper. "You know what else you can't lick?"

"I have no idea."

"Bet you can't lick your elbow neither."

"What? My elbow?"

"Go ahead and try it. You'll see."

Clifton shook his head and gave it a shot, feeling like a fool as he did so. And Swamper was right, it was impossible. "Okay, but why would you want to? How would you ever even think to try that?"

"You sit out in these woods by yourself for as long as I have, sometimes you have to invent ways to keep yourself entertained." He paused for a moment and then got up from his chair, stretching his lanky body toward the sky. "You feel like running some chess? We haven't played in forever."

"Sure."

Swamper's eyes lit up brighter still. He clapped his hands and then rubbed them together as if warming them by a fire. "Hot damn. I think I'm ready to beat the socks off you. You know, I even hitched a ride to the library in Samford a few months ago to find a book on chess. Read it over the winter. I got me some new strategy."

Clifton smiled. "Well, come on then. Bring it on."

Twenty minutes into the game, he could tell that Swamper had indeed done some studying. He was smarter with his pieces for one thing. And he was taking his time, really thinking about his strategy. But as Clifton moved his own pieces around the board, he felt his mind drifting to another place. Thinking about Julie. Thinking about the upcoming prom. Wondering what might happen *after* the prom.

He was in full thought, seeing the board in front of him but not really paying attention to what was happening. That is, he wasn't really paying attention until he heard Swamper call out, "Checkmate!" Clifton stared at the crown of the white queen sitting in front of him. The crown that Swamper had just lifted his finger from. He then looked up to see a proud smile across the old man's face. He beamed like a little boy who'd just brought home an A on a report card.

Clifton looked back down at the pieces and studied the board for a moment, a look of confusion on his face. His eyebrows scrunched together and he cocked his head to the side like a kitten seeing itself in a mirror for the first time.

Swamper slapped his knees with pleasure. "Told you I'd been studying."

Clifton looked up at Swamper, that same confused look on his face. His eyebrows were still wrinkled, his head still tilted. He then slid a black bishop from the far side of the board and took out Swamper's queen. "Sorry, old man. Not today."

Swamper stared at the board in utter amazement. He looked at his queen, which was now grouped on the edge of the table with his other captured pieces. He looked at her with a pained longing. It appeared he would have done anything, paid nearly any price, to have her back. "But . . . But I swear to God I checked . . . I double checked. How could I miss that?"

Clifton shrugged but didn't say anything. Six moves later, he slid his black queen diagonally and put Swamper in check. Two moves after that, with the aid of a bishop and knight, the white king was mated.

Swamper rapidly stood up from the table and smacked his open hands against the edge, rattling some of the pieces like bowling pins. "Goddamn son of a bitch." He grabbed the pouch of tobacco in his pants pocket and headed for the door. The glow of fading afternoon sunlight filtered through the window and lit up some of the fallen pieces, turning them a dull orange.

"Black wins again," said Clifton with a sly smile as he looked over his shoulder.

"Yeah, yeah, yeah," said Swamper as he opened the screen door and let it slap behind him. His voice was a bit muffled coming from the porch, but Clifton heard the click of a lighter and then Swamper say under his breath, "Black wins again, my ass."

Acknowledgments

I'd like to thank all of the following, who have helped me so much in one capacity or another. To my editor, Julia Richardson, who took a chance and believed in this novel before it was ever written. She saw the bigger picture right from the beginning, and also again at the end. To my son, Mason, who patiently listened, absorbed, and then told me, without hesitation, exactly what needed to be changed. To my wife, Jocelyn, for everything, but also for working so hard in the real world while I spend my days playing around in a fictitious one. To Joyce Taylor, who has repeatedly gone above and beyond the call of duty to help promote my work. To Keith Johnson, a discerning reader who provided significant insight concerning some of the more delicate issues within this book. And to his son, Kam, who gave me, unbeknown to him, a perfect detail. There were others who gave details, too, whether they realized it or not: Mrs. Jeri Phillips, Courtney Altizer, Kermit Moore, Brian Blankenship, and John Van Kirk all assisted in their own way, whether it was a story about bedbugs or a simple slip of the tongue. And thanks to my agent, Scott Miller, who gave me the initial nudge to write this book.

I'd also like to give a special thanks to the Virginia Center for the Creative Arts, which provided me time, space, and, most important, the solitude necessary to complete this novel. It's a unique and wonderful place.